PENGUIN CLASSICS

AN INTERNATIONAL EPISODE
AND OTHER STORIES

Henry James was born in 1843 in Washington Place, New York, of Scottish and Irish ancestry. His father was a prominent theologian and philosopher and his elder brother, William, was also famous as a philosopher. He attended schools in New York and later in London, Paris, and Geneva, entering the Law School at Harvard in 1862. In 1865 he began to contribute reviews and short stories to American journals. In 1875, after two prior visits to Europe, he settled for a year in Paris, where he met Flaubert, Turgenev, and other literary figures. However, the next year he moved to London, where he became such an inveterate diner-out that in the winter of 1878–9 he confessed to accepting 107 invitations. In 1898 he left London and went to live at Lamb House, Rye, Sussex. Henry James became naturalized in 1915, was awarded the O.M., and died early in 1916.

In addition to many short stories, plays, books of criticism, autobiography, and travel he wrote some twenty novels, the first published being *Roderick Hudson* (1875). They include *The Europeans*, *Washington Square*, *The Portrait of a Lady*, *The Bostonians*, *The Princess Casamassima*, *The Spoils of Poynton*, *The Awkward Age*, *The Wings of the Dove*, *The Ambassadors*, and *The Golden Bowl*.

Since 1968 Gorley Putt has been a Fellow of Christ's College, Cambridge, where he was also Senior Tutor. Previously he had been the United Kingdom and European representative of the Harkness Fellowship programme of the Commonwealth Fund of New York, offering postgraduate awards tenable at American universities. He became a Fellow of the Royal Society of Literature in 1952, was awarded the O.B.E. in 1966 and became Cavaliere of the Order of Merit of Italy in 1980. His publications include *Men Dressed as Seamen* (1943), *View from Atlantis* (1955), *A Reader's Guide to Henry James* (1966) and *The Golden Age of English Drama* (1981).

General Editor for the works of Henry James in the Penguin Classics: Geoffrey Moore.

Henry James

An International Episode and Other Stories

Edited with an introduction by
S. Gorley Putt

Penguin Books

Penguin Books Ltd, Harmondsworth, Middlesex, England
Viking Penguin Inc., 40 West 23rd Street, New York, New York 10010, U.S.A.
Penguin Books Australia Ltd, Ringwood, Victoria, Australia
Penguin Books Canada Ltd, 2801 John Street, Markham, Ontario, Canada L3R 1B4
Penguin Books (N.Z.) Ltd, 182–190 Wairau Road, Auckland 10, New Zealand

An International Episode first published in book form 1879
The Pension Beurepas first published in book form 1881
Lady Barberina first published in book form 1884
Published in Penguin Classics 1985

Introduction copyright © S. Gorley Putt, 1985
All rights reserved

Made and printed in Great Britain by
Richard Clay (The Chaucer Press) Ltd,
Bungay, Suffolk
Filmset in 9/11 Monophoto Photina by
Northumberland Press Ltd,
Gateshead, Tyne and Wear

Contents

Introduction

These three stories were published a hundred or so years ago. In accordance with Leon Edel's sensible habit of reprinting the tales as they first appeared in book form, the order of publication is as follows: *An International Episode* (published with *Daisy Miller*), 1878; *The Pension Beaurepas* (published with *Washington Square*), 1879; *Lady Barberina* (published in *Tales of Three Cities*), 1884. Yet the transatlantic balance has shifted so radically between then and now that the manners and attitudes of James's transatlantic pilgrims seem to be those of some distant millennium rather than of one short century's remove. What twentieth-century mother would whistle her son back to London at the news that he was becoming interested in an American heiress? Would it be an American or an English lady, nowadays, who was more likely to hope, in considering Anglo-American reciprocity, 'that an ultimate fusion was inevitable'? It may demand from a modern reader some effort of historical imagination to recapture that sense of fascinated outrage which once thrilled social conservatives on both sides of the Atlantic when they heard of yet another Anglo-American marriage. It may be helpful to recall that the fruit of one such union, solemnized in 1874, was Winston Churchill.

The young Henry James, who – to borrow a phrase from his wonderful travel letters – had gone 'reeling and moaning' through the storied streets of Rome, was the same man who, at the time of this group of tales, had announced in his critical study of Nathaniel Hawthorne (1879) that 'the flower of art blooms only where the soil is deep, that it takes a great deal of history to produce a little literature, that it needs a complex social history to set a writer in motion'. Something of the fresh propagandist enthusiasm of a story like *A Passionate Pilgrim*, written in 1870, had already been mildly moderated by the young writer's perception that 'the England of my visions', beneath whose 'acres of rain-deepened greenness a thousand honoured dead lay buried', could also shelter the not so honoured living who had added precious little to their heritage. Much, much later, when returning to his native New York in his sixties, he would discover that even the shallower soil of America could sprout a late growth of colourful pretentious weeds such as clustered around a fashionable hostess in the story *Crapy Cornelia* (1909), whose smile could

twinkle not only with the gleam of her lovely teeth, but with that of all her rings and brooches and bangles and other gew-gaws, to curl and spasmodically cluster as in emulation of her charming complicated yellow tresses, to surround the most animated of pink-and-white, or ruffled and ribboned, of frilled and festooned Dresden china shepherdesses with exactly the right system of curves and convolutions and other flourishes, a perfect bower of painted and gilded and moulded conceits.

The social criticism in our present group of tales is less savage; but it is there, and it gives liveliness and bite to what might otherwise have been too schematic a balancing of superficial national characteristics.

For although these three tales share that general transatlantic theme which was common to so much of James's work, from the earliest stories to the abundant late flowering in *The Ambassadors*, *The Wings of the Dove* and *The Golden Bowl*, each one has its independent point to make, each one presents characters vivid as human beings and not simply samples of national abstractions. The heroine of *An International Episode*, Bessie Alden, may seem to fit the preconceived pattern of an American charmer winning the devotion of an English peer: but it is because of the operation of her purely personal scale of values that, when invited to become Lady Lambeth, she decides that, on the whole, she would prefer not to. *The Pension Beaurepas* may contain, in the persons of the Ruck family, a caricature of hapless wealthy innocents abroad, the father having 'spent his whole time in buying and selling', while his wife and daughter 'have spent theirs, not in selling, but in buying; and they, on their side, know how to do nothing else'. But the contrasting figure of an indigent smug 'culture vulture', hovering with fraudulent enthusiasm over the European heritage, is *also* an American. In presenting the odious pretentiousness of Mrs Church, James has shuffled the cards as if to prove that jokers of this type are present in *both* national packs:

To care only for the best! To do the best, to know the best – to have, to desire, to recognize, only the best. That's what I have always done, in my quiet little way. I have gone through Europe on my devoted little errand, seeking, seeing, heeding, only the best. And it has not been for myself alone· it has been for my daughter ...

As for the substantial novelette *Lady Barberina*, it is true that the young English girl's 'character, like her figure, appeared mainly to have been formed by riding across country', and that the 'firm, tailor-made armour' of her class-conscious conditioning has formed a set of prejudices which ensure that, when transplanted to New York, she can 'neither assimilate nor be assimilated'. But the characters are well enough developed for us to appreciate the sad truth that the incompatibility of Mr Jackson with Lady Barberina Lemon will prove to be not so much that of an American husband with an aristocratic British wife as of a clever husband with a stupid wife.

Early James stories of this type have a deftness of dialogue and a brisk, amusing clarity of description, both quite without need of commentary, which may strike with surprise (and perhaps relief) a reader who has met only 'the later James' of the final period of his working life. Two general points may be illustrated from these slighter products. The first is a simple plea for tolerant acceptance of certain social assumptions of a century ago which strike an outmoded if not positively discordant note today. The second is more positive: there is an opportunity to detect even in these less ambitious works of art the abiding presence of James's compassionate concern for life's victims, whether they be victims of social or economic systems or simply of the unfairness of human life itself.

High social comedy of the type displayed here cannot function unless certain patterns of 'decent behaviour' are taken for granted, any more than tennis can be played without a net or without lines drawn on the court. Half the skill, the fun even, of many characters in James's 'international' tales consists simply in the degree to which they cheat or defy social expectations, whether American or European. We who tend to admit few, if any, conventional rules in the social games we now play may need to make a conscious effort to take seriously, even though we recognize them as hypocritical, some of the dividing-lines crossed by James's wanderers between social or national assumptions.

As for evidence of James's tenderness towards those who humbly oil the wheels of life or stand ineffectually aghast at man's inhumanity to man, it is a pleasure to recognize them even in his lesser works. The pretty young Newport girls 'swaying to and fro in rocking chairs ... and enjoying an enviable exemption from social cares' are a far cry from poor submissive Aurora Church who had lived 'at one time or another, in every *pension* in Europe'. They are all in another world from that inhabited by Lord Canterville, who, if his 'fortune was more ancient than abundant', was nevertheless 'visibly, incontestably, a personage'. To some extent they are all – Americans and Europeans, rich and poor alike – victims of the tribal dances they have been called upon to play. When James is affronted by vulgarity, by coarseness in human assessments, the affront may come from any nation or any class – in the form, perhaps, of 'the modern simper, which was the result of modern nerves'. The sort of young person he liked would prefer 'to do very simple things that are not at all simple'. As simple, perhaps, as that older James who came to see (in the words of *Crapy Cornelia* again), whether in the social or international context, that 'the best manners had been the best kindness'.

Christ's College,   S. GORLEY PUTT
Cambridge

An International Episode

I

Four years ago – in 1874 – two young Englishmen had occasion to go to the United States. They crossed the ocean at midsummer, and, arriving in New York on the first day of August, were much struck with the fervid temperature of that city. Disembarking upon the wharf, they climbed into one of those huge high-hung coaches which convey passengers to the hotels, and with a great deal of bouncing and bumping, took their course through Broadway. The midsummer aspect of New York is not perhaps the most favourable one; still, it is not without its picturesque and even brilliant side. Nothing could well resemble less a typical English street than the interminable avenue, rich in incongruities, through which our two travellers advanced – looking out on each side of them at the comfortable animation of the sidewalks, the high-coloured, hetero-geneous architecture, the huge white marble façades, glittering in the strong, crude light and bedizened with gilded lettering, the multifarious awnings, banners and streamers, the extraordinary number of omnibuses, horse-cars and other democratic vehicles, the vendors of cooling fluids, the white trousers and big straw-hats of the policemen, the tripping gait of the modish young persons on the pavement, the general brightness, newness, juvenility, both of people and things. The young men had exchanged few observa-tions; but in crossing Union Square, in front of the monument to Washington – in the very shadow, indeed, projected by the image of the *pater patriæ* – one of them remarked to the other, 'It seems a rum-looking place.'

'Ah, very odd, very odd,' said the other, who was the clever man of the two.

'Pity it's so beastly hot,' resumed the first speaker, after a pause.

'You know we are in a low latitude,' said his friend.

'I daresay,' remarked the other.

'I wonder,' said the second speaker, presently, 'if they can give one a bath.'

'I daresay not,' rejoined the other.

'Oh, I say!' cried his comrade.

This animated discussion was checked by their arrival at the hotel, which had been recommended to them by an American gentleman whose acquaintance they made – with whom, indeed, they became very intimate – on the steamer, and who had proposed to accompany them to the inn and introduce them, in a friendly way, to the proprietor. This plan, however, had been defeated by their friend's finding that his 'partner' was awaiting him on the wharf, and that his commercial associate desired him instantly to come and give his attention to certain telegrams received from St Louis. But the two Englishmen, with nothing but their national prestige and personal graces to recommend them, were very well received at the hotel, which had an air of capacious hospitality. They found that a bath was not unattainable, and were indeed struck with the facilities for prolonged and reiterated immersion with which their apartment was supplied. After bathing a good deal – more indeed than they had ever done before on a single occasion – they made their way into the dining-room of the hotel, which was a spacious restaurant, with a fountain in the middle, a great many tall plants in ornamental tubs, and an array of French waiters. The first dinner on land, after a sea-voyage, is under any circumstances a delightful occasion, and there was something particularly agreeable in the circumstances in which our young Englishmen found themselves. They were extremely good-natured young men; they were more observant than they appeared; in a sort of inarticulate, accidentally dissimulative fashion, they were highly appreciative. This was perhaps especially the case with the elder, who was also, as I have said, the man of talent. They sat down at a little table which was a very different affair from the great clattering see-saw in the saloon of the steamer. The wide doors and windows of the restaurant stood open, beneath large awnings, to a wide pavement, where there were other plants in tubs, and rows of spreading trees, and beyond which there was a large shady square, without any palings and with marble-paved walks. And above the vivid verdure rose other façades of white marble and of pale chocolate-coloured stone, squaring themselves against the deep blue sky. Here, outside, in the light and the shade and the heat, there was a great tinkling of the bells of innumerable street-cars, and a constant strolling and shuffling and rustling of many pedestrians, a large proportion of whom were young women in Pompadour-looking dresses. Within, the place was cool and vaguely-lighted; with the plash of water, the odour of flowers and the flitting of French waiters, as I have said, upon soundless carpets.

'It's rather like Paris, you know,' said the younger of our two travellers.

'It's like Paris – only more so,' his companion rejoined.

'I suppose it's the French waiters,' said the first speaker. 'Why don't they have French waiters in London?'

'Fancy a French waiter at a club,' said his friend.

The young Englishman stared a little, as if he could not fancy it. 'In Paris I'm very apt to dine at a place where there's an English waiter. Don't you know, what's-his-name's, close to the thing-umbob? They always set an English waiter at me. I suppose they think I can't speak French.'

'No more you can.' And the elder of the young Englishmen unfolded his napkin.

His companion took no notice whatever of this declaration. 'I say,' he resumed, in a moment, 'I suppose we must learn to speak American. I suppose we must take lessons.'

'I can't understand them,' said the clever man.

'What the deuce is *he* saying?' asked his comrade, appealing from the French waiter.

'He is recommending some soft shell crabs,' said the clever man.

And so, in desultory observation of the idiosyncrasies of the new society in which they found themselves, the young Englishmen proceeded to dine – going in largely, as the phrase is, for cooling draughts and dishes, of which their attendant offered them a very long list. After dinner they went out and slowly walked about the neighbouring streets. The early dusk of waning summer was coming on, but the heat was still very great. The pavements were hot even to the stout boot-soles of the British travellers, and the trees along the kerb-stone emitted strange exotic odours. The young men wandered through the adjoining square – that queer place without palings, and with marble walks arranged in black and white lozenges. There were a great many benches, crowded with shabby-looking people and the travellers remarked, very justly, that it was not much like Belgrave Square. On one side was an enormous hotel, lifting up into the hot darkness an immense array of open, brightly-lighted windows. At the base of this populous structure was an eternal jangle of horse-cars, and all round it, in the upper dusk, was a sinister hum of mosquitoes. The ground-floor of the hotel seemed to be a huge transparent cage, flinging a wide glare of gaslight into the street. of which it formed a sort of public adjunct, absorbing and emitting the passers-by promiscuously. The young Englishmen went in with every one else, from curiosity, and saw a couple of hundred men sitting on divans along a great marble-paved corridor, with their legs stretched out, together with several dozen more standing in a *queue*, as at the ticket-office of a railway station, before a brilliantly-illuminated counter, of vast extent. These latter persons, who carried portmanteaux in their hands, had a dejected, exhausted look: their garments were not very fresh, and they seemed to be rendering some mysterious tribute to a magnificent young man with a waxed moustache and a shirt front adorned with diamond buttons. who every now and then dropped an absent glance over their multitudinous patience. They were American citizens doing homage to an hotel-clerk.

'I'm glad he didn't tell us to go there,' said one of our Englishmen, alluding to their friend on the steamer, who had told them so many things. They walked up the Fifth Avenue, where, for instance, he had told them that all the first families lived. But the first families were out of town, and our young travellers had only the satisfaction of seeing some of the second – or perhaps even the third – taking the evening air upon balconies and high flights of doorsteps, in the streets which radiate from the more ornamental thoroughfare. They went a little way down one of these side-streets, and they saw young ladies in white dresses – charming-looking persons – seated in graceful attitudes on the chocolate-coloured steps. In one or two places these young ladies were conversing across the street with other young ladies seated in similar postures and costumes in front of the opposite houses. and in the warm night air their colloquial tones sounded strange in the ears of the young Englishmen. One of our friends, nevertheless – the younger one – intimated that he felt a disposition to intercept a few of these soft familiarities; but his companion observed, pertinently enough, that he had better be careful. 'We must not begin with making mistakes,' said his companion.

'But he told us, you know – he told us,' urged the young man, alluding again to the friend on the steamer.

'Never mind what he told us!' answered his comrade, who, if he had greater talents, was also apparently more of a moralist.

By bed-time – in their impatience to taste of a terrestrial couch again our seafarers went to bed early – it was still insufferably hot, and the buzz of the mosquitoes at the open windows might have passed for an audible crepitation of the temperature. 'We can't stand this, you know,' the young Englishmen said to each other; and they tossed about all night more boisterously than they had tossed upon the Atlantic billows. On the morrow, their first thought was that they would re-embark that day for England; and then it occurred to them that they might find an asylum nearer at hand. The cave of Æolus became their ideal of comfort, and they wondered where the Americans went when they wished to cool off. They had not the least idea, and they determined to apply for information to Mr J. L. Westgate. This was the name inscribed in a bold hand on the back of a letter carefully preserved in the pocket-book of our junior traveller. Beneath the address, in the left-hand corner of the envelope, were the words, 'Introducing Lord Lambeth and Percy Beaumont, Esq.' The letter had been given to the two Englishmen by a good friend of theirs in London, who had been in America two years previously and had singled out Mr J. L. Westgate from the many friends he had left there as the consignee, as it were, of his compatriots. 'He is a capital fellow,' the Englishman in London had said, 'and he has got an awfully pretty wife. He's tremendously hospitable – he will do everything in the world for you; and as he knows every one over there, it is quite needless I should give you any other introduction. He will make you see every one; trust to him for putting you into circulation. He has got a tremendously pretty wife.' It was natural that in the hour of tribulation Lord Lambeth and Mr Percy Beaumont should have bethought themselves of a gentleman whose attractions had been thus vividly depicted; all the more so that he lived in the Fifth Avenue and that the Fifth Avenue, as they had ascertained the night before, was contiguous to their hotel. 'Ten to one he'll be out of town,' said Percy Beaumont; 'but we can at least find out where he has gone, and we can immediately start in pursuit. He can't possibly have gone to a hotter place. you know.'

'Oh, there's only one hotter place,' said Lord Lambeth, 'and I hope he hasn't gone there.'

They strolled along the shady side of the street to the number indicated upon the precious letter. The house presented an imposing chocolate-coloured expanse, relieved by facings and window-cornices of florid sculpture, and by a couple of dusty rose-trees. which clambered over the balconies and the portico. This last-mentioned feature was approached by a monumental flight of steps.

'Rather better than a London house,' said Lord Lambeth, looking down from this altitude, after they had rung the bell.

'It depends upon what London house you mean,' replied his companion. 'You have a tremendous chance to get wet between the house-door and your carriage.'

'Well,' said Lord Lambeth, glancing at the burning heavens, 'I 'guess" it doesn't rain so much here!'

The door was opened by a long negro in a white jacket, who grinned familiarly when Lord Lambeth asked for Mr Westgate.

'He ain't at home, sir; he's down town at his o'fice.'

'Oh, at his office?' said the visitors. 'And when will he be at home?'

'Well, sir, when he goes out dis way in de mo'ning, he ain't liable to come home all day.'

This was discouraging; but the address of Mr Westgate's office was freely imparted by the intelligent black, and was taken down by Percy Beaumont in his pocket-book. The two gentlemen then returned, languidly, to their hotel, and sent for a hackney-coach; and in this commodious vehicle they rolled comfortably down town. They measured the whole length of Broadway again, and found it a path of fire; and then, deflecting to the left, they were deposited by their conductor before a fresh, light, ornamental structure, ten stories high, in a street crowded with keen-faced, light-limbed young men, who were running about very quickly and stopping each other eagerly at corners and in doorways. Passing into this brilliant building. they were introduced by one of the keen-faced young men – he was a charming fellow. in wonderful cream-coloured garments and a hat with a blue ribbon, who had evidently perceived them to be aliens and helpless – to a very snug hydraulic elevator, in which they took their place with many other persons, and which, shooting upward in its vertical socket, presently projected them into the seventh horizontal compartment of the edifice. Here, after brief delay, they found themselves face to face with the friend of their friend in London. His office was composed of several different rooms, and they waited very silently in one of these after they had sent in their letter and their cards. The letter was not one which it would take Mr Westgate very long to read, but he came out to speak to them more instantly than they could have expected; he had evidently jumped up from his work. He was a tall, lean personage, and was dressed all in fresh white linen; he had a thin, sharp, familiar face, with an expression that was at one and the same time sociable and businesslike, a quick, intelligent eye, and a large brown moustache, which concealed his mouth and made his chin, beneath it, look small. Lord Lambeth thought he looked tremendously clever.

'How do you do, Lord Lambeth – how do you do, sir?' he said, holding the open letter in his hand. 'I'm very glad to see you – I hope you're very well. You had better come in here – I think it's cooler'; and he led the way into another room, where there were law-books and papers, and windows wide open beneath striped awnings. Just opposite one of the windows, on a line with his eyes, Lord Lambeth observed the weather-vane of a church steeple. The uproar of the street sounded infinitely far below, and Lord Lambeth felt very high in the air. 'I say it's cooler,' pursued their host, 'but everything is relative. How do you stand the heat?'

'I can't say we like it,' said Lord Lambeth; 'but Beaumont likes it better than I.'

'Well, it won't last,' Mr Westgate very cheerfully declared; 'nothing unpleasant lasts over here. It was very hot when Captain Littledale was here; he did nothing but drink sherry-cobblers. He expresses some doubt in his letter whether I shall remember him – as if I didn't remember making six sherry-cobblers for him one day, in about twenty minutes. I hope you left him well; two years having elapsed since then.'

'Oh, yes, he's all right,' said Lord Lambeth.

'I am always very glad to see your countrymen,' Mr Westgate pursued. 'I thought it would be time some of you should be coming along. A friend of mine was saying to me only a day or two ago, "It's time for the water-melons and the Englishmen." '

'The Englishmen and the water-melons just now are about the same thing,' Percy Beaumont observed, wiping his dripping forehead.

'Ah, well, we'll put you on ice, as we do the melons. You must go down to Newport.'

'We'll go anywhere!' said Lord Lambeth.

'Yes, you want to go to Newport – that's what you want to do,' Mr Westgate affirmed. 'But let's see – when did you get here?'

'Only yesterday,' said Percy Beaumont.

'Ah, yes, by the "Russia". Where are you staying?'

'At the "Hanover", I think they call it.'

'Pretty comfortable?' inquired Mr Westgate.

'It seems a capital place, but I can't say we like the gnats,' said Lord Lambeth.

Mr Westgate stared and laughed. 'Oh, no, of course you don't like the gnats. We shall expect you to like a good many things over here, but we shan't insist upon your liking the gnats; though certainly you'll admit that, as gnats, they are fine, eh? But you oughtn't to remain in the city.'

'So we think,' said Lord Lambeth. 'If you would kindly suggest something –'

'Suggest something, my dear sir?' – and Mr Westgate looked at him, narrowing his eyelids. 'Open your mouth and shut your eyes! Leave it to me, and I'll put you through. It's a matter of national pride with me that all Englishmen should have a good time; and, as I have had considerable practice, I have learned to minister to their wants. I find they generally want the right thing. So just please to consider yourselves my property; and if any one should try to appropriate you, please to say, "Hands off; too late for the market." But let's see,' continued the American, in his slow, humorous voice, with a distinctness of utterance which appeared to his visitors to be part of a facetious intention – a strangely leisurely, speculative voice for a man evidently so busy and, as they felt, so professional – 'let's see; are you going to make something of a stay, Lord Lambeth?'

'Oh dear no,' said the young Englishman; 'my cousin was coming over on some business, so I just came across, at an hour's notice, for the lark.'

'Is it your first visit to the United States?'

'Oh dear, yes.'

'I was obliged to come on some business,' said Percy Beaumont, 'and I brought Lambeth with me.'

'And *you* have been here before, sir?'

'Never – never.'

'I thought, from your referring to business –' said Mr Westgate.

'Oh, you see I'm by way of being a barrister,' Percy Beaumont answered. 'I know some people that think of bringing a suit against one of your railways, and they asked me to come over and take measures accordingly.'

Mr Westgate gave one of his slow, keen looks again. 'What's your railroad?' he asked.

'The Tennessee Central.'

The American tilted back his chair a little, and poised it an instant. 'Well, I'm sorry you want to attack one of our institutions,' he said, smiling. 'But I guess you had better enjoy yourself *first!*'

'I'm certainly rather afraid I can't work in this weather,' the young barrister confessed.

'Leave that to the natives,' said Mr Westgate. 'Leave the Tennessee Central to me, Mr Beaumont. Some day we'll talk it over, and I guess I can make it square. But I didn't know you Englishmen ever did any work, in the upper classes.'

'Oh, we do a lot of work; don't we, Lambeth?' asked Percy Beaumont.

'I must certainly be at home by the 19th of September,' said the younger Englishman, irrelevantly, but gently.

'For the shooting, eh? or is it the hunting – or the fishing?' inquired his entertainer.

'Oh, I must be in Scotland,' said Lord Lambeth, blushing a little.

'Well, then,' rejoined Mr Westgate, 'you had better amuse yourself first, also. You must go down and see Mrs Westgate.'

'We should be so happy – if you would kindly tell us the train,' said Percy Beaumont.

'It isn't a train – it's a boat.'

'Oh, I see. And what is the name of – a – the – a – town?'

'It isn't a town, said Mr Westgate, laughing. 'It's a – well, what shall I call it? It's a watering-place. In short, it's Newport. You'll see what it is. It's cool; that's the principal thing. You will greatly oblige me by going down there and putting yourself into the hands of Mrs Westgate. It isn't perhaps for me to say it; but you couldn't be in better hands. Also in those of her sister, who is staying with her. She is very fond of Englishmen. She thinks there is nothing like them.'

'Mrs Westgate or – a – her sister?' asked Percy Beaumont, modestly, yet in the tone of an inquiring traveller.

'Oh, I mean my wife,' said Mr Westgate. 'I don't suppose my sister-in-law knows much about them. She has always led a very quiet life; she has lived in Boston.'

Percy Beaumont listened with interest. 'That, I believe,' he said, 'is the most – a – intellectual town?'

'I believe it is very intellectual. I don't go there much,' responded his host.

'I say, we ought to go there,' said Lord Lambeth to his companion.

'Oh, Lord Lambeth, wait till the great heat is over!' Mr Westgate interposed. 'Boston in this weather would be very trying; it's not the temperature for intellectual exertion. At Boston, you know, you have to pass an examination at the city limits; and when you come away they give you a kind of degree.'

Lord Lambeth stared, blushing a little; and Percy Beaumont stared a little also – but only with his fine natural complexion: glancing aside after a moment to see that his companion was not looking too credulous, for he had heard a great deal about American humour. 'I daresay it is very jolly,' said the younger gentleman.

'I daresay it is,' said Mr Westgate. 'Only I must impress upon you that at present – to-morrow morning, at an early hour – you will be expected at Newport. We have a house there; half the people in New York go there for the summer. I am not sure that at this very moment my wife can take you in; she has got a lot of people staying with her; I don't know who they all are; only she may have no room. But you can begin with the hotel, and meanwhile you can live at my house. In that way – simply sleeping at the hotel – you will find it tolerable. For the rest, you must make yourself at home at my

22

place. You mustn't be shy, you know; if you are only here for a month that will be a great waste of time. Mrs Westgate won't neglect you, and you had better not try to resist her. I know something about that. I expect you'll find some pretty girls on the premises. I shall write to my wife by this afternoon's mail, and to-morrow she and Miss Alden will look out for you. Just walk right in and make yourself comfortable. Your steamer leaves from this part of the city, and I will immediately send out and get you a cabin. Then, at half-past four o'clock, just call for me here, and I will go with you and put you on board. It's a big boat; you might get lost. A few days hence, at the end of the week, I will come down to Newport and see how you are getting on.'

The two young Englishmen inaugurated the policy of not resist-ing Mrs Westgate by submitting, with great docility and thankful-ness, to her husband. He was evidently a very good fellow, and he made an impression upon his visitors; his hospitality seemed to recommend itself, consciously – with a friendly wink, as it were – as if it hinted, judicially, that you could not possibly make a better bargain. Lord Lambeth and his cousin left their entertainer to his labours and returned to their hotel, where they spent three or four hours in their respective shower-baths. Percy Beaumont had sug-gested that they ought to see something of the town; but 'Oh, damn the town!' his noble kinsman had rejoined. They returned to Mr Westgate's office in a carriage, with their luggage, very punctually; but it must be reluctantly recorded that, this time, he kept them waiting so long that they felt themselves missing the steamer and were deterred only by an amiable modesty from dispensing with his attendance and starting on a hasty scramble to the wharf. But when at last he appeared, and the carriage plunged into the purlieus of Broadway, they jolted and jostled to such good purpose that they reached the huge white vessel while the bell for departure was still ringing and the absorption of passengers still active. It was indeed, as Mr Westgate had said, a big boat, and his leadership in the innumerable and interminable corridors and cabins, with which he seemed perfectly acquainted, and of which any one and every one appeared to have the *entrée*, was very grateful to the slightly bewildered voyagers. He showed them their state-room – a spacious apartment, embellished with gas-lamps, mirrors *en pied* and sculptured furniture – and then, long after they had been intimately convinced that the steamer was in motion and launched upon the unknown stream that they were about to navigate, he bade them a sociable farewell.

'Well, good-bye, Lord Lambeth,' he said. 'Good-bye, Mr Percy Beaumont; I hope you'll have a good time. Just let them do what they want with you. I'll come down by-and-by and look after you.'

2

The young Englishmen emerged from their cabin and amused themselves with wandering about the immense labyrinthine steamer, which struck them as an extraordinary mixture of a ship and an hotel. It was densely crowded with passengers, the larger number of whom appeared to be ladies and very young children; and in the big saloons, ornamented in white and gold, which followed each other in surprising succession, beneath the swinging gas-lights and among the small side-passages where the negro domestics of both sexes assembled with an air of philosophic leisure, every one was moving to and fro and exchanging loud and familiar observations. Eventually, at the instance of a discriminating black, our young men went and had some 'supper', in a wonderful place arranged like a theatre, where, in a gilded gallery upon which little boxes appeared to open, a large orchestra was playing operatic selections, and, below, people were handing about bills of fare, as if they had been programmes. All this was sufficiently curious; but the agreeable thing, later, was to sit out on one of the great white decks of the steamer, in the warm, breezy darkness, and, in the vague starlight, to make out the line of low, mysterious coast. The young Englishmen tried American cigars – those of Mr Westgate – and talked together as they usually talked, with many odd silences, lapses of logic and incongruities of transition; like people who have grown old together and learned to supply each other's missing phrases; or, more especially, like people thoroughly conscious of a common point of view, so that a style of conversation superficially lacking in finish might suffice for a reference to a fund of associations in the light of which everything was all right.

'We really seem to be going out to sea,' Percy Beaumont observed. 'Upon my word, we are going back to England. He has shipped us off again. I call that "real mean".'

'I suppose it's all right,' said Lord Lambeth. 'I want to see those pretty girls at Newport. You know he told us the place was an island; and aren't all islands in the sea?'

'Well,' resumed the elder traveller after a while, 'if his house is as good as his cigars, we shall do very well.'

'He seems a very good fellow,' said Lord Lambeth, as if this idea had just occurred to him.

'I say, we had better remain at the inn,' rejoined his companion, presently. 'I don't think I like the way he spoke of his house. I don't like stopping in the house with such a tremendous lot of women.'

'Oh, I don't mind,' said Lord Lambeth. And then they smoked awhile in silence. 'Fancy his thinking we do no work in England!' the young man resumed.

'I daresay he didn't really think so,' said Percy Beaumont.

'Well, I guess they don't know much about England over here!' declared Lord Lambeth, humorously. And then there was another long pause. 'He was devilish civil,' observed the young nobleman.

'Nothing, certainly, could have been more civil,' rejoined his companion.

'Littledale said his wife was great fun,' said Lord Lambeth.

'Whose wife – Littledale's?'

'This American's – Mrs Westgate. What's his name? J.L.'

Beaumont was silent a moment. 'What was fun to Littledale,' he said at last, rather sententiously, 'may be death to us.'

'What do you mean by that?' asked his kinsman. 'I am as good a man as Littledale.'

'My dear boy, I hope you won't begin to flirt,' said Percy Beaumont.

'I don't care. I daresay I shan't begin.'

'With a married woman, if she's bent upon it, it's all very well,' Beaumont expounded. 'But our friend mentioned a young lady – a sister, a sister-in-law. For God's sake, don't get entangled with her.'

'How do you mean, entangled?'

'Depend upon it she will try to hook you.'

'Oh, bother!' said Lord Lambeth.

'American girls are very clever,' urged his companion.

'So much the better,' the young man declared.

'I fancy they are always up to some game of that sort,' Beaumont continued.

'They can't be worse than they are in England,' said Lord Lambeth, judicially.

'Ah, but in England,' replied Beaumont, 'you have got your natural protectors. You have got your mother and sisters.'

'My mother and sisters –' began the young nobleman, with a certain energy. But he stopped in time, puffing at his cigar.

'Your mother spoke to me about it, with tears in her eyes,' said Percy Beaumont. 'She said she felt very nervous. I promised to keep you out of mischief.'

'You had better take care of yourself,' said the object of maternal and ducal solicitude.

'Ah,' rejoined the young barrister, 'I haven't the expectation of a hundred thousand a year – not to mention other attractions.'

'Well,' said Lord Lambeth, 'don't cry out before you're hurt!'

It was certainly very much cooler at Newport, where our travellers found themselves assigned to a couple of diminutive bedrooms in a far-away angle of an immense hotel. They had gone ashore in the early summer twilight, and had very promptly put themselves to bed; thanks to which circumstance and to their having, during the previous hours, in their commodious cabin, slept the sleep of youth and health, they began to feel, towards eleven o'clock, very alert and inquisitive. They looked out of their windows across a row of small green fields, bordered with low stone dykes, of rude construction, and saw a deep blue ocean lying beneath a deep blue sky and flecked now and then with scintillating patches of foam. A strong, fresh breeze came in through the curtainless casements and prompted our young men to observe, generously, that it didn't seem half a bad climate. They made other observations after they had emerged from their rooms in pursuit of breakfast – a meal of which they partook in a huge bare hall, where a hundred negroes, in white jackets, were shuffling about upon an uncarpeted floor; where the flies were superabundant and the tables and dishes covered over with a strange, voluminous integument of coarse blue gauze; and where several little boys and girls, who had risen late, were seated in fastidious solitude at the morning repast. These young persons had not the morning paper before them, but they were engaged in languid perusal of the bill of fare.

This latter document was a great puzzle to our friends, who, on reflecting that its bewildering categories had relation to breakfast alone, had an uneasy prevision of an encyclopædic dinner-list. They found a great deal of entertainment at the hotel, an enormous wooden structure, for the erection of which it seemed to them that the virgin forests of the West must have been terribly deflowered. It was perforated from end to end with immense bare corridors, through which a strong draught was blowing – bearing along wonderful figures of ladies in white morning-dresses and clouds of Valenciennes lace, who seemed to float down the long vistas with expanded furbelows, like angels spreading their wings. In front was a gigantic verandah, upon which an army might have encamped – a vast wooden terrace, with a roof as lofty as the nave of a cathedral. Here our young Englishmen enjoyed, as they supposed, a glimpse of American society, which was distributed over the measureless expanse in a variety of sedentary attitudes, and appeared to consist largely of pretty young girls, dressed as if for a *fête champêtre*, swaying to and fro in rocking-chairs, fanning themselves with large straw fans, and enjoying an enviable exemption from social cares. Lord Lambeth had a theory, which it might be interesting to trace to its origin, that it would be not only agreeable, but easily possible, to enter into relations with one of these young ladies; and his companion found occasion to check the young nobleman's colloquial impulses.

'You had better take care,' said Percy Beaumont, 'or you will have an offended father or brother pulling out a bowie-knife.'

'I assure you it is all right,' Lord Lambeth replied. 'You know the Americans come to these big hotels to make acquaintances.'

'I know nothing about it, and neither do you,' said his kinsman, who, like a clever man, had begun to perceive that the observation of American society demanded a readjustment of one's standard.

'Hang it, then, let's find out!' cried Lord Lambeth with some impatience. 'You know, I don't want to miss anything.'

'We will find out,' said Percy Beaumont, very reasonably. 'We will go and see Mrs Westgate and make all the proper inquiries.'

And so the two inquiring Englishmen, who had this lady's address inscribed in her husband's hand upon a card, descended from the verandah of the big hotel and took their way, according to direction, along a large straight road, past a series of fresh-looking villas, embosomed in shrubs and flowers and enclosed in an ingenious variety of wooden palings. The morning was brilliant and cool, the villas were smart and snug, and the walk of the young travellers was very entertaining. Everything looked as if it had received a coat of fresh paint the day before – the red roofs, the green shutters, the clean, bright browns and buffs of the house-fronts. The flower-beds on the little lawns seemed to sparkle in the radiant air, and the gravel in the short carriage-sweeps to flash and twinkle. Along the road came a hundred little basket-phaetons, in which, almost always, a couple of ladies were sitting — ladies in white dresses and long white gloves, holding the reins and looking at the two Englishmen, whose nationality was not elusive, through thick blue veils, tied tightly about their faces as if to guard their complexions. At last the young men came within sight of the sea again, and then, having interrogated a gardener over the paling of a villa, they turned into an open gate. Here they found themselves face to face with the ocean and with a very picturesque structure, resembling a magnified *chalet*, which was perched upon a green embankment just above it. The house had a verandah of extraordinary width all around it, and a great many doors and windows standing open to the verandah. These various apertures had, in common, such an accessible, hospitable air, such a breezy flutter, within, of light curtains, such expansive thresholds and reassuring interiors, that our friends hardly knew which was the regular entrance, and, after hesitating a moment, presented themselves at one of the windows. The room within was dark, but in a moment a graceful figure vaguely shaped itself in the rich-looking gloom, and a lady came to meet them. Then they saw that she had been seated at a table, writing, and that she had heard them and had got up. She stepped out into the light; she wore a frank, charming smile, with which she held out her hand to Percy Beaumont.

'Oh, you must be Lord Lambeth and Mr Beaumont,' she said. 'I have heard from my husband that you would come. I am extremely glad to see you.' And she shook hands with each of her visitors. Her visitors were a little shy, but they had very good manners; they responded with smiles and exclamations, and they apologised for not knowing the front door. The lady rejoined, with vivacity, that when she wanted to see people very much she did not insist upon those distinctions, and that Mr Westgate had written to her of his English friends in terms that made her really anxious. 'He said you were so terribly prostrated,' said Mrs Westgate.

'Oh, you mean by the heat?' replied Percy Beaumont. 'We were rather knocked up, but we feel wonderfully better. We had such a jolly – a – voyage down here. It's so very good of you to mind.'

'Yes, it's so very kind of you,' murmured Lord Lambeth.

Mrs Westgate stood smiling; she was extremely pretty. 'Well, I did mind,' she said; 'and I thought of sending for you this morning, to the Ocean House. I am very glad you are better, and I am charmed you have arrived. You must come round to the other side of the piazza.' And she led the way, with a light, smooth step, looking back at the young men and smiling.

The other side of the piazza was, as Lord Lambeth presently remarked, a very jolly place. It was of the most liberal proportions, and with its awnings, its fanciful chairs, its cushions and rugs, its view of the ocean, close at hand, tumbling along the base of the low cliffs whose level tops intervened in lawnlike smoothness, it formed a charming complement to the drawing-room. As such it was in course of use at the present moment; it was occupied by a social circle. There were several ladies and two or three gentlemen, to whom Mrs Westgate proceeded to introduce the distinguished strangers. She mentioned a great many names, very freely and distinctly: the young Englishmen, shuffling about and bowing, were rather bewildered. But at last they were provided with chairs – low wicker chairs, gilded and tied with a great many ribbons – and one of the ladies (a very young person, with a little snub nose and several dimples) offered Percy Beaumont a fan. The fan was also adorned with pink love-knots; but Percy Beaumont declined it, although he was very hot. Presently, however, it became cooler; the breeze from the sea was delicious, the view was charming, and the people sitting there looked exceedingly fresh and comfortable. Several of the ladies seemed to be young girls, and the gentlemen were slim, fair youths, such as our friends had seen the day before in New York. The ladies were working upon bands of tapestry, and one of the young men had an open book in his lap. Beaumont afterwards learned from one of the ladies that this young man had been reading aloud – that he was from Boston and was very fond of reading aloud. Beaumont said it was a great pity that they had interrupted him; he should like so much (from all he had heard) to hear a Bostonian read. Couldn't the young man be induced to go on?

'Oh no,' said his informant, very freely; 'he wouldn't be able to get the young ladies to attend to him now.'

There was something very friendly, Beaumont perceived, in the attitude of the company; they looked at the young Englishmen with an air of animated sympathy and interest; they smiled, brightly and unanimously, at everything either of the visitors said. Lord Lambeth and his companion felt that they were being made very welcome. Mrs Westgate seated herself between them, and, talking a great deal to each, they had occasion to observe that she was as pretty as their friend Littledale had promised. She was thirty years old, with the eyes and the smile of a girl of seventeen, and she was extremely light and graceful, elegant, exquisite. Mrs Westgate was extremely spontaneous. She was very frank and demonstrative, and appeared always – while she looked at you delightedly with her beautiful young eyes – to be making sudden confessions and concessions, after momentary hesitations.

'We shall expect to see a great deal of you,' she said to Lord Lambeth, with a kind of joyous earnestness. 'We are very fond of Englishmen here; that is, there are a great many we have been fond of. After a day or two you must come and stay with us; we hope you will stay a long time. Newport's a very nice place when you come really to know it, when you know plenty of people. Of course, you and Mr Beaumont will have no difficulty about that. Englishmen are very well received here; there are almost always two or three of them about. I think they always like it, and I must say I should think they would. They receive ever so much attention. I must say I think they sometimes get spoiled; but I am sure you and Mr Beaumont are proof against that. My husband tells me you are a friend of Captain Littledale; he was such a charming man. He made himself most agreeable here, and I am sure I wonder he didn't stay. It couldn't have been pleasanter for him in his own country. Though I suppose it is very pleasant in England, for English people. I don't know myself; I have been there very little. I have been a great deal abroad, but I am always on the Continent. I must say I'm extremely fond of Paris; you know we Americans always are; we go there when we die. Did you ever hear that before? that was said by a great wit. I mean the good Americans; but we are all good; you'll see that for yourself. All I know of England is London, and all I know of London is that place – on that little corner, you know, where you buy jackets – jackets with that coarse braid and those big buttons. They make very good jackets in London, I will do you the justice to say that. And some people like the hats; but about the hats I was always a heretic; I always got my hats in Paris. You can't wear an English hat – at least, I never could – unless you dress your hair *à l'Anglaise*; and I must say that is a talent I never possessed. In Paris they will make things to suit your peculiarities; but in England I think you like much more to have – how shall I say it? – one thing for everybody. I mean as regards dress. I don't know about other things; but I have always supposed that in other things everything was different. I mean according to the people – according to the classes, and all that. I am afraid you will think that I don't take a very favourable view; but you know you can't take a very favourable view in Dover Street, in the month of November. That has always been my fate. Do you know Jones's Hotel, in Dover Street? That's all I know of England. Of course, every one admits that the English hotels are your weak point. There was always the most frightful fog; I couldn't see to try my things on. When I got over to America – into the light – I usually found they were twice too big. The next time I mean to go in the season; I think I shall go next year. I want very much to take my sister; she has never been to England. I don't know whether you know what I mean by saying that the Englishmen who come here sometimes get spoiled. I mean that they take things as a matter of course – things that are done for them. Now, naturally, they are only a matter of course when the Englishmen are very nice. But, of course, they are almost always very nice. Of course, this isn't nearly such an interesting country as England; there are not nearly so many things to see, and we haven't your country life. I have never seen anything of your country life; when I am in Europe I am always on the Continent. But I have heard a great deal about it; I know that when you are among yourselves in the country you have the most beautiful time. Of course, we have nothing of that sort, we have nothing on that scale. I don't apologise, Lord Lambeth; some Americans are always apologising; you must have noticed that. We have the reputation of always boasting and bragging and waving the American flag; but I must say that what strikes me is that we are perpetually making excuses and trying to smooth things over. The American flag has quite gone out of fashion; it's very carefully folded up, like an old table-cloth. Why should we apologise? The English never apologise – do they? No, I must say I never apologise. You must take us as we come – with all our imperfections on our heads. Of course we haven't your country life, and your old ruins, and your great estates, and your leisure-class, and all that. But if we haven't, I should think you might find it a pleasant change – I think any country is pleasant where they have pleasant manners. Captain Littledale told me he had never seen such pleasant manners as at Newport; and he had been a great deal in European society. Hadn't he been in the diplomatic service? He told me the dream of his life was to get appointed to a diplomatic post in Washington. But he doesn't seem to have succeeded. I suppose that in England promotion – and all that sort of thing – is fearfully slow. With us, you know, it's a great deal too fast. You see I admit our drawbacks. But I must confess I think Newport is an ideal place. I don't know anything like it anywhere. Captain Littledale told me he didn't know anything like it anywhere. It's entirely different from most watering-places; it's a most charming life. I must say I think that when one goes to a foreign country, one ought to enjoy the differences. Of course there are differences; otherwise what did one come abroad for? Look for your pleasure in the differences, Lord Lambeth; that's the way to do it; and then I am sure you will find American society – at least Newport society – most charming and most interesting. I wish very much my husband were here; but he's dreadfully confined to New York. I suppose you think that's very strange – for a gentleman. Only you see we haven't any leisure-class.'

Mrs Westgate's discourse, delivered in a soft, sweet voice, flowed on like a miniature torrent and was interrupted by a hundred little smiles, glances and gestures, which might have figured the irregularities and obstructions of such a stream. Lord Lambeth listened to her with, it must be confessed, a rather ineffectual attention, although he indulged in a good many little murmurs and ejaculations of assent and deprecation. He had no great faculty for apprehending generalisations. There were some three or four indeed which, in the play of his own intelligence, he had originated, and which had seemed convenient at the moment; but at the present time he could hardly have been said to follow Mrs Westgate as she darted gracefully about in the sea of speculation. Fortunately she asked for no especial rejoinder, for she looked about at the rest of the company as well, and smiled at Percy Beaumont, on the other side of her, as if he too must understand her and agree with her. He was rather more successful than his companion; for besides being, as we know, cleverer, his attention was not vaguely distracted by close vicinity to a remarkably interesting young girl, with dark hair and blue eyes. This was the case with Lord Lambeth, to whom it occurred after a while that the young girl with blue eyes and dark hair was the pretty sister of whom Mrs Westgate had spoken. She presently turned to him with a remark which established her identity.

'It's a great pity you couldn't have brought my brother-in-law with you. It's a great shame he should be in New York in these days.'

'Oh yes; it's so very hot,' said Lord Lambeth.

'It must be dreadful,' said the young girl.

'I daresay he is very busy,' Lord Lambeth observed.

'The gentlemen in America work too much,' the young girl went on.

'Oh, do they? I daresay they like it,' said her interlocutor.

'I don't like it. One never sees them.'

'Don't you, really?' asked Lord Lambeth. 'I shouldn't have fancied that.'

'Have you come to study American manners?' asked the young girl.

'Oh, I don't know. I just came over for a lark. I haven't got long.' Here there was a pause, and Lord Lambeth began again. 'But Mr Westgate will come down here, will not he?'

'I certainly hope he will. He must help to entertain you and Mr Beaumont.'

Lord Lambeth looked at her a little with his handsome brown eyes. 'Do you suppose he would have come down with us, if we had urged him?'

Mr Westgate's sister-in-law was silent a moment, and then – 'I daresay he would,' she answered.

'Really!' said the young Englishman. 'He was immensely civil to Beaumont and me,' he added.

'He is a dear good fellow,' the young lady rejoined. 'And he is a perfect husband. But all Americans are that,' she continued, smiling.

'Really!' Lord Lambeth exclaimed again; and wondered whether all American ladies had such a passion for generalising as these two.

3

He sat there a good while: there was a great deal of talk; it was all very
friendly and lively and jolly. Every one present, sooner or later, said
something to him, and seemed to make a particular point of addressing him by name. Two or three other persons came in, and there was
a shifting of seats and changing of places; the gentlemen all entered
into intimate conversation with the two Englishmen, made them
urgent offers of hospitality and hoped they might frequently be of
service to them. They were afraid Lord Lambeth and Mr Beaumont
were not very comfortable at their hotel – that it was not, as one of
them said, 'so private as those dear little English inns of yours'. This
last gentlemen went on to say that unfortunately, as yet, perhaps,
privacy was not quite so easily obtained in America as might be
desired; still, he continued, you could generally get it by paying for
it; in fact you could get everything in America nowadays by paying
for it. American life was certainly growing a great deal more private;
it was growing very much like England. Everything at Newport, for
instance, was thoroughly private; Lord Lambeth would probably be
struck with that. It was also represented to the strangers that it
mattered very little whether their hotel was agreeable, as every one
would want them to make visits; they would stay with other people,
and, in any case, they would be a great deal at Mrs Westgate's. They
would find that very charming; it was the pleasantest house in
Newport. It was a pity Mr Westgate was always away; he was a man
of the highest ability – very acute, very acute. He worked like a horse
and he left his wife – well, to do about as she liked. He liked her to
enjoy herself, and she seemed to know how. She was extremely
brilliant, and a splendid talker. Some people preferred her sister; but
Miss Alden was very different; she was in a different style altogether.
Some people even thought her prettier, and, certainly, she was not
so sharp. She was more in the Boston style; she had lived a great
deal in Boston and she was very highly educated. Boston girls, it was
intimated, were more like English young ladies.

Lord Lambeth had presently a chance to test the truth of this proposition; for on the company rising in compliance with a suggestion from their hostess that they should walk down to the rocks and look at the sea, the young Englishman again found himself, as they strolled across the grass, in proximity to Mrs Westgate's sister. Though she was but a girl of twenty, she appeared to feel the obligation to exert an active hospitality; and this was perhaps the more to be noticed as she seemed by nature a reserved and retiring person, and had little of her sister's fraternising quality. She was perhaps rather too thin, and she was a little pale; but as she moved slowly over the grass, with her arms hanging at her sides, looking gravely for a moment at the sea and then brightly, for all her gravity, at him, Lord Lambeth thought her at least as pretty as Mrs Westgate, and reflected that if this was the Boston style the Boston style was very charming. He thought she looked very clever; he could imagine that she was highly educated; but at the same time she seemed gentle and graceful. For all her cleverness, however, he felt that she had to think a little what to say; she didn't say the first thing that came into her head; he had come from a different part of the world and from a different society, and she was trying to adapt her conversation. The others were scattering themselves near the rocks; Mrs Westgate had charge of Percy Beaumont.

'Very jolly place, isn't it?' said Lord Lambeth. 'It's a very jolly place to sit.'

'Very charming,' said the young girl; 'I often sit here; there are all kinds of cosy corners – as if they had been made on purpose.'

'Ah! I suppose you have had some of them made,' said the young man.

Miss Alden looked at him a moment. 'Oh no, we have had nothing made. It's pure nature.'

'I should think you would have a few little benches – rustic seats and that sort of thing. It might be so jolly to sit here you know,' Lord Lambeth went on.

'I am afraid we haven't so many of those things as you,' said the young girl, thoughtfully.

'I daresay you go in for pure nature as you were saying. Nature, over here, must be so grand, you know.' And Lord Lambeth looked about him.

The little coast-line hereabouts was very pretty, but it was not at all grand; and Miss Alden appeared to rise to a perception of this fact. 'I am afraid it seems to you very rough,' she said. 'It's not like the coast scenery in Kingsley's novels.'

'Ah, the novels always overdo it, you know,' Lord Lambeth rejoined. 'You must not go by the novels.'

They were wandering about a little on the rocks, and they stopped and looked down into a narrow chasm where the rising tide made a curious bellowing sound. It was loud enough to prevent their hearing each other, and they stood there for some moments in silence. The young girl looked at her companion, observing him attentively but covertly, as women, even when very young, know how to do. Lord Lambeth repaid observation; tall, straight and strong, he was handsome as certain young Englishmen, and certain young Englishmen almost alone, are handsome; with a perfect finish of feature and a look of intellectual repose and gentle good temper which seemed somehow to be consequent upon his well-cut nose and chin. And to speak of Lord Lambeth's expression of intel-lectual repose is not simply a civil way of saying that he looked stupid. He was evidently not a young man of an irritable imagina-tion; he was not, as he would himself have said, tremendously clever; but, though there was a kind of appealing dulness in his eye, he looked thoroughly reasonable and competent, and his appear-ance proclaimed that to be a nobleman, an athlete, and an excellent fellow, was a sufficiently brilliant combination of qualities. The young girl beside him, it may be attested without farther delay, thought him the handsomest young man she had ever seen; and Bessie Alden's imagination, unlike that of her companion, was irritable. He, however, was also making up his mind that she was uncommonly pretty.

'I daresay it's very gay here – that you have lots of balls and parties,' he said; for, if he was not tremendously clever, he rather prided himself on having, with women, a sufficiency of conversa-tion.

'Oh yes, there is a great deal going on,' Bessie Alden replied. 'There are not so many balls, but there are a good many other things. You will see for yourself; we live rather in the midst of it.'

'It's very kind of you to say that. But I thought you Americans were always dancing.'

'I suppose we dance a good deal; but I have never seen much of it. We don't do it much, at any rate, in summer. And I am sure,' said Bessie Alden, 'that we don't have so many balls as you have in England.'

'Really!' exclaimed Lord Lambeth. 'Ah, in England it all depends, you know.'

'You will not think much of our gaieties,' said the young girl, looking at him with a little mixture of interrogation and decision which was peculiar to her. The interrogation seemed earnest and the decision seemed arch; but the mixture, at any rate, was charming. 'Those things, with us, are much less splendid than in England.'

'I fancy you don't mean that,' said Lord Lambeth, laughing.

'I assure you I mean everything I say,' the young girl declared. 'Certainly, from what I have read about English society, it is very different.'

'Ah, well, you know,' said her companion, 'those things are often described by fellows who know nothing about them. You mustn't mind what you read.'

'Oh, I *shall* mind what I read!' Bessie Alden rejoined. 'When I read Thackeray and George Eliot, how can I help minding them?'

'Ah, well, Thackeray – and George Eliot,' said the young nobleman; 'I haven't read much of them.'

'Don't you suppose they know about society?' asked Bessie Alden.

'Oh, I daresay they know; they were so very clever. But those fashionable novels,' said Lord Lambeth, 'they are awful rot, you know.'

His companion looked at him a moment with her dark blue eyes, and then she looked down into the chasm where the water was tumbling about. 'Do you mean Mrs Gore, for instance?' she said presently, raising her eyes.

'I am afraid I haven't read that either,' was the young man's rejoinder, laughing a little and blushing. 'I am afraid you'll think I am not very intellectual.'

'Reading Mrs Gore is no proof of intellect. But I like reading everything about English life – even poor books. I am so curious about it.'

'Aren't ladies always curious?' asked the young man, jestingly.

But Bessie Alden appeared to desire to answer his question seriously. 'I don't think so – I don't think we are enough so – that we care about many things. So it's all the more of a compliment,' she added, 'that I should want to know so much about England.'

The logic here seemed a little close; but Lord Lambeth, conscious of a compliment, found his natural modesty just at hand. 'I am sure you know a great deal more than I do.'

'I really think I know a great deal – for a person who has never been there.'

'Have you really never been there?' cried Lord Lambeth. 'Fancy!'

'Never – except in imagination,' said the young girl.

'Fancy!' repeated her companion. 'But I daresay you'll go soon, won't you?'

'It's the dream of my life!' declared Bessie Alden, smiling.

'But your sister seems to know a tremendous lot about London,' Lord Lambeth went on.

The young girl was silent a moment. 'My sister and I are two very different persons,' she presently said. 'She has been a great deal in Europe. She has been in England several times. She has known a great many English people.'

'But you must have known some, too,' said Lord Lambeth.

'I don't think that I have ever spoken to one before. You are the first Englishman that – to my knowledge – I have ever talked with.'

Bessie Alden made this statement with a certain gravity – almost, as it seemed to Lord Lambeth, an impressiveness. Attempts at impressiveness always made him feel awkward, and he now began to laugh and swing his stick. 'Ah, you would have been sure to know!' he said. And then he added, after an instant – 'I'm sorry I am not a better specimen.'

The young girl looked away; but she smiled, laying aside her impressiveness. 'You must remember that you are only a beginning,' she said. Then she retraced her steps, leading the way back to the lawn, where they saw Mrs Westgate come towards them with Percy Beaumont still at her side. 'Perhaps I shall go to England next year.' Miss Alden continued; 'I want to, immensely. My sister is going to Europe, and she has asked me to go with her. If we go, I shall make her stay as long as possible in London.'

Ah, you must come in July,' said Lord Lambeth. 'That's the time when there is most going on.'

'I don't think I can wait till July,' the young girl rejoined. 'By the first of May I shall be very impatient.' They had gone farther, and Mrs Westgate and her companion were near them. 'Kitty,' said Miss Alden, 'I have given out that we are going to London next May. So please to conduct yourself accordingly.'

Percy Beaumont wore a somewhat animated – even a slightly irritated – air. He was by no means so handsome a man as his cousin, although in his cousin's absence he might have passed for a striking specimen of the tall, muscular, fair-bearded, clear-eyed Englishman. Just now Beaumont's clear eyes, which were small and of a pale grey colour, had a rather troubled light, and, after glancing at Bessie Alden while she spoke, he rested them upon his kinsman. Mrs Westgate meanwhile, with her superfluously pretty gaze, looked at every one alike.

'You had better wait till the time comes,' she said to her sister. 'Perhaps next May you won't care so much about London. Mr Beaumont and I,' she went on smiling at her companion, 'have had a tremendous discussion. We don't agree about anything. It's perfectly delightful.'

'Oh, I say, Percy!' exclaimed Lord Lambeth.

'I disagree,' said Beaumont, stroking down his black hair, 'even to the point of not thinking it delightful.'

'Oh, I say!' cried Lord Lambeth again.

'I don't see anything delightful in my disagreeing with Mrs Westgate,' said Percy Beaumont.

'Well, I do!' Mrs Westgate declared; and she turned to her sister. 'You know you have to go to town. The phaeton is there. You had better take Lord Lambeth.'

At this point Percy Beaumont certainly looked straight at his kinsman; he tried to catch his eye. But Lord Lambeth would not look at him; his own eyes were better occupied. 'I shall be very happy,' cried Bessie Alden. 'I am only going to some shops. But I will drive you about and show you the place.'

'An American woman who respects herself,' said Mrs Westgate, turning to Beaumont with her bright expository air, 'must buy something every day of her life. If she cannot do it herself, she must send out some member of her family for the purpose. So Bessie goes forth to fulfil my mission.'

The young girl had walked away, with Lord Lambeth by her side, to whom she was talking still; and Percy Beaumont watched them as they passed towards the house. 'She fulfils her own mission,' he presently said; 'that of being a very attractive young lady.'

'I don't know that I should say very attractive,' Mrs Westgate rejoined. 'She is not so much that as she is charming when you really know her. She is very shy.'

'Oh indeed?' said Percy Beaumont.

'Extremely shy,' Mrs Westgate repeated. 'But she is a dear good girl; she is a charming species of girl. She is not in the least a flirt; that isn't at all her line; she doesn't know the alphabet of that sort of thing. She is very simple – very serious. She has lived a great deal in Boston, with another sister of mine – the eldest of us – who married a Bostonian. She is very cultivated, not at all like me – I am not in the least cultivated. She has studied immensely and read everything; she is what they call in Boston "thoughtful".'

'A rum sort of girl for Lambeth to get hold of!' his lordship's kinsman privately reflected.

'I really believe,' Mrs Westgate continued, 'that the most charming girl in the world is a Boston superstructure upon a New York *fonds*; or perhaps a New York superstructure upon a Boston *fonds*. At any rate it's the mixture,' said Mrs Westgate, who continued to give Percy Beaumont a great deal of information.

Lord Lambeth got into a little basket-phaeton with Bessie Alden, and she drove him down the long avenue, whose extent he had measured on foot a couple of hours before, into the ancient town, as it was called in that part of the world, of Newport. The ancient town was a curious affair – a collection of fresh-looking little wooden houses, painted white, scattered over a hill-side and clustered about a long, straight street, paved with enormous cobble-stones. There were plenty of shops – a large proportion of which appeared to be those of fruit-vendors, with piles of huge water-melons and pumpkins stacked in front of them; and, drawn up before the shops, or bumping about on the cobble-stones, were innumerable other basket-phaetons freighted with ladies of high fashion, who greeted each other from vehicle to vehicle and con-

versed on the edge of the pavement in a manner that struck Lord
Lambeth as demonstrative – with a great many 'Oh, my dears', and
little quick exclamations and caresses. His companion went into
seventeen shops – he amused himself with counting them – and
accumulated, at the bottom of the phaeton, a pile of bundles that
hardly left the young Englishman a place for his feet. As she had
no groom nor footman, he sat in the phaeton to hold the ponies;
where, although he was not a particularly acute observer, he saw
much to entertain him – especially the ladies just mentioned, who
wandered up and down with the appearance of a kind of aimless
intentness, as if they were looking for something to buy, and who,
tripping in and out of their vehicles, displayed remarkably pretty
feet. It all seemed to Lord Lambeth very odd, and bright, and gay.
Of course, before they got back to the villa, he had had a great deal
of desultory conversation with Bessie Alden.

The young Englishmen spent the whole of that day and the whole
of many successive days in what the French call the *intimité* of their
new friends. They agreed that it was extremely jolly – that they had
never known anything more agreeable. It is not proposed to narrate
minutely the incidents of their sojourn on this charming shore;
though if it were convenient I might present a record of impressions
none the less delectable that they were not exhaustively analysed.
Many of them still linger in the minds of our travellers, attended by
a train of harmonious images – images of brilliant mornings on
lawns and piazzas that overlooked the sea; of innumerable pretty
girls; of infinite lounging and talking and laughing and flirting and
lunching and dining; of universal friendliness and frankness; of
occasions on which they knew every one and everything and had
an extraordinary sense of ease; of drives and rides in the late
afternoon, over gleaming beaches, on long sea-roads, beneath a sky
lighted up by marvellous sunsets; of tea-tables, on the return,
informal, irregular, agreeable; of evenings at open windows or on
the perpetual verandahs, in the summer starlight, above the warm
Atlantic. The young Englishmen were introduced to everybody,
entertained by everybody, intimate with everybody. At the end of
three days they had removed their luggage from the hotel, and had
gone to stay with Mrs Westgate – a step to which Percy Beaumont
at first offered some conscientious opposition. I call his opposition

conscientious because it was founded upon some talk that he had had, on the second day, with Bessie Alden. He had indeed had a good deal of talk with her, for she was not literally always in conversation with Lord Lambeth. He had meditated upon Mrs Westgate's account of her sister and he discovered, for himself, that the young lady was clever and appeared to have read a great deal. She seemed very nice, though he could not make out that, as Mrs Westgate had said, she was shy. If she was shy she carried it off very well.

'Mr Beaumont,' she had said, 'please tell me something about Lord Lambeth's family. How would you say it in England? – his position.'

'His position?' Percy Beaumont repeated.

'His rank – or whatever you call it. Unfortunately we haven't got a "Peerage", like the people in Thackeray.'

'That's a great pity,' said Beaumont. 'You would find it all set forth there so much better than I can do it.'

'He is a great noble, then?'

'Oh yes, he is a great noble.'

'Is he a peer?'

'Almost.'

'And has he any other title than Lord Lambeth?'

'His title is the Marquis of Lambeth,' said Beaumont; and then he was silent; Bessie Alden appeared to be looking at him with interest. 'He is the son of the Duke of Bayswater,' he added, presently.

'The eldest son?'

'The only son.'

'And are his parents living?'

'Oh yes; if his father were not living he would be a duke.'

'So that when his father dies,' pursued Bessie Alden, with more simplicity than might have been expected in a clever girl, 'he will become Duke of Bayswater?'

'Of course,' said Percy Beaumont. 'But his father is in excellent health.'

'And his mother?'

Beaumont smiled a little. 'The Duchess is uncommonly robust.'

'And has he any sisters?'

'Yes, there are two.'

And what are they called?'

'One of them is married. She is the Countess of Pimlico.'

'And the other?'

'The other is unmarried; she is plain Lady Julia.'

Bessie Alden looked at him a moment. 'Is she very plain?'

Beaumont began to laugh again. 'You would not find her so handsome as her brother,' he said; and it was after this that he attempted to dissuade the heir of the Duke of Bayswater from accepting Mrs Westgate's invitation. 'Depend upon it,' he said, 'that girl means to try for you.'

'It seems to me you are doing your best to make a fool of me,' the modest young nobleman answered.

'She has been asking me,' said Beaumont, 'all about your people and your possessions.'

'I am sure it is very good of her!' Lord Lambeth rejoined.

'Well, then,' observed his companion, 'if you go, you go with your eyes open.'

'Damn my eyes!' exclaimed Lord Lambeth. 'If one is to be a dozen times a day at the house, it is a great deal more convenient to sleep there. I am sick of travelling up and down this beastly Avenue.'

Since he had determined to go, Percy Beaumont would of course have been very sorry to allow him to go alone; he was a man of conscience, and he remembered his promise to the Duchess. It was obviously the memory of this promise that made him say to his companion a couple of days later that he rather wondered he should be so fond of that girl.

'In the first place, how do you know how fond I am of her?' asked Lord Lambeth. 'And in the second place, why shouldn't I be fond of her?'

'I shouldn't think she would be in your line.'

'What do you call my "line"? You don't set her down as "fast"?'

'Exactly so. Mrs Westgate tells me that there is no such thing as the "fast girl" in America; that it's an English invention and that the term has no meaning here.'

'All the better. It's an animal I detest.'

'You prefer a blue-stocking.'

'Is that what you call Miss Alden?'

'Her sister tells me,' said Percy Beaumont, 'that she is tremendously literary.'

'I don't know anything about that. She is certainly very clever.'

'Well, said Beaumont, 'I should have supposed you would have found that sort of thing awfully slow.'

'In point of fact ' Lord Lambeth rejoined, 'I find it uncommonly lively.'

After this, Percy Beaumont held his tongue; but on August 10th he wrote to the Duchess of Bayswater. He was, as I have said, a man of conscience, and he had a strong, incorruptible sense of the proprieties of life. His kinsman, meanwhile, was having a great deal of talk with Bessie Alden – on the red sea-rocks beyond the lawn; in the course of long island rides, with a slow return in the glowing twilight; on the deep verandah, late in the evening. Lord Lambeth, who had stayed at many houses, had never stayed at a house in which it was possible for a young man to converse so frequently with a young lady. This young lady no longer applied to Percy Beaumont for information concerning his lordship. She addressed herself directly to the young nobleman. She asked him a great many questions, some of which bored him a little; for he took no pleasure in talking about himself.

'Lord Lambeth,' said Bessie Alden, 'are you an hereditary legislator?'

'Oh, I say,' cried Lord Lambeth, 'don't make me call myself such names as that.'

'But you are a member of Parliament,' said the young girl.

'I don't like the sound of that either.'

'Doesn't your father sit in the House of Lords?' Bessie Alden went on.

'Very seldom,' said Lord Lambeth.

'Is it an important position?' she asked.

'Oh dear no,' said Lord Lambeth.

'I should think it would be very grand,' said Bessie Alden, 'to possess simply by an accident of birth the right to make laws for a great nation.'

'Ah, but one doesn't make laws. It's a great humbug.'

'I don't believe that,' the young girl declared. 'It must be a great

46

privilege, and I should think that if one thought of it in the right way – from a high point of view – it would be very inspiring.'

'The less one thinks of it the better,' Lord Lambeth affirmed.

'I think it's tremendous,' said Bessie Alden; and on another occasion she asked him if he had any tenantry. Hereupon it was that, as I have said, he was a little bored.

'Do you want to buy up their leases?' he asked.

'Well – have you got any livings?' she demanded.

'Oh, I say!' he cried. 'Have you got a clergyman that is looking out?' But she made him tell her that he had a Castle; he confessed to but one. It was the place in which he had been born and brought up, and, as he had an old-time liking for it, he was beguiled into describing it a little and saying it was really very jolly. Bessie Alden listened with great interest, and declared that she would give the world to see such a place. Whereupon – 'It would be awfully kind of you to come and stay there,' said Lord Lambeth. He took a vague satisfaction in the circumstance that Percy Beaumont had not heard him make the remark I have just recorded.

Mr Westgate, all this time, had not, as they said at Newport, 'come on'. His wife more than once announced that she expected him on the morrow; but on the morrow she wandered about a little, with a telegram in her jewelled fingers, declaring it was very tiresome that his business detained him in New York; that he could only hope the Englishmen were having a good time. 'I must say,' said Mrs Westgate, 'that it is no thanks to him if you are!' And she went on to explain, while she continued that slow-paced promenade which enabled her well-adjusted skirts to display themselves so advantageously, that unfortunately in America there was no leisure-class. It was Lord Lambeth's theory, freely propounded when the young men were together, that Percy Beaumont was having a very good time with Mrs Westgate, and that under the pretext of meeting for the purpose of animated discussion, they were indulging in practices that imparted a shade of hypocrisy to the lady's regret for her husband's absence.

'I assure you we are always discussing and differing,' said Percy Beaumont. 'She is awfully argumentative. American ladies certainly don't mind contradicting you. Upon my word I don't think I was ever treated so by a woman before. She's so devilish positive.'

Mrs Westgate's positive quality, however, evidently had its attractions; for Beaumont was constantly at his hostess's side. He detached himself one day to the extent of going to New York to talk over the Tennessee Central with Mr Westgate; but he was absent only forty-eight hours, during which, with Mr Westgate's assistance, he completely settled this piece of business. 'They certainly do things quickly in New York,' he observed to his cousin; and he added that Mr Westgate had seemed very uneasy lest his wife should miss her visitor – he had been in such an awful hurry to send him back to her. 'I'm afraid you'll never come up to an American husband – if that's what the wives expect,' he said to Lord Lambeth.

Mrs Westgate, however, was not to enjoy much longer the entertainment with which an indulgent husband had desired to keep her provided. On August 21st Lord Lambeth received a telegram from his mother, requesting him to return immediately to England; his father had been taken ill, and it was his filial duty to come to him.

The young Englishman was visibly annoyed. 'What the deuce does it mean?' he asked of his kinsman. 'What am I to do?'

Percy Beaumont was annoyed as well; he had deemed it his duty, as I have narrated, to write to the Duchess, but he had not expected that this distinguished woman would act so promptly upon his hint. 'It means,' he said, 'that your father is laid up. I don't suppose it's anything serious; but you have no option. Take the first steamer; but don't be alarmed.'

Lord Lambeth made his farewells; but the few last words that he exchanged with Bessie Alden are the only ones that have a place in our record. 'Of course I needn't assure you,' he said, 'that if you should come to England next year, I expect to be the first person that you inform of it.'

Bessie Alden looked at him a little and she smiled. 'Oh, if we come to London,' she answered, 'I should think you would hear of it.'

Percy Beaumont returned with his cousin, and his sense of duty compelled him, one windless afternoon, in mid-Atlantic, to say to Lord Lambeth that he suspected that the Duchess's telegram was in part the result of something he himself had written to her. 'I wrote to her – as I explicitly notified you I had promised to do – that you were extremely interested in a little American girl.'

Lord Lambeth was extremely angry, and he indulged for some

moments in the simple language of resentment. But I have said that he was a reasonable young man, and I can give no better proof of it than the fact that he remarked to his companion at the end of half-an-hour – 'You were quite right after all. I am very much interested in her. Only, to be fair,' he added, 'you should have told my mother also that she is not – seriously – interested in me.'

Percy Beaumont gave a little laugh. 'There is nothing so charming as modesty in a young man in your position. That speech is a capital proof that you are sweet on her.'

'She is not interested – she is not!' Lord Lambeth repeated.

'My dear fellow,' said his companion, 'you are very far gone.'

4

In point of fact, as Percy Beaumont would have said, Mrs Westgate disembarked on the 18th of May on the British coast. She was accompanied by her sister, but she was not attended by any other member of her family. To the deprivation of her husband's society Mrs Westgate was, however, habituated; she had made half-a-dozen journeys to Europe without him, and she now accounted for his absence, to interrogative friends on this side of the Atlantic, by allusion to the regrettable but conspicuous fact that in America there was no leisure-class. The two ladies came up to London and alighted at Jones's Hotel, where Mrs Westgate, who had made on former occasions the most agreeable impression at this establishment, received an obsequious greeting. Bessie Alden had felt much excited about coming to England; she had expected the 'associations' would be very charming, that it would be an infinite pleasure to rest her eyes upon the things she had read about in the poets and historians. She was very fond of the poets and historians, of the picturesque, of the past, of retrospect, of mementoes and reverberations of greatness; so that on coming into the great English world, where strangeness and familiarity would go hand in hand, she was prepared for a multitude of fresh emotions. They began very promptly – these tender, fluttering sensations; they began with the sight of the beautiful English landscape, whose dark richness was quickened and brightened by the season; with the carpeted fields and flowering hedge-rows, as she looked at them from the window of the train; with the spires of the rural churches, peeping above the rook-haunted tree-tops; with the oak-studded parks, the ancient homes, the cloudy light, the speech, the manners, the thousand differences. Mrs Westgate's impressions had of course much less novelty and keenness, and she gave but a wandering attention to her sister's ejaculations and rhapsodies.

'You know my enjoyment of England is not so intellectual as Bessie's,' she said to several of her friends in the course of her visit to this country. 'And yet if it is not intellectual, I can't say it is physical. I don't think I can quite say what it is, my enjoyment of England.' When once it was settled that the two ladies should come abroad and should spend a few weeks in England on their way to the Continent, they of course exchanged a good many allusions to their London acquaintance.

'It will certainly be much nicer having friends there,' Bessie Alden had said one day, as she sat on the sunny deck of the steamer, at her sister's feet, on a large blue rug.

'Whom do you mean by friends?' Mrs Westgate asked.

'All those English gentlemen whom you have known and entertained. Captain Littledale, for instance. And Lord Lambeth and Mr Beaumont,' added Bessie Alden.

'Do you expect them to give us a very grand reception?'

Bessie reflected a moment; she was addicted, as we know, to reflection. 'Well, yes.'

'My poor sweet child!' murmured her sister.

'What have I said that is so silly?' asked Bessie.

'You are a little too simple; just a little. It is very becoming, but it pleases people at your expense.'

'I am certainly too simple to understand you,' said Bessie.

'Shall I tell you a story?' asked her sister.

'If you would be so good. That is what they do to amuse simple people.'

Mrs Westgate consulted her memory, while her companion sat gazing at the shining sea. 'Did you ever hear of the Duke of Green-Erin?'

'I think not,' said Bessie.

'Well, it's no matter,' her sister went on.

'It's a proof of my simplicity.'

'My story is meant to illustrate that of some other people,' said Mrs Westgate. 'The Duke of Green-Erin is what they call in England a great swell; and some five years ago he came to America. He spent most of his time in New York, and in New York he spent his days and his nights at the Butterworths'. You have heard at least of the Butterworths. *Bien*. They did everything in the world for him – they turned themselves inside out. They gave him a dozen dinner-parties and balls, and were the means of his being invited to fifty more. At first he used to come into Mrs Butterworth's box at the opera in a tweed travelling-suit; but some one stopped that. At any rate, he had a beautiful time, and they parted the best friends in the world. Two years elapse, and the Butterworths come abroad and go to London. The first thing they see in all the papers – in England those things are in the most prominent place – is that the Duke of Green-Erin has arrived in town for the Season. They wait a little, and then Mr Butterworth – as polite as ever – goes and leaves a card. They wait a little more; the visit is not returned; they wait three weeks – *silence de mort* – the Duke gives no sign. The Butterworths see a lot of other people, put down the Duke of Green-Erin as a rude, ungrateful man, and forget all about him. One fine day they go to Ascot Races, and there they meet him face to face. He stares a moment and then comes up to Mr Butterworth, taking something from his pocket-book – something which proved to be a bank-note. "I'm glad to see you, Mr Butterworth," he says, "so that I can pay you that ten pounds I lost to you in New York. I saw the other day you remembered our bet; here are the ten pounds, Mr Butterworth. Good-bye, Mr Butterworth." And off he goes, and that's the last they see of the Duke of Green-Erin.'

'Is that your story?' asked Bessie Alden.

'Don't you think it's interesting?' her sister replied.

'I don't believe it,' said the young girl.

'Ah!' cried Mrs Westgate, 'you are not so simple after all. Believe it or not as you please; there is no smoke without fire.'

'Is that the way,' asked Bessie after a moment, 'that you expect your friends to treat you?'

'I defy them to treat me very ill, because I shall not give them the opportunity. With the best will in the world, in that case, they can't be very disobliging.'

Bessie Alden was silent a moment. 'I don't see what makes you talk that way,' she said. 'The English are a great people.'

'Exactly; and that is just the way they have grown great – by dropping you when you have ceased to be useful. People say they are not clever; but I think they are very clever.'

'You know you have liked them – all the Englishmen you have seen,' said Bessie.

'They have liked me,' her sister rejoined; 'it would be more correct to say that. And of course one likes that.'

Bessie Alden resumed for some moments her studies in sea-green. 'Well,' she said, 'whether they like me or not, I mean to like them. And happily,' she added, 'Lord Lambeth does not owe me ten pounds.'

During the first few days after their arrival at Jones's Hotel our charming Americans were much occupied with what they would have called looking about them. They found occasion to make a large number of purchases, and their opportunities for conversation were such only as were offered by the deferential London shopmen. Bessie Alden, even in driving from the station, took an immense fancy to the British metropolis, and, at the risk of exhibiting her as a young woman of vulgar tastes, it must be recorded that for a considerable period she desired no higher pleasure than to drive about the crowded streets in a Hansom cab. To her attentive eyes they were full of a strange picturesque life, and it is at least beneath the dignity of our historic muse to enumerate the trivial objects and incidents which this simple young lady from Boston found so entertaining. It may be freely mentioned, however, that whenever, after a round of visits in Bond Street and Regent Street, she was about to return with her sister to Jones's Hotel, she made an earnest request that they should be driven home by way of Westminster Abbey. She had begun by asking whether it would not be possible to take the Tower on the way to their lodgings; but it happened that at a more primitive stage of her culture Mrs Westgate had paid a visit to this venerable monument, which she spoke of ever afterwards, vaguely, as a dreadful disappointment; so that she expressed the liveliest disapproval of any attempt to combine historical researches with the purchase of hair-brushes and note-paper. The most she would consent to do in this line was to spend half-an-hour at Madame Tussaud's, where she saw several dusty wax effigies of members of the Royal Family. She told Bessie that if she wished to go to the Tower she must get some one else to take her. Bessie expressed hereupon an earnest disposition to go alone; but upon this proposal as well Mrs Westgate sprinkled cold water.

'Remember,' she said, 'that you are not in your innocent little Boston. It is not a question of walking up and down Beacon Street.'

Then she went on to explain that there were two classes of American girls in Europe – those that walked about alone and those that did not. 'You happen to belong, my dear,' she said to her sister, 'to the class that does not.'

'It is only,' answered Bessie, laughing, 'because you happen to prevent me.' And she devoted much private meditation to this question of effecting a visit to the Tower of London.

Suddenly it seemed as if the problem might be solved; the two ladies at Jones's Hotel received a visit from Willie Woodley. Such was the social appellation of a young American who had sailed from New York a few days after their own departure, and who, having the privilege of intimacy with them in that city, had lost no time, on his arrival in London, in coming to pay them his respects. He had, in fact, gone to see them directly after going to see his tailor; than which there can be no greater exhibition of promptitude on the part of a young American who has just alighted at the Charing Cross Hotel. He was a slim, pale youth, of the most amiable disposition, famous for the skill with which he led the 'German' in New York. Indeed, by the young ladies who habitually figured in this fashionable frolic he was believed to be 'the best dancer in the world'; it was in these terms that he was always spoken of, and that his identity was indicated. He was the gentlest, softest young man it was possible to meet; he was beautifully dressed – 'in the English style' – and he knew an immense deal about London. He had been at Newport during the previous summer, at the time of our young Englishman's visit, and he took extreme pleasure in the society of Bessie Alden, whom he always addressed as 'Miss Bessie'. She immediately arranged with him, in the presence of her sister, that he should conduct her to the scene of Lady Jane Grey's execution.

'You may do as you please,' said Mrs Westgate. 'Only – if you desire the information – it is not the custom here for young ladies to knock about London with young men.'

'Miss Bessie has waltzed with me so often,' observed Willie Woodley; 'she can surely go out with me in a Hansom.'

'I consider waltzing,' said Mrs Westgate, 'the most innocent pleasure of our time.'

'It's a compliment to our time!' exclaimed the young man, with a little laugh, in spite of himself.

'I don't see why I should regard what is done here,' said Bessie Alden. 'Why should I suffer the restrictions of a society of which I enjoy none of the privileges?'

'That's very good – very good,' murmured Willie Woodley.

'Oh, go to the Tower, and feel the axe, if you like!' said Mrs Westgate. 'I consent to your going with Mr Woodley; but I should not let you go with an Englishman.'

'Miss Bessie wouldn't care to go with an Englishman!' Mr Woodley declared, with a faint asperity that was, perhaps, not unnatural in a young man who, dressing in the manner that I have indicated, and knowing a great deal, as I have said, about London, saw no reason for drawing these sharp distinctions. He agreed upon a day with Miss Bessie – a day of that same week.

An ingenious mind might, perhaps, trace a connection between the young girl's allusion to her destitution of social privileges and a question she asked on the morrow as she sat with her sister at lunch.

'Don't you mean to write to – to any one?' said Bessie.

'I wrote this morning to Captain Littledale,' Mrs Westgate replied.

'But Mr Woodley said that Captain Littledale had gone to India.'

'He said he thought he had heard so; he knew nothing about it.'

For a moment Bessie Alden said nothing more; then, at last, 'And don't you intend to write to – to Mr Beaumont?' she inquired.

'You mean to Lord Lambeth,' said her sister.

'I said Mr Beaumont because he was so good a friend of yours.'

Mrs Westgate looked at the young girl with sisterly candour. 'I don't care two straws for Mr Beaumont.'

'You were certainly very nice to him.'

'I am nice to every one,' said Mrs Westgate, simply.

'To every one but me,' rejoined Bessie, smiling.

Her sister continued to look at her; then, at last, 'Are you in love with Lord Lambeth?' she asked.

The young girl stared a moment, and the question was apparently too humorous even to make her blush. 'Not that I know of,' she answered.

'Because if you are,' Mrs Westgate went on, 'I shall certainly not send for him.'

'That proves what I said,' declared Bessie, smiling – 'that you are not nice to me.'

'It would be a poor service, my dear child,' said her sister.

'In what sense? There is nothing against Lord Lambeth, that I know of.'

Mrs Westgate was silent a moment. 'You *are* in love with him, then?'

Bessie stared again; but this time she blushed a little. 'Ah! if you won't be serious,' she answered, 'we will not mention him again.'

For some moments Lord Lambeth was not mentioned again, and it was Mrs Westgate who, at the end of this period, reverted to him. 'Of course I will let him know we are here; because I think he would be hurt – justly enough – if we should go away without seeing him. It is fair to give him a chance to come and thank me for the kindness we showed him. But I don't want to seem eager.'

'Neither do I,' said Bessie, with a little laugh.

'Though I confess,' added her sister, 'that I am curious to see how he will behave.'

'He behaved very well at Newport.'

'Newport is not London. At Newport he could do as he liked; but here, it is another affair. He has to have an eye to consequences.'

'If he had more freedom, then, at Newport,' argued Bessie, 'it is the more to his credit that he behaved well; and if he has to be so careful here, it is possible he will behave even better.'

'Better – better,' repeated her sister. 'My dear child, what is your point of view?'

'How do you mean – my point of view?'

'Don't you care for Lord Lambeth – a little?'

This time Bessie Alden was displeased; she slowly got up from table, turning her face away from her sister. 'You will oblige me by not talking so,' she said.

Mrs Westgate sat watching her for some moments as she moved slowly about the room and went and stood at the window. 'I will write to him this afternoon,' she said at last.

'Do as you please!' Bessie answered; and presently she turned round. 'I am not afraid to say that I like Lord Lambeth. I like him very much.'

'He is not clever,' Mrs Westgate declared.

'Well, there have been clever people whom I have disliked,' said Bessie Alden; 'so that I suppose I may like a stupid one. Besides, Lord Lambeth is not stupid.'

'Not so stupid as he looks!' exclaimed her sister, smiling.

'If I were in love with Lord Lambeth, as you said just now, it would be bad policy on your part to abuse him.'

'My dear child, don't give me lessons in policy!' cried Mrs Westgate. 'The policy I mean to follow is very deep.'

The young girl began to walk about the room again; then she stopped before her sister. 'I have never heard in the course of five minutes,' she said, 'so many hints and innuendoes. I wish you would tell me in plain English what you mean.'

'I mean that you may be much annoyed.'

'That is still only a hint,' said Bessie.

Her sister looked at her, hesitating an instant. 'It will be said of you that you have come after Lord Lambeth – that you followed him.'

Bessie Alden threw back her pretty head like a startled hind, and a look flashed into her face that made Mrs Westgate rise from her chair. 'Who says such things as that?' she demanded.

'People here.'

'I don't believe it,' said Bessie.

'You have a very convenient faculty of doubt. But my policy will be, as I say, very deep. I shall leave you to find out this kind of thing for yourself.'

Bessie fixed her eyes on her sister, and Mrs Westgate thought for a moment there were tears in them. 'Do they talk that way here?' she asked.

'You will see. I shall leave you alone.'

'Don't leave me alone,' said Bessie Alden. 'Take me away.'

'No; I want to see what you make of it,' her sister continued.

'I don't understand.'

'You will understand after Lord Lambeth has come,' said Mrs Westgate, with a little laugh.

The two ladies had arranged that on this afternoon Willie Woodley should go with them to Hyde Park, where Bessie Alden expected to derive much entertainment from sitting on a little green chair, under the green trees, beside Rotten Row. The want of a suitable escort had hitherto rendered this pleasure inaccessible; but no escort, now, for such an expedition, could have been more suitable than their devoted young countryman, whose mission in life, it might almost be said, was to find chairs for ladies, and who appeared on the stroke of half-past five with a white camellia in his button-hole.

'I have written to Lord Lambeth, my dear,' said Mrs Westgate to her sister, on coming into the room where Bessie Alden, drawing on her long grey gloves, was entertaining their visitor.

Bessie said nothing, but Willie Woodley exclaimed that his lordship was in town; he had seen his name in the *Morning Post*.

'Do you read the *Morning Post*?' asked Mrs Westgate.

'Oh yes; it's great fun,' Willie Woodley affirmed.

'I want so to see it,' said Bessie, 'there is so much about it in Thackeray.'

'I will send it to you every morning,' said Willie Woodley.

He found them what Bessie Alden thought excellent places, under the great trees, beside the famous avenue whose humours had been made familiar to the young girl's childhood by the pictures in *Punch*. The day was bright and warm, and the crowd of riders and spectators and the great procession of carriages were proportionately dense and brilliant. The scene bore the stamp of the London Season at its height, and Bessie Alden found more entertainment in it than she was able to express to her companions. She sat silent, under her parasol, and her imagination, according to its wont, let itself loose into the great changing assemblage of striking and suggestive figures. They stirred up a host of old impressions and preconceptions, and she found herself fitting a history to this person and a theory to that, and making a place for them all in her little private museum of types. But if she said little, her sister on one side and Willie Woodley on the other expressed themselves in lively alternation.

'Look at that green dress with blue flounces,' said Mrs Westgate. '*Quelle toilette!*'

'That's the Marquis of Blackborough,' said the young man – 'the one in the white coat. I heard him speak the other night in the House of Lords; it was something about ramrods; he called them *wamwods*. He's an awful swell.'

'Did you ever see anything like the way they are pinned back?' Mrs Westgate resumed. 'They never know where to stop.'

'They do nothing but stop,' said Willie Woodley. 'It prevents them from walking. Here comes a great celebrity – Lady Beatrice Bellevue. She's awfully fast; see what little steps she takes.'

'Well, my dear,' Mrs Westgate pursued, 'I hope you are getting some ideas for your *couturière?*'

'I am getting plenty of ideas,' said Bessie, 'but I don't know that my *couturière* would appreciate them.'

Willie Woodley presently perceived a friend on horseback, who drove up beside the barrier of the Row and beckoned to him. He went forward and the crowd of pedestrians closed about him, so that for some ten minutes he was hidden from sight. At last he reappeared, bringing a gentleman with him – a gentleman whom Bessie at first supposed to be his friend dismounted. But at a second glance she found herself looking at Lord Lambeth, who was shaking hands with her sister.

'I found him over there,' said Willie Woodley, 'and I told him you were here.'

And then Lord Lambeth, touching his hat a little, shook hands with Bessie. 'Fancy your being here!' he said. He was blushing and smiling; he looked very handsome, and he had a kind of splendour that he had not had in America. Bessie Alden's imagination, as we know, was just then in exercise; so that the tall young Englishman, as he stood there looking down at her, had the benefit of it. 'He is handsomer and more splendid than anything I have ever seen,' she said to herself. And then she remembered that he was a Marquis, and she thought he looked like a Marquis.

'Really, you know,' he cried, 'you ought to have let a man know you were here!'

'I wrote to you an hour ago,' said Mrs Westgate.

'Doesn't all the world know it?' asked Bessie, smiling.

'I assure you I didn't know it!' cried Lord Lambeth. 'Upon my honour I hadn't heard of it. Ask Woodley now; had I, Woodley?'

'Well, I think you are rather a humbug,' said Willie Woodley.

'You don't believe that – do you, Miss Alden?' asked his lordship. 'You don't believe I'm a humbug, eh?'

'No,' said Bessie, 'I don't.'

'You are too tall to stand up, Lord Lambeth,' Mrs Westgate observed. 'You are only tolerable when you sit down. Be so good as to get a chair.'

He found a chair and placed it sidewise, close to the two ladies. 'If I hadn't met Woodley I should never have found you,' he went on. 'Should I, Woodley?'

'Well, I guess not,' said the young American.

'Not even with my letter?' asked Mrs Westgate.

'Ah, well, I haven't got your letter yet; I suppose I shall get it this evening. It was awfully kind of you to write.'

'So I said to Bessie,' observed Mrs Westgate.

'Did she say so, Miss Alden?' Lord Lambeth inquired. 'I daresay you have been here a month.'

'We have been here three,' said Mrs Westgate.

'Have you been here three months?' the young man asked again of Bessie.

'It seems a long time,' Bessie answered.

'I say, after that you had better not call me a humbug!' cried Lord Lambeth. 'I have only been in town three weeks; but you must have been hiding away. I haven't seen you anywhere.'

'Where should you have seen us – where should we have gone?' asked Mrs Westgate.

'You should have gone to Hurlingham,' said Willie Woodley.

'No, let Lord Lambeth tell us,' Mrs Westgate insisted.

'There are plenty of places to go to,' said Lord Lambeth – 'each one stupider than the other. I mean people's houses; they send you cards.'

'No one has sent us cards,' said Bessie.

'We are very quiet,' her sister declared. 'We are here as travellers.'

'We have been to Madame Tussaud's,' Bessie pursued.

'Oh, I say!' cried Lord Lambeth.

'We thought we should find your image there,' said Mrs Westgate – 'yours and Mr Beaumont's.'

'In the Chamber of Horrors?' laughed the young man.

'It did duty very well for a party,' said Mrs Westgate. 'All the women were *décolletées*, and many of the figures looked as if they could speak if they tried.'

'Upon my word,' Lord Lambeth rejoined, 'you see people at

London parties that look as if they couldn't speak if they tried.'

'Do you think Mr Woodley could find us Mr Beaumont?' asked Mrs Westgate.

Lord Lambeth stared and looked round him. 'I daresay he could. Beaumont often comes here. Don't you think you could find him, Woodley? Make a dive into the crowd.'

'Thank you; I have had enough diving,' said Willie Woodley. 'I will wait till Mr Beaumont comes to the surface.'

'I will bring him to see you,' said Lord Lambeth; 'where are you staying?'

'You will find the address in my letter – Jones's Hotel.'

'Oh, one of those places just out of Piccadilly? Beastly hole, isn't it?' Lord Lambeth inquired.

'I believe it's the best hotel in London,' said Mrs Westgate.

'But they give you awful rubbish to eat, don't they?' his lordship went on.

'Yes,' said Mrs Westgate.

'I always feel so sorry for the people that come up to town and go to live in those places,' continued the young man. 'They eat nothing but poison.'

'Oh, I say!' cried Willie Woodley.

'Well, how do you like London, Miss Alden?' Lord Lambeth asked, unperturbed by this ejaculation.

'I think it's grand,' said Bessie Alden.

'My sister likes it, in spite of the "poison"!' Mrs Westgate exclaimed.

'I hope you are going to stay a long time.'

'As long as I can,' said Bessie.

'And where is Mr Westgate?' asked Lord Lambeth of this gentleman's wife.

'He's where he always is – in that tiresome New York.'

'He must be tremendously clever,' said the young man.

'I suppose he is,' said Mrs Westgate.

Lord Lambeth sat for nearly an hour with his American friends; but it is not our purpose to relate their conversation in full. He addressed a great many remarks to Bessie Alden, and finally turned towards her altogether, while Willie Woodley entertained Mrs

Westgate. Bessie herself said very little; she was on her guard, thinking of what her sister had said to her at lunch. Little by little, however, she interested herself in Lord Lambeth again, as she had done at Newport; only it seemed to her that here he might become more interesting. He would be an unconscious part of the antiquity, the impressiveness, the picturesqueness of England; and poor Bessie Alden, like many a Yankee maiden, was terribly at the mercy of picturesqueness.

'I have often wished I were at Newport again,' said the young man. 'Those days I spent at your sister's were awfully jolly.'

'We enjoyed them very much; I hope your father is better.'

'Oh dear, yes. When I got to England, he was out grouse-shooting. It was what you call in America a gigantic fraud. My mother had got nervous. My three weeks at Newport seemed like a happy dream.'

'America certainly is very different from England,' said Bessie.

'I hope you like England better, eh?' Lord Lambeth rejoined, almost persuasively.

'No Englishman can ask that seriously of a person of another country.'

Her companion looked at her for a moment. 'You mean it's a matter of course?'

'If I were English,' said Bessie, 'it would certainly seem to me a matter of course that every one should be a good patriot.'

'Oh dear, yes; patriotism is everything,' said Lord Lambeth, not quite following, but very contented. 'Now, what are you going to do here?'

'On Thursday I am going to the Tower.'

'The Tower?'

'The Tower of London. Did you never hear of it?'

'Oh yes, I have been there,' said Lord Lambeth. 'I was taken there by my governess, when I was six years old. It's a rum idea, your going there.'

'Do give me a few more rum ideas,' said Bessie. 'I want to see everything of that sort. I am going to Hampton Court, and to Windsor, and to the Dulwich Gallery.'

Lord Lambeth seemed greatly amused. 'I wonder you don't go to the Rosherville Gardens.'

'Are they interesting?' asked Bessie.

'Oh, wonderful!'

'Are they very old? That's all I care for,' said Bessie.

'They are tremendously old; they are all falling to ruins.'

'I think there is nothing so charming as an old ruinous garden,' said the young girl. 'We must certainly go there.'

Lord Lambeth broke out into merriment. 'I say, Woodley,' he cried, 'here's Miss Alden wants to go to the Rosherville Gardens!'

Willie Woodley looked a little blank; he was caught in the fact of ignorance of an apparently conspicuous feature of London life. But in a moment he turned it off. 'Very well,' he said, 'I'll write for a permit.'

Lord Lambeth's exhilaration increased. "Gad, I believe you Americans would go anywhere!' he cried.

'We wish to go to Parliament,' said Bessie. 'That's one of the first things.'

'Oh, it would bore you to death!' cried the young man.

'We wish to hear you speak.'

'I never speak – except to young ladies,' said Lord Lambeth, smiling.

Bessie Alden looked at him awhile; smiling, too, in the shadow of her parasol. 'You are very strange,' she murmured. 'I don't think I approve of you.'

'Ah, now, don't be severe, Miss Alden!' said Lord Lambeth, smiling still more. 'Please don't be severe. I want you to like me – awfully.'

'To like you awfully? You must not laugh at me, then, when I make mistakes. I consider it my right – as a free-born American – to make as many mistakes as I choose.'

'Upon my word, I didn't laugh at you,' said Lord Lambeth.

'And not only that,' Bessie went on; 'but I hold that all my mistakes shall be set down to my credit. You must think the better of me for them.'

'I can't think better of you than I do,' the young man declared.

Bessie Alden looked at him a moment again. 'You certainly speak very well to young ladies. But why don't you address the House? – isn't that what they call it?'

'Because I have nothing to say,' said Lord Lambeth.

'Haven't you a great position?' asked Bessie Alden.

He looked a moment at the back of his glove. 'I'll set that down,' he said, 'as one of your mistakes – to your credit.' And, as if he disliked talking about his position, he changed the subject. 'I wish you would let me go with you to the Tower, and to Hampton Court, and to all those other places.'

'We shall be most happy,' said Bessie.

'And of course I shall be delighted to show you the Houses of Parliament – some day that suits you. There are a lot of things I want to do for you. I want you to have a good time. And I should like very much to present some of my friends to you, if it wouldn't bore you. Then it would be awfully kind of you to come down to Branches.'

'We are much obliged to you, Lord Lambeth,' said Bessie. 'What is Branches?'

'It's a house in the country. I think you might like it.'

Willie Woodley and Mrs Westgate, at this moment, were sitting in silence, and the young man's ear caught these last words of Lord Lambeth's. 'He's inviting Miss Bessie to one of his castles,' he murmured to his companion.

Mrs Westgate, foreseeing what she mentally called 'complications', immediately got up; and the two ladies, taking leave of Lord Lambeth, returned, under Mr Woodley's conduct, to Jones's Hotel.

5

Lord Lambeth came to see them on the morrow, bringing Percy Beaumont with him – the latter having instantly declared his intention of neglecting none of the usual offices of civility. This declaration, however, when his kinsman informed him of the advent of their American friends, had been preceded by another remark.

'Here they are, then, and you are in for it.'

'What am I in for?' demanded Lord Lambeth.

'I will let your mother give it a name. With all respect to whom,' added Percy Beaumont, 'I must decline on this occasion to do any more police duty. Her Grace must look after you herself.'

'I will give her a chance,' said her Grace's son, a trifle grimly. 'I shall make her go and see them.'

'She won't do it, my boy.'

'We'll see if she doesn't,' said Lord Lambeth.

But if Percy Beaumont took a sombre view of the arrival of the two ladies at Jones's Hotel, he was sufficiently a man of the world to offer them a smiling countenance. He fell into animated conversation, at least, that was animated on her side – with Mrs Westgate, while his companion made himself agreeable to the younger lady. Mrs Westgate began confessing and protesting, declaring and expounding.

'I must say London is a great deal brighter and prettier just now than it was when I was here last – in the month of November. There is evidently a great deal going on, and you seem to have a good many flowers. I have no doubt it is very charming for all you people, and that you amuse yourselves immensely. It is very good of you to let Bessie and me come and sit and look at you. I suppose you will think I am very satirical, but I must confess that that's the feeling I have in London.'

'I am afraid I don't quite understand to what feeling you allude,' said Percy Beaumont.

'The feeling that it's all very well for you English people. Every-thing is beautifully arranged for you.'

'It seems to me it is very well for some Americans, sometimes,' rejoined Beaumont.

'For some of them, yes – if they like to be patronised. But I must say I don't like to be patronised. I may be very eccentric and undisciplined and unreasonable; but I confess I never was fond of patronage. I like to associate with people on the same terms as I do in my own country; that's a peculiar taste that I have. But here people seem to expect something else – Heaven knows what! I am afraid you will think I am very ungrateful, for I certainly have received a great deal of attention. The last time I was here, a lady sent me a message that I was at liberty to come and see her.'

'Dear me, I hope you didn't go,' observed Percy Beaumont.

'You are deliciously *naïf*, I must say that for you!' Mrs Westgate exclaimed. 'It must be a great advantage to you here in London. I suppose that if I myself had a little more *naïveté*, I should enjoy it more. I should be content to sit on a chair in the Park, and see the people pass, and be told that this is the Duchess of Suffolk, and that is the Lord Chamberlain, and that I must be thankful for the privilege of beholding them. I daresay it is very wicked and critical of me to ask for anything else. But I was always critical, and I freely confess to the sin of being fastidious. I am told there is some remarkably superior second-rate society provided here for strangers. *Merci!* I don't want any superior second-rate society. I want the society that I have been accustomed to.'

'I hope you don't call Lambeth and me second-rate,' Beaumont interposed.

'Oh, I am accustomed to you!' said Mrs Westgate. 'Do you know that you English sometimes make the most wonderful speeches? The first time I came to London, I went out to dine – as I told you, I have received a great deal of attention. After dinner, in the drawing-room, I had some conversation with an old lady; I assure you I had. I forget what we talked about; but she presently said, in allusion to something we were discussing, "Oh, you know, the aristocracy do so-and-so; but in one's own class of life it is very different." In one's own class of life! What is a poor unprotected

American woman to do in a country where she is liable to have that sort of thing said to her?'

'You seem to get hold of some very queer old ladies; I compliment you on your acquaintance!' Percy Beaumont exclaimed. 'If you are trying to bring me to admit that London is an odious place, you'll not succeed. I'm extremely fond of it, and I think it the jolliest place in the world.'

'*Pour vous autres.* I never said the contrary,' Mrs Westgate retorted. I make use of this expression because both interlocutors had begun to raise their voices. Percy Beaumont naturally did not like to hear his country abused, and Mrs Westgate, no less naturally, did not like a stubborn debater.

'Hallo!' said Lord Lambeth; 'what are they up to now?' And he came away from the window, where he had been standing with Bessie Alden.

'I quite agree with a very clever countrywoman of mine,' Mrs Westgate continued, with charming ardour, though with imperfect relevancy. She smiled at the two gentlemen for a moment with terrible brightness, as if to toss at their feet – upon their native heath – the gauntlet of defiance. 'For me, there are only two social positions worth speaking of – that of an American lady and that of the Emperor of Russia.'

'And what do you do with the American gentlemen?' asked Lord Lambeth.

'She leaves them in America!' said Percy Beaumont.

On the departure of their visitors, Bessie Alden told her sister that Lord Lambeth would come the next day, to go with them to the Tower, and that he had kindly offered to bring his 'trap', and drive them thither. Mrs Westgate listened in silence to this communication, and for some time afterwards she said nothing. But at last, 'If you had not requested me the other day not to mention it,' she began, 'there is something I should venture to ask you.' Bessie frowned a little; her dark blue eyes were more dark than blue. But her sister went on. 'As it is, I will take the risk. You are not in love with Lord Lambeth: I believe it, perfectly. Very good. But is there, by chance, any danger of your becoming so? It's a very simple question; don't take offence. I have a particular reason,' said Mrs Westgate, 'for wanting to know.'

Bessie Alden for some moments said nothing; she only looked displeased. 'No; there is no danger,' she answered at last, curtly.

'Then I should like to frighten them,' declared Mrs Westgate, clasping her jewelled hands.

'To frighten whom?'

'All these people; Lord Lambeth's family and friends.'

'How should you frighten them?' asked the young girl.

'It wouldn't be I – it would be you. It would frighten them to think that you should absorb his lordship's young affections.'

Bessie Alden, with her clear eyes still overshadowed by her dark brows, continued to interrogate. 'Why should that frighten them?'

Mrs Westgate poised her answer with a smile before delivering it. 'Because they think you are not good enough. You are a charming girl, beautiful and amiable, intelligent and clever, and as *bien-élevée* as it is possible to be; but you are not a fit match for Lord Lambeth.'

Bessie Alden was immensely disgusted. 'Where do you get such extraordinary ideas?' she asked. 'You have said some strange things lately. My dear Kitty, where do you collect them?'

Kitty was evidently enamoured of her idea. 'Yes, it would put them on pins and needles, and it wouldn't hurt you. Mr Beaumont is already most uneasy; I could soon see that.'

The young girl meditated a moment. 'Do you mean that they spy upon him – that they interfere with him?'

'I don't know what power they have to interfere, but I know that a British mamma may worry her son's life out.'

It has been intimated that, as regards certain disagreeable things, Bessie Alden had a fund of scepticism. She abstained on the present occasion from expressing disbelief, for she wished not to irritate her sister. But she said to herself that Kitty had been misinformed – that this was a traveller's tale. Though she was a girl of a lively imagination, there could in the nature of things be, to her sense, no reality in the idea of her belonging to a vulgar category. What she said aloud was – 'I must say that in that case I am very sorry for Lord Lambeth.'

Mrs Westgate, more and more exhilarated by her scheme, was smiling at her again. 'If I could only believe it was safe!' she exclaimed. 'When you begin to pity him, I, on my side, am afraid.'

'Afraid of what?'

'Of your pitying him too much.'

Bessie Alden turned away impatiently; but at the end of a minute she turned back. 'What if I should pity him too much?' she asked.

Mrs Westgate hereupon turned away, but after a moment's reflection she also faced her sister again. 'It would come, after all, to the same thing,' she said.

Lord Lambeth came the next day with his trap, and the two ladies, attended by Willie Woodley, placed themselves under his guidance and were conveyed eastward, through some of the duskier portions of the metropolis, to the great turreted donjon which overlooks the London shipping. They all descended from their vehicle and entered the famous enclosure; and they secured the services of a venerable beefeater, who, though there were many other claimants for legendary information, made a line exclusive party of them and marched them through courts and corridors, through armouries and prisons. He delivered his usual peripatetic discourse, and they stopped and stared, and peeped and stooped, according to the official admonitions. Bessie Alden asked the old man in the crimson doublet a great many questions; she thought it a most fascinating place. Lord Lambeth was in high good-humour; he was constantly laughing; he enjoyed what he would have called the lark. Willie Woodley kept looking at the ceilings and tapping the walls with the knuckle of a pearl-grey glove; and Mrs Westgate, asking at frequent intervals to be allowed to sit down and wait till they came back, was as frequently informed that they would never come back. To a great many of Bessie's questions – chiefly on collateral points of English history – the ancient warder was naturally unable to reply; whereupon she always appealed to Lord Lambeth. But his lordship was very ignorant. He declared that he knew nothing about that sort of thing, and he seemed greatly diverted at being treated as an authority.

'You can't expect every one to know as much as you,' he said.

'I should expect you to know a great deal more,' declared Bessie Alden.

'Women always know more than men about names and dates, and that sort of thing,' Lord Lambeth rejoined. 'There was Lady Jane

Grey we have just been hearing about, who went in for Latin and Greek and all the learning of her age.'

'*You* have no right to be ignorant, at all events,' said Bessie.

'Why haven't I as good a right as any one else?'

'Because you have lived in the midst of all these things.'

'What things do you mean? Axes and blocks and thumb-screws?'

'All these historical things. You belong to an historical family.'

'Bessie is really too historical,' said Mrs Westgate, catching a word of this dialogue.

'Yes, you are too historical,' said Lord Lambeth, laughing, but thankful for a formula. 'Upon my honour, you are too historical!'

He went with the ladies a couple of days later to Hampton Court, Willie Woodley being also of the party. The afternoon was charming, the famous horse-chestnuts were in blossom, and Lord Lambeth, who quite entered into the spirit of the cockney excursionist, declared that it was a jolly old place. Bessie Alden was in ecstasies; she went about murmuring and exclaiming.

'It's too lovely,' said the young girl, 'it's too enchanting; it's too exactly what it ought to be!'

At Hampton Court the little flocks of visitors are not provided with an official bellwether, but are left to browse at discretion upon the local antiquities. It happened in this manner that, in default of another informant, Bessie Alden, who on doubtful questions was able to suggest a great many alternatives, found herself again applying for intellectual assistance to Lord Lambeth. But he again assured her that he was utterly helpless in such matters – that his education had been sadly neglected.

'And I am sorry it makes you unhappy,' he added in a moment.

'You are very disappointing, Lord Lambeth,' she said.

'Ah, now, don't say that!' he cried. 'That's the worst thing you could possibly say.'

'No,' she rejoined; 'it is not so bad as to say that I had expected nothing of you.'

'I don't know. Give me a notion of the sort of thing you expected.'

'Well,' said Bessie Alden, 'that you would be more what I should like to be – what I should try to be – in your place.'

'Ah, my place!' exclaimed Lord Lambeth; 'you are always talking about my place.'

The young girl looked at him; he thought she coloured a little; and for a moment she made no rejoinder.

'Does it strike you that I am always talking about your place?' she asked.

'I am sure you do it a great honour,' he said, fearing he had been uncivil.

'I have often thought about it,' she went on after a moment. 'I have often thought about your being an hereditary legislator. An hereditary legislator ought to know a great many things.'

'Not if he doesn't legislate.'

'But you will legislate; it's absurd your saying you won't. You are very much looked up to here – I am assured of that.'

'I don't know that I ever noticed it.'

'It is because you are used to it, then. You ought to fill the place.'

'How do you mean, to fill it?' asked Lord Lambeth.

'You ought to be very clever and brilliant, and to know almost everything.'

Lord Lambeth looked at her a moment. 'Shall I tell you something?' he asked. 'A young man in my position, as you call it –'

'I didn't invent the term,' interposed Bessie Alden. 'I have seen it in a great many books.'

'Hang it, you are always at your books! A fellow in my position, then, does very well, whatever he does. That's about what I mean to say.'

'Well, if your own people are content with you,' said Bessie Alden, laughing, 'it is not for me to complain. But I shall always think that, properly, you should have a great mind – a great character.'

'Ah, that's very theoretic!' Lord Lambeth declared. 'Depend upon it, that's a Yankee prejudice.'

'Happy the country,' said Bessie Alden, 'where even people's prejudices are so elevated!'

'Well, after all,' observed Lord Lambeth, 'I don't know that I am such a fool as you are trying to make me out.'

'I said nothing so rude as that; but I must repeat that you are disappointing.'

'My dear Miss Alden,' exclaimed the young man, 'I am the best fellow in the world!'

'Ah, if it were not for that!' said Bessie Alden, with a smile.

Mrs Westgate had a good many more friends in London than she pretended, and before long she had renewed acquaintance with most of them. Their hospitality was extreme, so that, one thing leading to another, she began, as the phrase is, to go out. Bessie Alden, in this way, saw something of what she found it a great satisfaction to call to herself English society. She went to balls and danced, she went to dinners and talked, she went to concerts and listened (at concerts Bessie always listened), she went to exhibitions and wondered. Her enjoyment was keen and her curiosity insatiable, and, grateful in general for all her opportunities, she especially prized the privilege of meeting certain celebrated persons – authors and artists, philosophers and statesmen – of whose renown she had been a humble and distant beholder, and who now, as a part of the habitual furniture of London drawing-rooms, struck her as stars fallen from the firmament and become palpable – revealing also, sometimes, on contact, qualities not to have been predicted of bodies sidereal. Bessie, who knew so many of her contemporaries by reputation, had a good many personal disappointments; but, on the other hand, she had innumerable satisfactions and enthusiasms, and she communicated the emotions of either class to a dear friend, of her own sex, in Boston, with whom she was in voluminous correspondence. Some of her reflections, indeed, she attempted to impart to Lord Lambeth, who came almost every day to Jones's Hotel, and whom Mrs Westgate admitted to be really devoted. Captain Littledale, it appeared, had gone to India; and of several others of Mrs Westgate's ex-pensioners – gentlemen who, as she said, had made, in New York, a club-house of her drawing-room – no tidings were to be obtained; but Lord Lambeth was certainly attentive enough to make up for the accidental absences, the short memories, all the other irregularities, of every one else. He drove them in the Park, he took them to visit private collections of pictures, and having a house of his own, invited them to dinner. Mrs Westgate, following the fashion of many of her compatriots, caused herself and her sister to be presented at the English Court by her diplomatic representative – for it was in this manner that she alluded to the American Minister to England, inquiring what on earth he was put there for, if not to make the proper arrangements for one's going to a Drawing Room.

Lord Lambeth declared that he hated Drawing Rooms, but he participated in the ceremony on the day on which the two ladies at Jones's Hotel repaired to Buckingham Palace in a remarkable coach which his lordship had sent to fetch them. He had on a gorgeous uniform, and Bessie Alden was particularly struck with his appearance – especially when on her asking him, rather foolishly as she felt, if he were a loyal subject, he replied that he was a loyal subject to *her*. This declaration was emphasised by his dancing with her at a royal ball to which the two ladies afterwards went, and was not impaired by the fact that she thought he danced very ill. He seemed to her wonderfully kind; she asked herself, with growing vivacity, why he should be so kind. It was his disposition – that seemed the natural answer. She had told her sister that she liked him very much, and now that she liked him more she wondered why. She liked him for his disposition; to this question as well that seemed the natural answer. When once the impressions of London life began to crowd thickly upon her she completely forgot her sister's warning about the cynicism of public opinion. It had given her great pain at the moment; but there was no particular reason why she should remember it; it corresponded too little with any sensible reality; and it was disagreeable to Bessie to remember disagreeable things. So she was not haunted with the sense of a vulgar imputation. She was not in love with Lord Lambeth – she assured herself of that. It will immediately be observed that when such assurances become necessary the state of a young lady's affections is already ambiguous; and indeed Bessie Alden made no attempt to dissimulate – to herself, of course – a certain tenderness that she felt for the young nobleman. She said to herself that she liked the type to which he belonged – the simple, candid, manly, healthy English temperament. She spoke to herself of him as women speak of young men they like – alluded to his bravery (which she had never in the least seen tested), to his honesty and gentlemanliness; and was not silent upon the subject of his good looks. She was perfectly conscious, moreover, that she liked to think of his more adventitious merits – that her imagination was excited and gratified by the sight of a handsome young man endowed with such large opportunities – opportunities she hardly knew for what, but, as she supposed, for doing great things – for setting an example, for exerting an influence, for conferring happiness, for encouraging the arts. She had a kind of ideal of conduct for a young man who should find himself in this magnificent position, and she tried to adapt it to Lord Lambeth's deportment, as you might attempt to fit a silhouette in cut paper upon a shadow projected upon a wall. But Bessie Alden's silhouette refused to coincide with his lordship's image; and this want of harmony sometimes vexed her more than she thought reasonable. When he was absent it was of course less striking – then he seemed to her a sufficiently graceful combination of high responsibilities and amiable qualities. But when he sat there within sight, laughing and talking with his customary good humour and simplicity, she measured it more accurately, and she felt acutely that if Lord Lambeth's position was heroic, there was but little of the hero in the young man himself. Then her imagination wandered away from him – very far away; for it was an incontestable fact that at such moments he seemed distinctly dull. I am afraid that while Bessie's imagination was thus invidiously roaming, she cannot have been herself a very lively companion; but it may well have been that these occasional fits of indifference seemed to Lord Lambeth a part of the young girl's personal charm. It had been a part of this charm from the first that he felt that she judged him and measured him more freely and irresponsibly – more at her ease and her leisure, as it were – than several young ladies with whom he had been on the whole about as intimate. To feel this, and yet to feel that she also liked him, was very agreeable to Lord Lambeth. He fancied he had compassed that gratification so desirable to young men of title and fortune – being liked for himself. It is true that a cynical counsellor might have whispered to him, 'Liked for yourself? Yes; but not so very much!' He had, at any rate, the constant hope of being liked more.

It may seem, perhaps, a trifle singular – but it is nevertheless true – that Bessie Alden, when he struck her as dull, devoted some time, on grounds of conscience, to trying to like him more. I say on grounds of conscience, because she felt that he had been extremely 'nice' to her sister, and because she reflected that it was no more than fair that she should think as well of him as he thought of her. This effort was possibly sometimes not so successful as it might have been, for the result of it was occasionally a vague irritation, which expressed itself in hostile criticism of several British institutions. Bessie Alden went to some entertainments at which she met Lord Lambeth; but she went to others at which his lordship was neither actually nor potentially present; and it was chiefly on these latter occasions that she encountered those literary and artistic celebrities of whom mention has been made. After a while she reduced the matter to a principle. If Lord Lambeth should appear anywhere, it was a symbol that there would be no poets and philosophers; and in consequence – for it was almost a strict consequence – she used to enumerate to the young man these objects of her admiration.

'You seem to be awfully fond of that sort of people,' said Lord Lambeth one day, as if the idea had just occurred to him.

'They are the people in England I am most curious to see,' Bessie Alden replied.

'I suppose that's because you have read so much,' said Lord Lambeth, gallantly.

'I have not read so much. It is because we think so much of them at home.'

'Oh, I see!' observed the young nobleman. 'In Boston.'

'Not only in Boston; everywhere,' said Bessie. 'We hold them in great honour; they go to the best dinner-parties.'

'I daresay you are right. I can't say I know many of them.'

'It's a pity you don't,' Bessie Alden declared. 'It would do you good.'

'I daresay it would,' said Lord Lambeth, very humbly. 'But I must say I don't like the looks of some of them.'

'Neither do I – of some of them. But there are all kinds, and many of them are charming.'

'I have talked with two or three of them,' the young man went on, 'and I thought they had a kind of fawning manner.'

'Why should they fawn?' Bessie Alden demanded.

'I'm sure I don't know. Why, indeed?'

'Perhaps you only thought so,' said Bessie.

'Well, of course,' rejoined her companion, 'that's a kind of thing that can't be proved.'

'In America they don't fawn,' said Bessie.

'Ah! well, then, they must be better company.'

Bessie was silent a moment. 'That is one of the things I don't like about England,' she said; 'your keeping the distinguished people apart.'

'How do you mean, apart?'

'Why, letting them come only to certain places. You never see them.'

Lord Lambeth looked at her a moment. 'What people do you mean?'

'The eminent people – the authors and artists – the clever people.'

'Oh, there are other eminent people besides those!' said Lord Lambeth.

'Well, you certainly keep them apart,' repeated the young girl.

'And there are other clever people,' added Lord Lambeth, simply.

Bessie Alden looked at him, and she gave a light laugh. 'Not many,' she said.

On another occasion – just after a dinner-party – she told him that there was something else in England she did not like.

'Oh, I say!' he cried; 'haven't you abused us enough?'

'I have never abused you at all,' said Bessie; 'but I don't like your *precedence*.'

'It isn't my precedence!' Lord Lambeth declared, laughing.

'Yes, it is yours – just exactly yours; and I think it's odious,' said Bessie.

'I never saw such a young lady for discussing things! Has some one had the impudence to go before you?' asked his lordship.

'It is not the going before me that I object to,' said Bessie; 'it is their thinking that they have a right to do it – a right that I should recognise.'

'I never saw such a young lady as you are for not "recognising". I have no doubt the thing is beastly, but it saves a lot of trouble.'

'It makes a lot of trouble. It's horrid!' said Bessie.

'But how would you have the first people go?' asked Lord Lambeth. 'They can't go last.'

'Whom do you mean by the first people?'

'Ah, if you mean to question first principles!' said Lord Lambeth.

'If those are your first principles, no wonder some of your arrangements are horrid,' observed Bessie Alden, with a very pretty ferocity. 'I am a young girl, so of course I go last; but imagine what

Kitty must feel on being informed that she is not at liberty to budge until certain other ladies have passed out!'

'Oh, I say, she is not "informed"!' cried Lord Lambeth. 'No one would do such a thing as that.'

'She is made to feel it,' the young girl insisted – 'as if they were afraid she would make a rush for the door. No, you have a lovely country,' said Bessie Alden, 'but your precedence is horrid.'

'I certainly shouldn't think your sister would like it,' rejoined Lord Lambeth, with even exaggerated gravity. But Bessie Alden could induce him to enter no formal protest against this repulsive custom, which he seemed to think an extreme convenience.

6

Percy Beaumont all this time had been a very much less frequent visitor at Jones's Hotel than his noble kinsman; he had in fact called but twice upon the two American ladies. Lord Lambeth, who often saw him, reproached him with his neglect, and declared that although Mrs Westgate had said nothing about it, he was sure that she was secretly wounded by it. 'She suffers too much to speak,' said Lord Lambeth.

'That's all gammon,' said Percy Beaumont; 'there's a limit to what people can suffer!' And, though sending no apologies to Jones's Hotel, he undertook in a manner to explain his absence. 'You are always there,' he said; 'and that's reason enough for my not going.'

'I don't see why. There is enough for both of us.'

'I don't care to be a witness of your – your reckless passion,' said Percy Beaumont.

Lord Lambeth looked at him with a cold eye, and for a moment said nothing. 'It's not so obvious as you might suppose,' he rejoined, dryly, 'considering what a demonstrative beggar I am.'

'I don't want to know anything about it – nothing whatever,' said Beaumont. 'Your mother asks me every time she sees me whether I believe you are really lost – and Lady Pimlico does the same. I prefer to be able to answer that I know nothing about it – that I never go there. I stay away for consistency's sake. As I said the other day, they must look after you themselves.'

'You are devilish considerate,' said Lord Lambeth. 'They never question me.'

'They are afraid of you. They are afraid of irritating you and making you worse. So they go to work very cautiously, and, somewhere or other, they get their information. They know a great deal about you. They know that you have been with those ladies to the dome of St Paul's and – where was the other place? – to the Thames Tunnel.'

'If all their knowledge is as accurate as that, it must be very valuable,' said Lord Lambeth.

'Well, at any rate, they know that you have been visiting the "sights of the metropolis". They think – very naturally, as it seems to me – that when you take to visiting the sights of the metropolis with a little American girl, there is serious cause for alarm.' Lord Lambeth responded to this intimation by scornful laughter, and his companion continued, after a pause: 'I said just now I didn't want to know anything about the affair; but I will confess that I am curious to learn whether you propose to marry Miss Bessie Alden.'

On this point Lord Lambeth gave his interlocutor no immediate satisfaction; he was musing, with a frown. 'By Jove,' he said, 'they go rather too far. They *shall* find me dangerous – I promise them.'

Percy Beaumont began to laugh. 'You don't redeem your promises. You said the other day you would make your mother call.'

Lord Lambeth continued to meditate. 'I asked her to call,' he said, simply.

'And she declined?'

'Yes, but she shall do it yet.'

'Upon my word,' said Percy Beaumont, 'if she gets much more frightened I believe she will.' Lord Lambeth looked at him, and he went on. 'She will go to the girl herself.'

'How do you mean, she will go to her?'

'She will beg her off, or she will bribe her. She will take strong measures.'

Lord Lambeth turned away in silence, and his companion watched him take twenty steps and then slowly return. 'I have invited Mrs Westgate and Miss Alden to Branches,' he said, 'and this evening I shall name a day.'

'And shall you invite your mother and your sisters to meet them?'

'Explicitly!'

'That will set the Duchess off,' said Percy Beaumont. 'I suspect she will come.'

'She may do as she pleases.'

Beaumont looked at Lord Lambeth. 'You do really propose to marry the little sister, then?'

'I like the way you talk about it!' cried the young man. 'She won't gobble me down; don't be afraid.'

'She won't leave you on your knees,' said Percy Beaumont. 'What *is* the inducement?'

'You talk about proposing – wait till I have proposed,' Lord Lambeth went on.

'That's right, my dear fellow; think about it,' said Percy Beaumont.

'She's a charming girl,' pursued his lordship.

'Of course she's a charming girl. I don't know a girl more charming, intrinsically. But there are other charming girls nearer home.'

'I like her spirit,' observed Lord Lambeth, almost as if he were trying to torment his cousin.

'What's the peculiarity of her spirit?'

'She's not afraid, and she says things out, and she thinks herself as good as any one. She is the only girl I have ever seen that was not dying to marry me.'

'How do you know that, if you haven't asked her?'

'I don't know how; but I know it.'

'I am sure she asked me questions enough about your property and your titles,' said Beaumont.

'She has asked me questions, too; no end of them,' Lord Lambeth admitted. 'But she asked for information, don't you know.'

'Information? Ay, I'll warrant she wanted it. Depend upon it that she is dying to marry you just as much and just as little as all the rest of them.'

'I shouldn't like her to refuse me – I shouldn't like that.'

'If the thing would be so disagreeable, then, both to you and to her, in Heaven's name leave it alone,' said Percy Beaumont.

Mrs Westgate, on her side, had plenty to say to her sister about the rarity of Mr Beaumont's visits and the non-appearance of the Duchess of Bayswater. She professed, however, to derive more satisfaction from this latter circumstance than she could have done from the most lavish attentions on the part of this great lady. 'It is most marked,' she said, 'most marked. It is a delicious proof that we have made them miserable. The day we dined with Lord Lambeth I was really sorry for the poor fellow.' It will have been gathered that the entertainment offered by Lord Lambeth to his American friends had not been graced by the presence of his anxious mother. He had invited several choice spirits to meet them; but the ladies of his immediate family were to Mrs Westgate's sense – a sense, possibly, morbidly acute – conspicuous by their absence.

'I don't want to express myself in a manner that you dislike,' said Bessie Alden; 'but I don't know why you should have so many theories about Lord Lambeth's poor mother. You know a great many young men in New York without knowing their mothers.'

Mrs Westgate looked at her sister, and then turned away. 'My dear Bessie, you are superb!' she said.

'One thing is certain,' the young girl continued. 'If I believed I were a cause of annoyance – however unwitting – to Lord Lambeth's family, I should insist –'

'Insist upon my leaving England,' said Mrs Westgate.

'No, not that. I want to go to the National Gallery again; I want to see Stratford-on-Avon and Canterbury Cathedral. But I should insist upon his coming to see us no more.'

'That would be very modest and very pretty of you – but you wouldn't do it now.'

'Why do you say "now"?' asked Bessie Alden. 'Have I ceased to be modest?'

'You care for him too much. A month ago, when you said you didn't, I believe it was quite true. But at present, my dear child,' said Mrs Westgate, 'you wouldn't find it quite so simple a matter never to see Lord Lambeth again. I have seen it coming on.'

'You are mistaken,' said Bessie. 'You don't understand.'

'My dear child, don't be perverse,' rejoined her sister.

'I know him better, certainly, if you mean that,' said Bessie. 'And I like him very much. But I don't like him enough to make trouble for him with his family. However, I don't believe in that.'

'I like the way you say "however"!' Mrs Westgate exclaimed. 'Come, you would not marry him?'

'Oh no,' said the young girl.

Mrs Westgate, for a moment, seemed vexed. 'Why not, pray?' she demanded.

'Because I don't care to,' said Bessie Alden.

The morning after Lord Lambeth had had, with Percy Beaumont, that exchange of ideas which has just been narrated, the ladies at Jones's Hotel received from his lordship a written invitation to pay their projected visit to Branches Castle on the following Tuesday.

'I think I have made up a very pleasant party,' the young nobleman said. 'Several people whom you know, and my mother and sisters, who have so long been regrettably prevented from making your acquaintance.' Bessie Alden lost no time in calling her sister's attention to the injustice she had done the Duchess of Bayswater, whose hostility was now proved to be a vain illusion.

'Wait till you see if she comes,' said Mrs Westgate. 'And if she is to meet us at her son's house the obligation was all the greater for her to call upon us.'

Bessie had not to wait long, and it appeared that Lord Lambeth's mother now accepted Mrs Westgate's view of her duties. On the morrow, early in the afternoon, two cards were brought to the apartment of the American ladies – one of them bearing the name of the Duchess of Bayswater and the other that of the Countess of Pimlico. Mrs Westgate glanced at the clock. 'It is not yet four,' she said; 'they have come early; they wish to see us. We will receive them.' And she gave orders that her visitors should be admitted. A few moments later they were introduced, and there was a solemn exchange of amenities. The Duchess was a large lady, with a fine fresh colour; the Countess of Pimlico was very pretty and elegant.

The Duchess looked about her as she sat down – looked not especially at Mrs Westgate. 'I dare say my son has told you that I have been wanting to come and see you,' she observed.

'You are very kind,' said Mrs Westgate, vaguely – her conscience not allowing her to assent to this proposition – and indeed not permitting her to enunciate her own with any appreciable emphasis.

'He says you were so kind to him in America,' said the Duchess.

'We are very glad,' Mrs Westgate replied, 'to have been able to make him a little more – a little less – a little more comfortable.'

'I think he stayed at your house,' remarked the Duchess of Bayswater, looking at Bessie Alden.

'A very short time,' said Mrs Westgate.

'Oh!' said the Duchess; and she continued to look at Bessie, who was engaged in conversation with her daughter.

'Do you like London?' Lady Pimlico had asked of Bessie, after looking at her a good deal – at her face and her hands, her dress and her hair.

'Very much indeed,' said Bessie.

'Do you like this hotel?'

'It is very comfortable,' said Bessie.

'Do you like stopping at hotels?' inquired Lady Pimlico, after a pause.

'I am very fond of travelling,' Bessie answered, 'and I suppose hotels are a necessary part of it. But they are not the part I am fondest of.'

'Oh, I hate travelling!' said the Countess of Pimlico, and transferred her attention to Mrs Westgate.

'My son tells me you are going to Branches,' the Duchess presently resumed.

'Lord Lambeth has been so good as to ask us,' said Mrs Westgate, who perceived that her visitor had now begun to look at her, and who had her customary happy consciousness of a distinguished appearance. The only mitigation of her felicity on this point was that, having inspected her visitor's own costume, she said to herself, 'She won't know how well I am dressed!'

'He has asked me to go, but I am not sure I shall be able,' murmured the Duchess.

'He had offered us the p— the prospect of meeting you,' said Mrs Westgate.

'I hate the country at this season,' responded the Duchess.

Mrs Westgate gave a little shrug. 'I think it is pleasanter than London.'

But the Duchess's eyes were absent again; she was looking very fixedly at Bessie. In a moment she slowly rose, walked to a chair that stood empty at the young girl's right hand, and silently seated herself. As she was a majestic, voluminous woman, this little transaction had, inevitably, an air of somewhat impressive intention. It diffused a certain awkwardness, which Lady Pimlico, as a sympathetic daughter, perhaps desired to rectify in turning to Mrs Westgate.

'I daresay you go out a great deal,' she observed.

'No, very little. We are strangers, and we didn't come here for society.'

'I see,' said Lady Pimlico. 'It's rather nice in town just now.'

'It's charming,' said Mrs Westgate. 'But we only go to see a few people – whom we like.'

'Of course one can't like every one,' said Lady Pimlico.

'It depends upon one's society,' Mrs Westgate rejoined.

The Duchess, meanwhile, had addressed herself to Bessie. 'My son tells me the young ladies in America are so clever.'

'I am glad they made such a good impression on him,' said Bessie, smiling.

The Duchess was not smiling; her large fresh face was very tranquil. 'He is very susceptible,' she said. 'He thinks every one clever, and sometimes they are.'

'Sometimes,' Bessie assented, smiling still.

The Duchess looked at her a little and then went on – 'Lambeth is very susceptible, but he is very volatile, too.'

'Volatile?' asked Bessie.

'He is very inconstant. It won't do to depend on him.'

'Ah!' said Bessie; 'I don't recognise that description. We have depended on him greatly – my sister and I – and he has never disappointed us.'

'He will disappoint you yet,' said the Duchess.

Bessie gave a little laugh, as if she were amused at the Duchess's persistency. 'I suppose it will depend on what we expect of him.'

'The less you expect the better,' Lord Lambeth's mother declared.

'Well,' said Bessie, 'we expect nothing unreasonable.'

The Duchess, for a moment, was silent, though she appeared to have more to say. 'Lambeth says he has seen so much of you,' she presently began.

'He has been to see us very often – he has been very kind,' said Bessie Alden.

'I daresay you are used to that. I am told there is a great deal of that in America.'

'A great deal of kindness?' the young girl inquired, smiling.

'Is that what you call it? I know you have different expressions.'

'We certainly don't always understand each other,' said Mrs Westgate, the termination of whose interview with Lady Pimlico allowed her to give her attention to their elder visitor.

'I am speaking of the young men calling so much upon the young ladies,' the Duchess explained.

'But surely in England,' said Mrs Westgate, 'the young ladies don't call upon the young men?'

84

'Some of them do – almost!' Lady Pimlico declared. 'When the young men are a great *parti*.'

'Bessie, you must make a note of that,' said Mrs Westgate. 'My sister,' she added, 'is a model traveller. She writes down all the curious facts she hears, in a little book she keeps for the purpose.'

The Duchess was a little flushed; she looked all about the room, while her daughter turned to Bessie. 'My brother told us you were wonderfully clever,' said Lady Pimlico.

'He should have said my sister,' Bessie answered – 'when she says such things as that.'

'Shall you be long at Branches?' the Duchess asked, abruptly, of the young girl.

'Lord Lambeth has asked us for three days,' said Bessie.

'I shall go,' the Duchess declared, 'and my daughter too.'

'That will be charming!' Bessie rejoined.

'Delightful!' murmured Mrs Westgate.

'I shall expect to see a deal of you,' the Duchess continued. 'When I go to Branches I monopolise my son's guests.'

'They must be most happy,' said Mrs Westgate, very graciously.

'I want immensely to see it – to see the Castle,' said Bessie to the Duchess. 'I have never seen one – in England at least; and you know we have none in America.'

'Ah! you are fond of castles?' inquired her Grace.

'Immensely!' replied the young girl. 'It has been the dream of my life to live in one.'

The Duchess looked at her a moment, as if she hardly knew how to take this assurance, which, from her Grace's point of view, was either very artless or very audacious. 'Well,' she said, rising, 'I will show you Branches myself.' And upon this the two great ladies took their departure.

'What did they mean by it?' asked Mrs Westgate, when they were gone.

'They meant to be polite,' said Bessie, 'because we are going to meet them.'

'It is too late to be polite,' Mrs Westgate replied, almost grimly. 'They meant to overawe us by their fine manners and their grandeur, and to make you *lâcher prise*.'

'*Lâcher prise?* What strange things you say!' murmured Bessie Alden.

'They meant to snub us, so that we shouldn't dare to go to Branches,' Mrs Westgate continued.

'On the contrary,' said Bessie, 'the Duchess offered to show me the place herself.'

'Yes, you may depend upon it she won't let you out of her sight. She will show you the place from morning till night.'

'You have a theory for everything,' said Bessie.

'And you apparently have none for anything.'

'I saw no attempt to "overawe" us,' said the young girl. 'Their manners were not fine.'

'They were not even good!' Mrs Westgate declared.

Bessie was silent awhile, but in a few moments she observed that she had a very good theory. 'They came to look at me!' she said, as if this had been a very ingenious hypothesis. Mrs Westgate did it justice; she greeted it with a smile and pronounced it most brilliant; while in reality she felt that the young girl's scepticism, or her charity, or, as she had sometimes called it, appropriately, her idealism, was proof against irony. Bessie, however, remained meditative all the rest of that day and well on into the morrow.

On the morrow, before lunch, Mrs Westgate had occasion to go out for an hour, and left her sister writing a letter. When she came back she met Lord Lambeth at the door of the hotel, coming away. She thought he looked slightly embarrassed; he was certainly very grave. 'I am sorry to have missed you. Won't you come back?' she asked.

'No,' said the young man, 'I can't. I have seen your sister. I can never come back.' Then he looked at her a moment, and took her hand. 'Good-bye, Mrs Westgate,' he said. 'You have been very kind to me.' And with what she thought a strange, sad look in his handsome young face, he turned away.

She went in and she found Bessie still writing her letter; that is, Mrs Westgate perceived she was sitting at the table with the pen in her hand and not writing. 'Lord Lambeth has been here,' said the elder lady at last.

Then Bessie got up and showed her a pale, serious face. She bent this face upon her sister for some time, confessing silently and, a little pleading. 'I told him,' she said at last, 'that we could not go to Branches.'

Mrs Westgate displayed just a spark of irritation. 'He might have waited,' she said with a smile, 'till one had seen the Castle.' Later, an hour afterwards, she said, 'Dear Bessie, I wish you might have accepted him.'

'I couldn't,' said Bessie, gently.

'He is a dear good fellow,' said Mrs Westgate.

'I couldn't,' Bessie repeated.

'If it is only,' her sister added, 'because those women will think that they succeeded – that they paralysed us!'

Bessie Alden turned away; but presently she added, 'They were interesting; I should have liked to see them again.'

'So should I!' cried Mrs Westgate, significantly.

'And I should have liked to see the Castle,' said Bessie. 'But now we must leave England,' she added.

Her sister looked at her. 'You will not wait to go to the National Gallery?'

'Not now.'

'Nor to Canterbury Cathedral?'

Bessie reflected a moment. 'We can stop there on our way to Paris,' she said.

Lord Lambeth did not tell Percy Beaumont that the contingency he was not prepared at all to like had occurred; but Percy Beaumont, on hearing that the two ladies had left London, wondered with some intensity what had happened; wondered, that is, until the Duchess of Bayswater came, a little, to his assistance. The two ladies went to Paris, and Mrs Westgate beguiled the journey to that city by repeating several times, 'That's what I regret; they will think they petrified us.' But Bessie Alden seemed to regret nothing.

The Pension Beaurepas

I

I was not rich – on the contrary; and I had been told the Pension
Beaurepas was cheap. I had, moreover, been told that a boarding-
house is a capital place for the study of human nature. I had a fancy
for a literary career, and a friend of mine had said to me, 'If you
mean to write you ought to go and live in a boarding-house; there
is no other such place to pick up material.' I had read something
of this kind in a letter addressed by Stendhal to his sister; 'I have
a passionate desire to know human nature, and have a great mind
to live in a boarding-house, where people cannot conceal their real
characters.' I was an admirer of *La Chartreuse de Parme*, and it
appeared to me that one could not do better than follow in the
footsteps of its author. I remembered, too, the magnificent boarding-
house in Balzac's Père Goriot, – the '*pension bourgeoise des deux sexes
et autres*', kept by Madam Vauquer, *née* De Conflans. Magnificent,
I mean, as a piece of portraiture; the establishment, as an establishment, was certainly sordid enough, and I hoped for better things
from the Pension Beaurepas. This institution was one of the most
esteemed in Geneva, and, standing in a little garden of its own, not
far from the lake, had a very homely, comfortable, sociable aspect.
The regular entrance was, as one might say, at the back, which
looked upon the street, or rather upon a little *place*, adorned like
every place in Geneva, great or small, with a fountain. This fact was
not prepossessing, for on crossing the threshold you found yourself
more or less in the kitchen, encompassed with culinary odours.
This, however, was no great matter, for at the Pension Beaurepas
there was no attempt at gentility or at concealment of the domestic
machinery. The latter was of a very simple sort. Madame Beaurepas
was an excellent little old woman – she was very far advanced in
life, and had been keeping a pension for forty years – whose only
faults were that she was slightly deaf, that she was fond of a
surreptitious pinch of snuff, and that, at the age of seventy-three,
she wore flowers in her cap. There was a tradition in the house that

she was not so deaf as she pretended; that she feigned this infirmity in order to possess herself of the secrets of her lodgers. But I never subscribed to this story; I am convinced that Madame Beaurepas had outlived the period of indiscreet curiosity. She was a phil-osopher, on a matter-of-fact basis; she had been having lodgers for forty years, and all that she asked of them was that they should pay their bills, make use of the door-mat, and fold their napkins. She cared very little for their secrets. 'J'en ai vus de toutes les couleurs,' she said to me. She had quite ceased to care for individuals; she cared only for types, for categories. Her large observation had made her acquainted with a great number, and her mind was a complete collection of 'heads'. She flattered herself that she knew at a glance where to pigeon-hole a new-comer, and if she made any mistakes her deportment never betrayed them. I think that, as regards indivi-duals, she had neither likes nor dislikes; but she was capable of expressing esteem or contempt for a species. She had her own ways, I suppose, of manifesting her approval, but her manner of indicating the reverse was simple and unvarying. 'Je trouve que c'est déplacé!' – this exhausted her view of the matter. If one of her inmates had put arsenic into the *pot-au-feu*, I believe Madame Beaurepas would have contented herself with remarking that the proceeding was out of place. The line of misconduct to which she most objected was an undue assumption of gentility; she had no patience with boarders who gave themselves airs. 'When people come *chez moi*, it is not to cut a figure in the world; I have never had that illusion,' I remember hearing her say; 'and when you pay seven francs a day, *tout compris*, it comprises everything but the right to look down upon the others. But there are people who, the less they pay, the more they take themselves *au sérieux*. My most difficult boarders have always been those who have had the little rooms.'

Madame Beaurepas had a niece, a young woman of some forty odd years; and the two ladies, with the assistance of a couple of thick-waisted, red-armed peasant women, kept the house going. If on your exits and entrances you peeped into the kitchen, it made very little difference; for Célestine, the cook, had no pretension to be an invisible functionary or to deal in occult methods. She was always at your service, with a grateful grin: she blacked your boots; she trudged off to fetch a cab; she would have carried your baggage, if you had allowed her, on her broad little back. She was always tramping in and out, between her kitchen and the fountain in the place, where it often seemed to me that a large part of the preparation for our dinner went forward – the wringing out of towels and table-cloths, the washing of potatoes and cabbages, the scouring of saucepans and cleansing of water-bottles. You enjoyed, from the door-step, a perpetual back view of Célestine and of her large, loose, woollen ankles, as she craned, from the waist, over into the fountain and dabbled in her various utensils. This sounds as if life went on in a very make-shift fashion at the Pension Beaurepas – as if the tone of the establishment were sordid. But such was not at all the case. We were simply very *bourgeois*; we practised the good old Genevese principle of not sacrificing to appearances. This is an excellent principle – when you have the reality. We had the reality at the Pension Beaurepas: we had it in the shape of soft, short beds, equipped with fluffy *duvets*; of admirable coffee, served to us in the morning by Célestine in person, as we lay recumbent on these downy couches; of copious, wholesome, succulent dinners, conformable to the best provincial traditions. For myself, I thought the Pension Beaurepas picturesque, and this, with me, at that time was a great word. I was young and ingenuous; I had just come from America. I wished to perfect myself in the French tongue, and I innocently believed that it flourished by Lake Leman. I used to go to lectures at the Academy, and come home with a violent appetite. I always enjoyed my morning walk across the long bridge (there was only one, just there, in those days) which spans the deep blue out-gush of the lake, and up the dark, steep streets of the old Calvinistic city. The garden faced this way, toward the lake and the old town; and this was the pleasantest approach to the house. There was a high wall, with a double gate in the middle, flanked by a couple of ancient massive posts; the big rusty *grille* contained some old-fashioned iron-work. The garden was rather mouldy and weedy, tangled and untended; but it contained a little thin-flowing fountain, several green benches, a rickety little table of the same complexion, and three orange-trees, in tubs, which were deposited as effectively as possible in front of the windows of the *salon*.

2

As commonly happens in boarding-houses, the rustle of petticoats was, at the Pension Beaurepas, the most familiar form of the human tread. There was the usual allotment of economical widows and old maids, and to maintain the balance of the sexes there were only an old Frenchman and a young American. It hardly made the matter easier that the old Frenchman came from Lausanne. He was a native of that estimable town, but he had once spent six months in Paris, he had tasted of the tree of knowledge; he had got beyond Lausanne, whose resources he pronounced inadequate. Lausanne, as he said, *'manquait d'agréments'*. When obliged, for reasons which he never specified, to bring his residence in Paris to a close, he had fallen back on Geneva; he had broken his fall at the Pension Beaurepas. Geneva was, after all, more like Paris, and at a Genevese boarding-house there was sure to be plenty of Americans with whom one could talk about the French metropolis. M. Pigeonneau was a little lean man, with a large, narrow nose, who sat a great deal in the garden, reading with the aid of a large magnifying glass a volume from the *cabinet de lecture*.

One day, a fortnight after my arrival at the Pension Beaurepas, I came back rather earlier than usual from my academic session; it wanted half an hour of the midday breakfast. I went into the salon with the design of possessing myself of the day's *Galignani* before one of the little English old maids should have removed it to her virginal bower – a privilege to which Madame Beaurepas frequently alluded as one of the attractions of the establishment. In the salon I found a newcomer, a tall gentleman in a high black hat, whom I immediately recognised as a compatriot. I had often seen him, or his equivalent, in the hotel-parlours of my native land. He apparently supposed himself to be at the present moment in a hotel-parlour; his hat was on his head, or, rather, half off it – pushed back from his forehead, and rather suspended than poised. He stood before a table on which old newspapers were scattered, one of which he had taken up and, with his eye-glass on his nose, was holding out at arm's-length. It was that honourable but extremely diminutive sheet, the *Journal de Genève*, a newspaper of about the size of a pocket-handkerchief. As I drew near, looking for my *Galignani*, the tall gentleman gave me, over the top of his eye-glass, a somewhat solemn stare. Presently, however, before I had time to lay my hand on the object of my search, he silently offered me the *Journal de Genève*.

'It appears,' he said, 'to be the paper of the country.'

'Yes,' I answered, 'I believe it's the best.'

He gazed at it again, still holding it at arm's-length, as if it had been a looking-glass. 'Well,' he said, 'I suppose it's natural a small country should have small papers. You could wrap it up, mountains and all, in one of our dailies!'

I found my *Galignani* and went off with it into the garden, where I seated myself on a bench in the shade. Presently I saw the tall gentleman in the hat appear in one of the open windows of the salon, and stand there with his hands in his pockets and his legs a little apart. He looked very much bored, and – I don't know why – I immediately began to feel sorry for him. He was not at all a picturesque personage; he looked like a jaded, faded man of business. But after a little he came into the garden and began to stroll about; and then his restless, unoccupied carriage, and the vague, unacquainted manner in which his eyes wandered over the place seemed to make it proper that, as an older resident, I should exercise a certain hospitality. I said something to him, and he came and sat down beside me on my bench, clasping one of his long knees in his hands.

'When is it this big breakfast of theirs comes off?' he inquired. 'That's what I call it – the little breakfast and the big breakfast. I never thought I should live to see the time when I should care to eat two breakfasts. But a man's glad to do anything, over here.'

'For myself,' I observed, 'I find plenty to do.'

He turned his head and glanced at me with a dry, deliberate, kind-looking eye. 'You're getting used to the life, are you?'

'I like the life very much,' I answered, laughing.

'How long have you tried it?'

'Do you mean in this place?'

'Well, I mean anywhere. It seems to me pretty much the same all over.'

'I have been in this house only a fortnight,' I said.

'Well, what should you say, from what you have seen?' my companion asked.

'Oh,' said I, 'you can see all there is immediately. It's very simple.'

'Sweet simplicity, eh? I'm afraid my two ladies will find it too simple.'

'Everything is very good,' I went on. 'And Madame Beaurepas is a charming old woman. And then it's very cheap.'

'Cheap, is it?' my friend repeated meditatively.

'Doesn't it strike you so?' I asked. I thought it very possible he had not inquired the terms. But he appeared not to have heard me; he sat there, clasping his knee and blinking, in a contemplative manner, at the sunshine.

'Are you from the United States, sir?' he presently demanded, turning his head again.

'Yes, sir,' I replied; and I mentioned the place of my nativity.

'I presumed,' he said, 'that you were American or English. I'm from the United States myself; from New York city. Many of our people here?'

'Not so many as, I believe, there have sometimes been. There are two or three ladies.'

'Well,' my interlocutor declared, 'I am very fond of ladies' society. I think when it's superior there's nothing comes up to it. I've got two ladies here myself; I must make you acquainted with them.'

I rejoined that I should be delighted, and I inquired of my friend whether he had been long in Europe.

'Well, it seems precious long,' he said, 'but my time's not up yet. We have been here fourteen weeks and a half.'

'Are you travelling for pleasure?' I asked.

My companion turned his head again and looked at me – looked at me so long in silence that I at last also turned and met his eyes.

'No, sir,' he said presently. 'No, sir,' he repeated, after a considerable interval.

'Excuse me,' said I, for there was something so solemn in his tone that I feared I had been indiscreet.

He took no notice of my ejaculation; he simply continued to look at me. 'I'm travelling,' he said, at last, 'to please the doctors. They seemed to think they would like it.'

'Ah, they sent you abroad for your health?'

'They sent me abroad because they were so confoundedly muddled they didn't know what else to do.'

'That's often the best thing,' I ventured to remark.

'It was a confession of weakness; they wanted me to stop plaguing them. They didn't know enough to cure me, and that's the way they thought they would get round it. I wanted to be cured – I didn't want to be transported. I hadn't done any harm.'

I assented to the general proposition of the inefficiency of doctors, and asked my companion if he had been seriously ill.

'I didn't sleep,' he said, after some delay.

'Ah, that's very annoying. I suppose you were over-worked.'

'I didn't eat; I took no interest in my food.'

'Well, I hope you both eat and sleep now,' I said.

'I couldn't hold a pen,' my neighbour went on. 'I couldn't sit still. I couldn't walk from my house to the cars – and it's only a little way. I lost my interest in business.'

'You needed a holiday,' I observed.

'That's what the doctors said. It wasn't so very smart of them. I had been paying strict attention to business for twenty-three years.'

'In all that time you have never had a holiday?' I exclaimed, with horror.

My companion waited a little. 'Sundays,' he said at last.

'No wonder, then, you were out of sorts.'

'Well, sir,' said my friend, 'I shouldn't have been where I was three years ago if I had spent my time travelling round Europe. I was in a very advantageous position. I did a very large business. I was considerably interested in lumber.' He paused, turned his head, and looked at me a moment. 'Have you any business interests yourself?' I answered that I had none, and he went on again, slowly, softly, deliberately. 'Well, sir, perhaps you are not aware that business in the United States is not what it was a short time since. Business interests are very insecure. There seems to be a general falling-off. Different parties offer different explanations of the fact, but so far as I am aware none of their observations have set things going again.' I ingeniously intimated that if business was dull, the time was good for coming away; whereupon my neighbour threw back his head and stretched his legs a while. 'Well, sir, that's one view of the matter certainly. There's something to be said for that. These things should be looked at all round. That's the ground my wife took. That's the ground,' he added in a moment 'that a lady would naturally take'; and he gave a little dry laugh.

'You think it's slightly illogical,' I remarked.

'Well, sir, the ground I took was that the worse a man's business is, the more it requires looking after. I shouldn't want to go out to take a walk – not even to go to church – if my house was on fire. My firm is not doing the business it was; it's like a sick child, it requires nursing. What I wanted the doctors to do was to fix me up, so that I could go on at home. I'd have taken anything they'd have given me, and as many times a day. I wanted to be right there; I had my reasons; I have them still. But I came off, all the same,' said my friend, with a melancholy smile.

I was a great deal younger than he, but there was something so simple and communicative in his tone, so expressive of a desire to fraternise, and so exempt from any theory of human differences, that I quite forgot his seniority, and found myself offering him paternal advice. 'Don't think about all that,' said I. 'Simply enjoy yourself, amuse yourself, get well. Travel about and see Europe. At the end of a year, by the time you are ready to go home, things will have improved over there, and you will be quite well and happy.'

My friend laid his hand on my knee; he looked at me for some moments, and I thought he was going to say, 'You are very young!' But he said presently, '*You* have got used to Europe any way!'

3

At breakfast I encountered his ladies – his wife and daughter. They were placed, however, at a distance from me, and it was not until the *pensionnaires* had dispersed, and some of them, according to custom, had come out into the garden, that he had an opportunity of making me acquainted with them.

'Will you allow me to introduce you to my daughter?' he said, moved apparently by a paternal inclination to provide this young lady with social diversion. She was standing with her mother, in one of the paths, looking about with no great complacency, as I imagined, at the homely characteristics of the place, and old M. Pigeonneau was hovering near, hesitating apparently between the desire to be urbane and the absence of a pretext. 'Mrs Ruck – Miss Sophy Ruck,' said my friend, leading me up.

Mrs Ruck was a large, plump, light coloured person, with a smooth fair face, a somnolent eye, and an elaborate coiffure. Miss Sophy was a girl of one and twenty, very small and very pretty – what I suppose would have been called a lively brunette. Both of these ladies were attired in black silk dresses, very much trimmed; they had an air of the highest elegance.

'Do you think highly of this pension?' inquired Mrs Ruck, after a few preliminaries.

'It's a little rough, but it seems to me comfortable,' I answered.

'Does it take a high rank in Geneva?' Mrs Ruck pursued.

'I imagine it enjoys a very fair fame,' I said, smiling.

'I should never dream of comparing it to a New York boarding-house,' said Mrs Ruck.

'It's quite a different style,' her daughter observed. Miss Ruck had folded her arms; she was holding her elbows with a pair of white little hands, and she was tapping the ground with a pretty little foot.

'We hardly expected to come to a pension,' said Mrs Ruck. 'But we thought we would try; we had heard so much about Swiss pensions. I was saying to Mr Ruck that I wondered whether this was a favourable specimen. I was afraid we might have made a mistake.'

'We knew some people who had been here; they thought everything of Madame Beaurepas,' said Miss Sophy. 'They said she was a real friend.'

'Mr and Mrs Parker – perhaps you have heard her speak of them,' Mrs Ruck pursued.

'Madame Beaurepas has had a great many Americans; she is very fond of Americans,' I replied.

'Well, I must say I should think she would be, if she compares them with some others.'

'Mother is always comparing,' observed Miss Ruck.

'Of course I am always comparing,' rejoined the elder lady. 'I never had a chance till now; I never knew my privileges. Give me an American!' And Mrs Ruck indulged in a little laugh.

'Well, I must say there are some things I like over here,' said Miss Sophy, with courage. And indeed I could see that she was a young woman of great decision.

'You like the shops – that's what you like,' her father affirmed.

The young lady addressed herself to me, without heeding this remark. 'I suppose you feel quite at home here.'

'Oh, he likes it; he has got used to the life!' exclaimed Mr Ruck.

'I wish you'd teach Mr Ruck,' said his wife. 'It seems as if he couldn't get used to anything.'

'I'm used to you, my dear,' the husband retorted, giving me a humorous look.

'He's intensely restless,' continued Mrs Ruck. 'That's what made me want to come to a pension. I thought he would settle down more.'

'I don't think I *am* used to you, after all,' said her husband.

In view of a possible exchange of conjugal repartee I took refuge in conversation with Miss Ruck, who seemed perfectly able to play her part in any colloquy. I learned from this young lady that, with her parents, after visiting the British islands, she had been spending a month in Paris, and that she thought she should have died when she left that city. 'I hung out of the carriage, when we left the hotel,' said Miss Ruck, 'I assure you I did. And mother did, too.'

'Out of the other window, I hope,' said I.

'Yes, one out of each window,' she replied, promptly. 'Father had hard work, I can tell you. We hadn't half finished; there were ever so many places we wanted to go to.'

'Your father insisted on coming away?'

'Yes; after we had been there about a month he said he had enough. He's fearfully restless; he's very much out of health. Mother and I said to him that if he was restless in Paris he needn't hope for peace anywhere. We don't mean to leave him alone till he takes us back.' There was an air of keen resolution in Miss Ruck's pretty face, of lucid apprehension of desirable ends, which made me, as she pronounced these words, direct a glance of covert compassion toward her poor recalcitrant father. He had walked away a little with his wife, and I saw only his back and his stooping, patient-looking shoulders, whose air of acute resignation was thrown into relief by the voluminous tranquillity of Mrs Ruck. 'He will have to take us back in September, any way,' the young girl pursued; 'he will have to take us back to get some things we have ordered.'

'Have you ordered a great many things?' I asked, jocosely.

'Well, I guess we have ordered *some*. Of course we wanted to take advantage of being in Paris – ladies always do. We have left the principal things till we go back. Of course that is the principal interest, for ladies. Mother said she should feel so shabby, if she just passed through. We have promised all the people to be back in September, and I never broke a promise yet. So Mr Ruck has got to make his plans accordingly.'

'And what are his plans?'

'I don't know; he doesn't seem able to make any. His great idea was to get to Geneva, but now that he has got here he doesn't seem to care. It's the effect of ill health. He used to be so bright; but now he is quite subdued. It's about time he should improve, any way. We went out last night to look at the jewellers' windows – in that street behind the hotel. I had always heard of those jewellers' windows. We saw some lovely things, but it didn't seem to rouse father. He'll get tired of Geneva sooner than he did of Paris.'

'Ah,' said I, 'there are finer things here than the jewellers' windows. We are very near some of the most beautiful scenery in Europe.'

'I suppose you mean the mountains. Well, we have seen plenty of mountains at home. We used to go to the mountains every summer. We are familiar enough with the mountains. Aren't we, mother?' the young lady demanded, appealing to Mrs Ruck, who, with her husband, had drawn near again.

'Aren't we what?' inquired the elder lady.

'Aren't we familiar with the mountains?'

'Well, I hope so,' said Mrs Ruck.

Mr Ruck, with his hands in his pockets, gave me a sociable wink. 'There's nothing much you can tell them!' he said.

The two ladies stood face to face a few moments, surveying each other's garments. 'Don't you want to go out?' the young girl at last inquired of her mother.

'Well, I think we had better; we have got to go up to that place.'

'To what place?' asked Mr Ruck.

'To that jeweller's – to that big one.'

'They all seemed big enough; they were too big!' And Mr Ruck gave me another wink.

'That one where we saw the blue cross,' said his daughter.

'Oh, come, what do you want of that blue cross?' poor Mr Ruck demanded.

'She wants to hang it on a black velvet ribbon and tie it round her neck,' said his wife.

'A black velvet ribbon? No, I thank you!' cried the young lady. 'Do you suppose I would wear that cross on a black velvet ribbon? On a nice little gold chain, if you please – a little narrow gold chain, like an old-fashioned watch-chain. That's the proper thing for that blue cross. I know the sort of chain I mean; I'm going to look for one. When I want a thing,' said Miss Ruck, with decision, 'I can generally find it.'

'Look here, Sophy,' her father urged, 'you don't want that blue cross.'

'I do want it – I happen to want it.' And Sophy glanced at me with ⁊ little laugh.

Her laugh, which in itself was pretty, suggested that there were various relations in which one might stand to Miss Ruck; but I think I was conscious of a certain satisfaction in not occupying the paternal one. 'Don't worry the poor child,' said her mother.

'Come on, mother,' said Miss Ruck.

'We are going to look about a little,' explained the elder lady to me, by way of taking leave.

'I know what that means,' remarked Mr Ruck, as his companions moved away. He stood looking at them a moment, while he raised his hand to his head, behind, and stood rubbing it a little, with a movement that displaced his hat. (I may remark in parenthesis that I never saw a hat more easily displaced than Mr Ruck's.) I supposed he was going to say something querulous, but I was mistaken. Mr Ruck was unhappy, but he was very good-natured. 'Well, they want to pick up something,' he said. 'That's the principal interest, for ladies.'

4

Mr Ruck distinguished me, as the French say. He honoured me with
his esteem, and, as the days elapsed, with a large portion of his
confidence. Sometimes he bored me a little, for the tone of his
conversation was not cheerful, tending as it did almost exclusively
to a melancholy dirge over the financial prostration of our common
country. 'No, sir, business in the United States is not what it once
was,' he found occasion to remark several times a day. 'There's not
the same spring – there's not the same hopeful feeling. You can see
it in all departments.' He used to sit by the hour in the little garden
of the pension, with a roll of American newspapers in his lap and
his high hat pushed back, swinging one of his long legs and reading
the *New York Herald*. He paid a daily visit to the American banker's,
on the other side of the Rhône, and remained there a long time,
turning over the old papers on the green velvet table in the middle
of the Salon des Étrangers and fraternising with chance compatriots. But in spite of these diversions his time hung heavily upon his
hands. I used sometimes to propose to him to take a walk; but he
had a mortal horror of pedestrianism, and regarded my own taste
for it as a morbid form of activity. 'You'll kill yourself, if you don't
look out,' he said, 'walking all over the country. I don't want to walk
round that way; I ain't a postman!' Briefly speaking, Mr Ruck had
few resources. His wife and daughter, on the other hand, it was to
be supposed, were possessed of a good many that could not be
apparent to an unobtrusive young man. They also sat a great deal
in the garden or in the salon, side by side, with folded hands,
contemplating material objects, and were remarkably independent
of most of the usual feminine aids to idleness – light literature,
tapestry, the use of the piano. They were, however, much fonder
of locomotion than their companion, and I often met them in the
Rue du Rhône and on the quays, loitering in front of the jewellers'
windows. They might have had a cavalier in the person of old M.
Pigeonneau, who possessed a high appreciation of their charms, but

who, owing to the absence of a common idiom, was deprived of the pleasures of intimacy. He knew no English, and Mrs Ruck and her daughter had, as it seemed, an incurable mistrust of the beautiful tongue which, as the old man endeavoured to impress upon them, was pre-eminently the language of conversation.

'They have a *tournure de princesse* – a *distinction suprême*,' he said to me. 'One is surprised to find them in a little pension, at seven francs a day.'

'Oh, they don't come for economy,' I answered. 'They must be rich.'

'They don't come for my *beaux yeux* – for mine,' said M. Pigeonneau, sadly. 'Perhaps it's for yours, young man. Je vous recommande la mère.'

I reflected a moment. 'They came on account of Mr Ruck – because at hotels he's so restless.'

M. Pigeonneau gave me a knowing nod. 'Of course he is, with such a wife as that! – a *femme superbe*. Madame Ruck is preserved in perfection – a miraculous *fraîcheur*. I like those large, fair, quiet women; they are often, *dans l'intimité*, the most agreeable. I'll warrant you that at heart Madame Ruck is a finished coquette.'

'I rather doubt it,' I said.

'You suppose her cold? Ne vous y fiez pas!'

'It is a matter in which I have nothing at stake.'

'You young Americans are droll,' said M. Pigeonneau; 'you never have anything at stake! But the little one, for example; I'll warrant you she's not cold. She is admirably made.'

'She is very pretty.'

' "She is very pretty!" Vous dites cela d'un ton! When you pay compliments to Mademoiselle Ruck, I hope that's not the way you do it.'

'I don't pay compliments to Mademoiselle Ruck.'

'Ah, decidedly,' said M. Pigeonneau, 'you young Americans are droll!'

I should have suspected that these two ladies would not especially commend themselves to Madame Beaurepas; that as a *maîtresse de salon*, which she in some degree aspired to be, she would have found them wanting in a certain flexibility of deportment. But I should have gone quite wrong; Madame Beaurepas had no fault at all to find with her new pensionnaires. 'I have no observation whatever to make about them,' she said to me one evening. 'I see nothing in those ladies which is at all *déplacé*. They don't complain of anything; they don't meddle; they take what's given them; they leave me tranquil. The Americans are often like that. Often, but not always,' Madame Beaurepas pursued. 'We are to have a specimen tomorrow of a very different sort.'

'An American?' I inquired.

'Two *Américaines* – a mother and a daughter. There are Americans and Americans: when you are *difficiles*, you are more so than any one, and when you have pretensions – ah, *par exemple*, it's serious. I foresee that with this little lady everything will be serious, beginning with her *café au lait*. She has been staying at the Pension Chamousset – my *concurrent*, you know, farther up the street; but she is coming away because the coffee is bad. She holds to her coffee, it appears. I don't know what liquid Madame Chamousset may have invented, but we will do the best we can for her. Only, I know she will make me *des histoires* about something else. She will demand a new lamp for the salon; *vous allez voir cela*. She wishes to pay but eleven francs a day for herself and her daughter, *tout compris*; and for their eleven francs they expect to be lodged like princesses. But she is very "ladylike" – isn't that what you call it in English? Oh, *pour cela*, she is ladylike!'

I caught a glimpse on the morrow of this ladylike person, who was arriving at her new residence as I came in from a walk. She had come in a cab, with her daughter and her luggage; and, with an air of perfect softness and serenity, she was disputing the fare as she stood among her boxes, on the steps. She addressed her cabman in a very English accent, but with extreme precision and correctness. 'I wish to be perfectly reasonable, but I don't wish to encourage you in exorbitant demands. With a franc and a half you are sufficiently paid. It is not the custom at Geneva to give a *pour-boire* for so short a drive. I have made inquiries, and I find it is not the custom, even in the best families. I am a stranger, yes, but I always adopt the custom of the native families. I think it my duty toward the natives.'

'But I am a native, too, *moi!*' said the cabman, with an angry laugh.

'You seem to me to speak with a German accent,' continued the lady. 'You are probably from Basel. A franc and a half is sufficient. I see you have left behind the little red bag which I asked you to hold between your knees; you will please to go back to the other house and get it. Very well, if you are impolite I will make a complaint of you to-morrow at the administration. Aurora, you will find a pencil in the outer pocket of my embroidered satchel; please to write down his number, – 87; do you see it distinctly? – in case we should forget it.'

The young lady addressed as 'Aurora' – a slight, fair girl, holding a large parcel of umbrellas – stood at hand while this allocution went forward, but she apparently gave no heed to it. She stood looking about her, in a listless manner, at the front of the house, at the corridor, at Célestine tucking up her apron in the door-way, at me as I passed in amid the disseminated luggage; her mother's parsimonious attitude seeming to produce in Miss Aurora neither sympathy nor embarrassment. At dinner the two ladies were placed on the same side of the table as myself, below Mrs Ruck and her daughter, my own position being on the right of Mr Ruck. I had therefore little observation of Mrs Church – such I learned to be her name – but I occasionally heard her soft, distinct voice.

'White wine, if you please; we prefer white wine. There is none on the table? Then you will please to get some, and to remember to place a bottle of it always here, between my daughter and myself.'

'That lady seems to know what she wants,' said Mr Ruck, 'and she speaks so I can understand her. I can't understand every one, over here. I should like to make that lady's acquaintance. Perhaps she knows what I want, too; it seems hard to find out. But I don't want any of their sour white wine; that's one of the things I don't want. I expect she'll be an addition to the pension.'

Mr Ruck made the acquaintance of Mrs Church that evening in the parlour, being presented to her by his wife, who presumed on the rights conferred upon herself by the mutual proximity, at table, to the two ladies. I suspected that in Mrs Church's view Mrs Ruck presumed too far. The fugitive from the Pension Chamousset, as M. Pigeonneau called her, was a little fresh, plump, comely woman, looking less than her age, with a round, bright, serious face. She was very simply and frugally dressed, not at all in the manner of Mr Ruck's companions, and she had an air of quiet distinction which was an excellent defensive weapon. She exhibited a polite disposition to listen to what Mr Ruck might have to say, but her manner was equivalent to an intimation that what she valued least in boarding-house life was its social opportunities. She had placed herself near a lamp, after carefully screwing it and turning it up, and she had opened in her lap, with the assistance of a large embroidered marker, an octavo volume, which I perceived to be in German. To Mrs Ruck and her daughter she was evidently a puzzle, with her economical attire and her expensive culture. The two younger ladies, however, had begun to fraternise very freely, and Miss Ruck presently went wandering out of the room with her arm round the waist of Miss Church. It was a very warm evening; the long windows of the salon stood wide open into the garden, and, inspired by the balmy darkness, M. Pigeonneau and Mademoiselle Beaurepas, a most obliging little woman, who lisped and always wore a huge cravat, declared they would organise a *fête de nuit*. They engaged in this undertaking, and the fête developed itself, consisting of half a dozen red paper lanterns, hung about on the trees, and of several glasses of *sirop*, carried on a tray by the stout-armed Célestine. As the festival deepened to its climax I went out into the garden, where M. Pigeonneau was master of ceremonies.

'But where are those charming young ladies,' he cried, 'Miss Ruck and the new-comer, *l'aimable transfuge*? Their absence has been remarked, and they are wanting to the brilliancy of the occasion. *Voyez* I have selected a glass of syrup – a generous glass – for Mademoiselle Ruck, and I advise you, my young friend, if you wish to make a good impression, to put aside one which you may offer to the other young lady. What is her name? Miss Church. I see; it's a singular name. There is a church in which I would willingly worship!'

Mr Ruck presently came out of the salon, having concluded his interview with Mrs Church. Through the open window I saw the latter lady sitting under the lamp with her German octavo, while Mrs Ruck, established, empty-handed, in an arm-chair near her, gazed at her with an air of fascination.

'Well, I told you she would know what I want,' said Mr Ruck. 'She says I want to go up to Appenzell, wherever that is; that I want to drink whey and live in a high latitude – what did she call it? – a high altitude. She seemed to think we ought to leave for Appenzell to-morrow; she'd got it all fixed. She says this ain't a high enough lat – a high enough altitude. And she says I mustn't go too high, either; that would be just as bad; she seems to know just the right figure. She says she'll give me a list of the hotels where we must stop, on the way to Appenzell. I asked her if she didn't want to go with us, but she says she'd rather sit still and read. I expect she's a big reader.'

The daughter of this accomplished woman now reappeared, in company with Miss Ruck, with whom she had been strolling through the outlying parts of the garden.

'Well,' said Miss Ruck, glancing at the red paper lanterns, 'are they trying to stick the flower-pots into the trees?'

'It's an illumination in honour of our arrival,' the other young girl rejoined. 'It's a triumph over Madame Chamousset.'

'Meanwhile, at the Pension Chamousset,' I ventured to suggest, 'they have put out their lights; they are sitting in darkness, lamenting your departure.'

She looked at me, smiling; she was standing in the light that came from the house. M. Pigeonneau, meanwhile, who had been awaiting his chance, advanced to Miss Ruck with his glass of syrup. 'I have kept it for you, mademoiselle,' he said; 'I have jealously guarded it. It is very delicious!'

Miss Ruck looked at him and his syrup, without making any motion to take the glass. 'Well, I guess it's sour,' she said in a moment; and she gave a little shake of her head.

M. Pigeonneau stood staring, with his syrup in his hand; then he slowly turned away. He looked about at the rest of us, as if to appeal from Miss Ruck's insensibility, and went to deposit his rejected tribute on a bench.

'Won't you give it to me?' asked Miss Church, in faultless French. 'J'adore le sirop, moi.'

M. Pigeonneau came back with alacrity, and presented the glass with a very low bow. 'I adore good manners,' murmured the old man.

This incident caused me to look at Miss Church with quickened interest. She was not strikingly pretty, but in her charming, irregular face there was something brilliant and ardent. Like her mother, she was very simply dressed.

'She wants to go to America, and her mother won't let her,' said Miss Sophy to me, explaining her companion's situation.

'I am very sorry – for America,' I answered, laughing.

'Well, I don't want to say anything against your mother, but I think it's shameful,' Miss Ruck pursued.

'Mamma has very good reasons; she will tell you them all.'

'Well, I'm sure I don't want to hear them,' said Miss Ruck. 'You have got a right to go to your own country; every one has a right to go to their own country.'

'Mamma is not very patriotic,' said Aurora Church, smiling.

'Well, I call that dreadful,' her companion declared. 'I have heard that there are some Americans like that, but I never believed it.'

'There are all sorts of Americans,' I said, laughing.

'Aurora's one of the right sort,' rejoined Miss Ruck, who had apparently become very intimate with her new friend.

'Are you very patriotic?' I asked of the young girl.

'She's right down homesick,' said Miss Sophy; 'she's dying to go. If I were you my mother would have to take me.'

'Mamma is going to take me to Dresden.'

'Well, I declare I never heard of anything so dreadful!' cried Miss Ruck. 'It's like something in a story.'

'I never heard there was anything very dreadful in Dresden,' I interposed.

Miss Ruck looked at me a moment. 'Well, I don't believe *you* are a good American,' she replied, 'and I never supposed you were. You had better go in there and talk to Mrs Church.'

'Dresden is really very nice, isn't it?' I asked of her companion.

'It isn't nice if you happen to prefer New York,' said Miss Sophy. 'Miss Church prefers New York. Tell him you are dying to see New York; it will make him angry,' she went on.

'I have no desire to make him angry,' said Aurora, smiling.

'It is only Miss Ruck who can do that,' I rejoined. 'Have you been a long time in Europe?'

'Always.'

'I call that wicked!' Miss Sophy declared.

'You might be in a worse place,' I continued. 'I find Europe very interesting.'

Miss Ruck gave a little laugh. 'I was saying that you wanted to pass for a European.'

'Yes, I want to pass for a Dalmatian.'

Miss Ruck looked at me a moment. 'Well, you had better not come home,' she said. 'No one will speak to you.'

'Were you born in these countries?' I asked of her companion.

'Oh, no; I came to Europe when I was a small child. But I remember America a little, and it seems delightful.'

'Wait till you see it again. It's just too lovely,' said Miss Sophy.

'It's the grandest country in the world,' I added.

Miss Ruck began to toss her head. 'Come away, my dear,' she said. 'If there's a creature I despise it's a man that tries to say funny things about his own country.'

'Don't you think one can be tired of Europe?' Aurora asked, lingering.

'Possibly – after many years.'

'Father was tired of it after three weeks,' said Miss Ruck.

'I have been here sixteen years,' her friend went on, looking at me with a charming intentness, as if she had a purpose in speaking. 'It used to be for my education. I don't know what it's for now.'

'She's beautifully educated,' said Miss Ruck. 'She knows four languages.'

'I am not very sure that I know English.'

'You should go to Boston!' cried Miss Sophy. 'They speak splendidly in Boston.'

'C'est mon rêve,' said Aurora, still looking at me.

'Have you been all over Europe,' I asked – 'in all the different countries?'

She hesitated a moment. 'Everywhere that there's a *pension*. Mamma is devoted to *pensions*. We have lived, at one time or another, in every *pension* in Europe.'

'Well, I should think you had seen about enough,' said Miss Ruck.

'It's a delightful way of seeing Europe,' Aurora rejoined, with her brilliant smile. 'You may imagine how it has attached me to the different countries. I have such charming souvenirs! There is a *pension* awaiting us now at Dresden, – eight francs a day, without wine. That's rather dear. Mamma means to make them give us wine. Mamma is a great authority on *pensions*; she is known, that way, all over Europe. Last winter we were in Italy, and she discovered one at Piacenza, – four francs a day. We made economies.'

'Your mother doesn't seem to mingle much,' observed Miss Ruck, glancing through the window at the scholastic attitude of Mrs Church.

'No, she doesn't mingle, except in the native society. Though she lives in *pensions*, she detests them.'

'Why does she live in them?' asked Miss Sophy, rather resentfully.

'Oh, because we are so poor; it's the cheapest way to live. We have tried having a cook, but the cook always steals. Mamma used to set me to watch her; that's the way I passed my *jeunesse* – my *belle jeunesse*. We are frightfully poor,' the young girl went on, with the same strange frankness – a curious mixture of girlish grace and conscious cynicism. 'Nous n'avons pas le sou. That's one of the reasons we don't go back to America; mamma says we can't afford to live there.'

'Well, any one can see that you're an American girl,' Miss Ruck remarked, in a consolatory manner. 'I can tell an American girl a mile off. You've got the American style.'

'I'm afraid I haven't the American *toilette*,' said Aurora, looking at the other's superior splendour.

'Well, your dress was cut in France; any one can see that.'

'Yes,' said Aurora, with a laugh, 'my dress was cut in France – at Avranches.'

'Well, you've got a lovely figure, any way,' pursued her companion.

'Ah,' said the young girl, 'at Avranches, too, my figure was admired.' And she looked at me askance, with a certain coquetry. But I was an innocent youth, and I only looked back at her, wondering. She was a great deal nicer than Miss Ruck, and yet Miss Ruck would not have said that. 'I try to be like an American girl,' she continued; 'I do my best, though mamma doesn't at all encourage it. I am very patriotic. I try to copy them, though mamma has brought me up *à la française*; that is, as much as one can in *pensions*. For instance, I have never been out of the house without mamma; oh, never, never. But sometimes I despair; American girls are so wonderfully frank. I can't be frank, like that. I am always afraid. But I do what I can, as you see. Excusez du peu!'

I thought this young lady at least as outspoken as most of her unexpatriated sisters; there was something almost comical in her despondency. But she had by no means caught, as it seemed to me, the American tone. Whatever her tone was, however, it had a fascination; there was something dainty about it, and yet it was decidedly audacious.

The young ladies began to stroll about the garden again, and I enjoyed their society until M. Pigeonneau's festival came to an end.

5

Mr Ruck did not take his departure to Appenzell on the morrow, in spite of the eagerness to witness such an event which he had attributed to Mrs Church. He continued, on the contrary, for many days after, to hang about the garden, to wander up to the banker's and back again, to engage in desultory conversation with his fellow-boarders, and to endeavour to assuage his constitutional restlessness by perusal of the American journals. But on the morrow I had the honour of making Mrs Church's acquaintance. She came into the salon, after the midday breakfast, with her German octavo under her arm, and she appealed to me for assistance in selecting a quiet corner.

'Would you very kindly,' she said, 'move that large fauteuil a little more this way? Not the largest; the one with the little cushion. The fauteuils here are very insufficient; I must ask Madame Beaurepas for another. Thank you; a little more to the left, please; that will do. Are you particularly engaged?' she inquired, after she had seated herself. 'If not, I should like to have some conversation with you. It is some time since I have met a young American of your – what shall I call it? – your affiliations. I have learned your name from Madame Beaurepas; I think I used to know some of your people. I don't know what has become of all my friends. I used to have a charming little circle at home, but now I meet no one I know. Don't you think there is a great difference between the people one meets and the people one would like to meet? Fortunately, sometimes,' added my interlocutress graciously, 'it's quite the same. I suppose you are a specimen, a favourable specimen,' she went on, 'of young America. Tell me, now, what is young America thinking of in these days of ours? What are its feelings, its opinions, its aspirations? What is its *ideal*?' I had seated myself near Mrs Church, and she had pointed this interrogation with the gaze of her bright little eyes. I felt it embarrassing to be treated as a favourable specimen of young America, and to be expected to answer for the great republic.

Observing my hesitation, Mrs Church clasped her hands on the open page of her book and gave an intense, melancholy smile. '*Has* it an ideal?' she softly asked. 'Well, we must talk of this,' she went on, without insisting. 'Speak, for the present, for yourself simply. Have you come to Europe with any special design?'

'Nothing to boast of,' I said. 'I am studying a little.'

'Ah, I am glad to hear that. You are gathering up a little European culture; that's what we lack, you know, at home. No individual can do much, of course. But you must not be discouraged; every little counts.'

'I see that you, at least, are doing your part,' I rejoined gallantly, dropping my eyes on my companion's learned volume.

'Yes, I frankly admit that I am fond of study. There is no one, after all, like the Germans. That is, for facts. For opinions I by no means always go with them. I form my opinions myself. I am sorry to say, however,' Mrs Church continued, 'that I can hardly pretend to diffuse my acquisitions. I am afraid I am sadly selfish; I do little to irrigate the soil. I belong – I frankly confess it – to the class of absentees.'

'I had the pleasure, last evening,' I said, 'of making the acquaintance of your daughter. She told me you had been a long time in Europe.'

Mrs Church smiled benignantly. 'Can one ever be too long? We shall never leave it.'

'Your daughter won't like that,' I said, smiling too.

'Has she been taking you into her confidence? She is a more sensible young lady than she sometimes appears. I have taken great pains with her; she is really – I may be permitted to say it – superbly educated.'

'She seemed to me a very charming girl,' I rejoined. 'And I learned that she speaks four languages.'

'It is not only that,' said Mrs Church, in a tone which suggested that this might be a very superficial species of culture. 'She has made what we call *de fortes études* – such as I suppose you are making now. She is familiar with the results of modern science; she keeps pace with the new historical school.'

'Ah,' said I, 'she has gone much farther than I!'

'You doubtless think I exaggerate, and you force me, therefore, to mention the fact that I am able to speak of such matters with a certain intelligence.'

'That is very evident,' I said. 'But your daughter thinks you ought to take her home.' I began to fear, as soon as I had uttered these words, that they savoured of treachery to the young lady, but I was reassured by seeing that they produced on her mother's placid countenance no symptom whatever of irritation.

'My daughter has her little theories,' Mrs Church observed, 'she has, I may say, her illusions. And what wonder! What would youth be without its illusions? Aurora has a theory that she would be happier in New York, in Boston, in Philadelphia, than in one of the charming old cities in which our lot is cast. But she is mistaken, that is all. We must allow our children their illusions, must we not? But we must watch over them.'

Although she herself seemed proof against discomposure, I found something vaguely irritating in her soft, sweet positiveness.

'American cities,' I said, 'are the paradise of young girls.'

'Do you mean,' asked Mrs Church, 'that the young girls who come from those places are angels?'

'Yes,' I said, resolutely.

'This young lady – what is her odd name? – with whom my daughter has formed a somewhat precipitate acquaintance: is Miss Ruck an angel? But I won't force you to say anything uncivil. It would be too cruel to make a single exception.'

'Well,' said I, 'at any rate, in America young girls have an easier lot. They have much more liberty.'

My companion laid her hand for an instant on my arm. 'My dear young friend, I know America, I know the conditions of life there, so well. There is perhaps no subject on which I have reflected more than on our national idiosyncrasies.'

'I am afraid you don't approve of them,' said I, a little brutally.

Brutal indeed my proposition was, and Mrs Church was not prepared to assent to it in this rough shape. She dropped her eyes on her book, with an air of acute meditation. Then, raising them, 'We are very crude,' she softly observed – 'we are very crude.' Lest even this delicately-uttered statement should seem to savour of the vice that she deprecated, she went on to explain. 'There are two classes of minds, you know – those that hold back, and those that push forward. My daughter and I are not pushers; we move with little steps. We like the old, trodden paths; we like the old, old world.'

'Ah,' said I, 'you know what you like; there is a great virtue in that.'

'Yes, we like Europe; we prefer it. We like the opportunities of Europe; we like the *rest*. There is so much in that, you know. The world seems to me to be hurrying, pressing forward so fiercely, without knowing where it is going. "Whither?" I often ask, in my little quiet way. But I have yet to learn that any one can tell me.'

'You're a great conservative,' I observed, while I wondered whether I myself could answer this inquiry.

Mrs Church gave me a smile which was equivalent to a confession. 'I wish to retain a *little* – just a little. Surely, we have done so much, we might rest a while; we might pause. That is all my feeling – just to stop a little, to wait! I have seen so many changes. I wish to draw in, to draw in – to hold back, to hold back.'

'You shouldn't hold your daughter back!' I answered, laughing and getting up. I got up, not by way of terminating our interview, for I perceived Mrs Church's exposition of her views to be by no means complete, but in order to offer a chair to Miss Aurora, who at this moment drew near. She thanked me and remained standing, but without at first, as I noticed, meeting her mother's eye.

'You have been engaged with your new acquaintance, my dear?' this lady inquired.

'Yes, mamma dear,' said the young girl, gently.

'Do you find her very edifying?'

Aurora was silent a moment; then she looked at her mother. 'I don't know, mamma; she is very fresh.'

I ventured to indulge in a respectful laugh. 'Your mother has another word for that. But I must not,' I added, 'be crude.'

'Ah, vous m'en voulez?' inquired Mrs Church. 'And yet I can't pretend I said it in jest. I feel it too much. We have been having a little social discussion,' she said to her daughter. 'There is still so much to be said. And I wish,' she continued, turning to me, 'that I could give you our point of view. Don't you wish, Aurora, that we could give him our point of view?'

'Yes, mamma,' said Aurora.

'We consider ourselves very fortunate in our point of view, don't we, dearest?' mamma demanded.

'Very fortunate, indeed, mamma.'

'You see we have acquired an insight into European life,' the elder lady pursued. 'We have our place at many a European fireside. We find so much to esteem – so much to enjoy. Do we not, my daughter?'

'So very much, mamma,' the young girl went on, with a sort of inscrutable submissiveness. I wondered at it; it offered so strange a contrast to the mocking freedom of her tone the night before; but while I wondered, I was careful not to let my perplexity take precedence of my good manners.

'I don't know what you ladies may have found at European firesides,' I said, 'but there can be very little doubt what you have left there.'

Mrs Church got up, to acknowledge my compliment. 'We have spent some charming hours. And that reminds me that we have just now such an occasion in prospect. We are to call upon some Genevese friends – the family of the Pasteur Galopin. They are to go with us to the old library at the Hôtel de Ville, where there are some very interesting documents of the period of the Reformation; we are promised a glimpse of some manuscripts of poor Servetus, the antagonist and victim, you know, of Calvin. Here, of course, one can only speak of Calvin under one's breath, but some day, when we are more private,' and Mrs Church looked round the room, 'I will give you my view of him. I think it has a touch of originality. Aurora is familiar with, are you not, my daughter, familiar with my view of Calvin?'

'Yes, mamma,' said Aurora, with docility, while the two ladies went to prepare for their visit to the Pasteur Galopin.

6

'She has demanded a new lamp; I told you she would!' This communication was made me by Madame Beaurepas a couple of days later. 'And she has asked for a new *tapis de lit*, and she has requested me to provide Célestine with a pair of light shoes. I told her that, as a general thing, cooks are not shod with satin. That poor Célestine!'

'Mrs Church may be exacting,' I said, 'but she is a clever little woman.'

'A lady who pays but five francs and a half shouldn't be too clever. C'est déplacé. I don't like the type.'

'What type do you call Mrs Church's?'

'Mon Dieu,' said Madame Beaurepas, 'c'est une de ces mamans comme vous en avez, qui promènent leur fille.'

'She is trying to marry her daughter? I don't think she's of that sort.'

But Madame Beaurepas shrewdly held to her idea. 'She is trying it in her own way; she does it very quietly. She doesn't want an American; she wants a foreigner. And she wants a *mari sérieux*. But she is travelling over Europe in search of one. She would like a magistrate.'

'A magistrate?'

'A *gros bonnet* of some kind; a professor or a deputy.'

'I am very sorry for the poor girl,' I said, laughing.

'You needn't pity her too much; she's a sly thing.'

'Ah, for that, no!' I exclaimed. 'She's a charming girl.'

Madame Beaurepas gave an elderly grin. 'She has hooked you, eh? But the mother won't have you.'

I developed my idea, without heeding this insinuation. 'She's a charming girl, but she is a little odd. It's a necessity of her position. She is less submissive to her mother than she has to pretend to be. That's in self-defence; it's to make her life possible.'

'She wishes to get away from her mother,' continued Madame Beaurepas. 'She wishes to *courir les champs*.'

'She wishes to go to America, her native country.'

'Precisely. And she will certainly go.'

'I hope so!' I rejoined.

'Some fine morning – or evening – she will go off with a young man; probably with a young American.'

'Allons donc!' said I, with disgust.

'That will be quite America enough,' pursued my cynical hostess. 'I have kept a boarding-house for forty years. I have seen that type.'

'Have such things as that happened *chez vous?*' I asked.

'Everything has happened *chez moi*. But nothing has happened more than once. Therefore this won't happen here. It will be at the next place they go to, or the next. Besides, here there is no young American *pour la partie* – none except you, monsieur. You are susceptible, but you are too reasonable.'

'It's lucky for you I am reasonable,' I answered. 'It's thanks to that fact that you escape a scolding.'

One morning, about this time, instead of coming back to breakfast at the *pension*, after my lectures at the Academy, I went to partake of this meal with a fellow-student, at an ancient eating-house in the collegiate quarter. On separating from my friend, I took my way along that charming public walk known in Geneva as the Treille, a shady terrace, of immense elevation, overhanging a portion of the lower town. There are spreading trees and well-worn benches, and over the tiles and chimneys of the *ville basse* there is a view of the snow-crested Alps. On the other side, as you turn your back to the view, the promenade is overlooked by a row of tall, sober-faced *hôtels*, the dwellings of the local aristocracy. I was very fond of the place, and often resorted to it to stimulate my sense of the picturesque. Presently, as I lingered there on this occasion, I became aware that a gentleman was seated not far from where I stood, with his back to the Alpine chain, which this morning was brilliant and distinct, and a newspaper, unfolded, in his lap. He was not reading, however; he was staring before him in gloomy contemplation. I don't know whether I recognised first the newspaper or its proprietor; one, in either case, would have helped me to identify the other. One was the *New York Herald*; the other, of course, was Mr Ruck. As I drew nearer, he transferred his eyes from the stony, high-featured masks of the gray old houses on the other side of the terrace, and I knew by the expression of his face just how he had been feeling about these distinguished abodes. He had made up his mind that their proprietors were a dusky, narrow-minded, unsociable company; plunging their roots into a superfluous past. I endeavoured, therefore, as I sat down beside him, to suggest something more impersonal.

'That's a beautiful view of the Alps,' I observed.

'Yes,' said Mr Ruck, without moving, 'I've examined it. Fine thing, in its way – fine thing. Beauties of nature – that sort of thing. We came up on purpose to look at it.'

'Your ladies, then, have been with you?'

'Yes; they are just walking round. They're awfully restless. They keep saying I'm restless, but I'm as quiet as a sleeping child to them. It takes,' he added in a moment, drily, 'the form of shopping.'

'Are they shopping now?'

'Well, if they ain't, they're trying to. They told me to sit here a while, and they'd just walk round. I generally know what that means. But that's the principal interest for ladies,' he added, retracting his irony. 'We thought we'd come up here and see the cathedral; Mrs Church seemed to think it a dead loss that we shouldn't see the cathedral, especially as we hadn't seen many yet. And I had to come up to the banker's any way. Well, we certainly saw the cathedral. I don't know as we are any the better for it, and I don't know as I should know it again. But we saw it, any way. I don't know as I should want to go there regularly; but I suppose it will give us, in conversation, a kind of hold on Mrs Church, eh? I guess we want something of that kind. Well,' Mr Ruck continued, 'I stepped in at the banker's to see if there wasn't something, and they handed me out a Herald.

'I hope the Herald is full of good news,' I said.

'Can't say it is. D—d bad news.'

'Political,' I inquired, 'or commercial?'

'Oh, hang politics! It's business, sir. There ain't any business. It's all gone to,' – and Mr Ruck became profane. 'Nine failures in one day. What do you say to that?'

'I hope they haven't injured you,' I said.

'Well, they haven't helped me much. So many houses on fire, that's all. If they happen to take place in your own street, they don't increase the value of your property. When mine catches, I suppose they'll write and tell me – one of these days, when they've got nothing else to do. I didn't get a blessed letter this morning; I suppose they think I'm having such a good time over here it's a pity to disturb me. If I could attend to business for about half an hour, I'd find out something. But I can't, and it's no use talking. The state of my health was never so unsatisfactory as it was about five o'clock this morning.'

'I am very sorry to hear that,' I said, 'and I recommend you strongly not to think of business.'

'I don't,' Mr Ruck replied. 'I'm thinking of cathedrals; I'm think-ing of the beauties of nature. Come,' he went on, turning round on the bench and leaning his elbow on the parapet, 'I'll think of those mountains over there; they *are* pretty, certainly. Can't you get over there?'

'Over where?'

'Over to those hills. Don't they run a train right up?'

'You can go to Chamouni,' I said. 'You can go to Grindelwald and Zermatt and fifty other places. You can't go by rail, but you can drive.'

'All right, we'll drive – and not in a one-horse concern, either. Yes, Chamouni is one of the places we put down. I hope there are a few nice shops in Chamouni.' Mr Ruck spoke with a certain quickened emphasis, and in a tone more explicitly humorous than he commonly employed. I thought he was excited, and yet he had not the appearance of excitement. He looked like a man who has simply taken, in the face of disaster, a sudden, somewhat imagina-tive, resolution not to 'worry'. He presently twisted himself about on his bench again and began to watch for his companions. 'Well, they *are* walking round,' he resumed; 'I guess they've hit on some-thing, somewhere. And they've got a carriage waiting outside of that archway, too. They seem to do a big business in archways here, don't they. They like to have a carriage to carry home the things – those ladies of mine. Then they're sure they've got them.' The ladies, after this, to do them justice, were not very long in appearing. They came toward us, from under the archway to which Mr Ruck had somewhat invidiously alluded, slowly and with a rather exhausted step and expression. My companion looked at them a moment, as they advanced. 'They're tired,' he said softly. 'When they're tired, like that, it's very expensive.'

'Well,' said Mrs Ruck, 'I'm glad you've had some company.' Her husband looked at her, in silence, through narrowed eyelids, and I suspected that this gracious observation on the lady's part was prompted by a restless conscience.

Miss Sophy glanced at me with her little straightforward air of defiance. 'It would have been more proper if *we* had had the company. Why didn't you come after us, instead of sitting there?' she asked of Mr Ruck's companion.

'I was told by your father,' I explained, 'that you were engaged in sacred rites.' Miss Ruck was not gracious, though I doubt whether it was because her conscience was better than her mother's.

'Well, for a gentleman there is nothing so sacred as ladies' society,' replied Miss Ruck, in the manner of a person accustomed to giving neat retorts.

'I suppose you refer to the cathedral,' said her mother. 'Well, I must say, we didn't go back there. I don't know what it may be of a Sunday, but it gave me a chill.'

'We discovered the loveliest little lace-shop,' observed the young girl, with a serenity that was superior to bravado.

Her father looked at her a while; then turned about again, leaning on the parapet, and gazed away at the 'hills'.

'Well, it was certainly cheap,' said Mrs Ruck, also contemplating the Alps.

'We are going to Chamouni,' said her husband. 'You haven't any occasion for lace at Chamouni.'

'Well, I'm glad to hear you have decided to go somewhere,' rejoined his wife. 'I don't want to be a fixture at a boarding-house.'

'You can wear lace anywhere,' said Miss Ruck, 'if you put it on right. That's the great thing, with lace. I don't think they know how to wear lace in Europe. I know how I mean to wear mine; but I mean to keep it till I get home.'

Her father transferred his melancholy gaze to her elaborately-appointed little person; there was a great deal of very new-looking detail in Miss Ruck's appearance. Then, in a tone of voice quite out of consonance with his facial despondency, 'Have you purchased a great deal?' he inquired.

'I have purchased enough for you to make a fuss about.'

'He can't make a fuss about that,' said Mrs Ruck.

'Well, you'll see!' declared the young girl with a little sharp laugh.

But her father went on, in the same tone: 'Have you got it in your pocket? Why don't you put it on – why don't you hang it round you?'

'I'll hang it round *you*, if you don't look out!' cried Miss Sophy.

'Don't you want to show it to this gentleman?' Mr Ruck continued.

'Mercy, how you do talk about that lace?' said his wife.

'Well, I want to be lively. There's every reason for it; we're going to Chamouni.'

'You're restless; that's what's the matter with you.' And Mrs Ruck got up.

'No, I ain't,' said her husband. 'I never felt so quiet; I feel as peaceful as a little child.'

Mrs Ruck, who had no sense whatever of humour, looked at her daughter and at me. 'Well, I hope you'll improve,' she said.

'Send in the bills,' Mr Ruck went on, rising to his feet. 'Don't hesitate, Sophy. I don't care what you do now. In for a penny, in for a pound.'

Miss Ruck joined her mother, with a little toss of her head, and we followed the ladies to the carriage. 'In your place,' said Miss Sophy to her father, 'I wouldn't talk so much about pennies and pounds before strangers.'

Poor Mr Ruck appeared to feel the force of this observation, which, in the consciousness of a man who had never been 'mean', could hardly fail to strike a responsive chord. He coloured a little, and he was silent; his companions got into their vehicle, the front seat of which was adorned with a large parcel. Mr Ruck gave the parcel a little poke with his umbrella, and then, turning to me with a rather grimly penitential smile, 'After all,' he said, 'for the ladies that's the principal interest.'

7

Old M. Pigeonneau had more than once proposed to me to take a walk, but I had hitherto been unable to respond to so alluring an invitation. It befell, however, one afternoon, that I perceived him going forth upon a desultory stroll, with a certain lonesomeness of demeanour that attracted my sympathy. I hastily overtook him, and passed my hand into his venerable arm, a proceeding which produced in the good old man so jovial a sense of comradeship that he ardently proposed we should bend our steps to the English Garden; no locality less festive was worthy of the occasion. To the English Garden, accordingly, we went; it lay beyond the bridge, beside the lake. It was very pretty and very animated; there was a band playing in the middle, and a considerable number of persons sitting under the small trees, on benches and little chairs, or strolling beside the blue water. We joined the strollers, we observed our companions, and conversed on obvious topics. Some of these last, of course, were the pretty women who embellished the scene, and who, in the light of M. Pigeonneau's comprehensive criticism, appeared surprisingly numerous. He seemed bent upon our making up our minds as to which was the prettiest, and as this was an innocent game I consented to play at it.

Suddenly M. Pigeonneau stopped, pressing my arm with the liveliest emotion. 'La voilà, la voilà, the prettiest!' he quickly murmured, 'coming toward us, in a blue dress, with the other.' It was at the other I was looking, for the other, to my surprise, was our interesting fellow-pensioner, the daughter of a vigilant mother. M. Pigeonneau, meanwhile, had redoubled his exclamations; he had recognised Miss Sophy Ruck. 'Oh, la belle rencontre, nos aimables convives; the prettiest girl in the world, in effect!'

We immediately greeted and joined the young ladies, who, like ourselves, were walking arm in arm and enjoying the scene.

'I was citing you with admiration to my friend, even before I had recognised you,' said M. Pigeonneau to Miss Ruck.

'I don't believe in French compliments,' remarked this young lady, presenting her back to the smiling old man.

'Are you and Miss Ruck walking alone?' I asked of her companion. 'You had better accept of M. Pigeonneau's gallant protection, and of mine.'

Aurora Church had taken her hand out of Miss Ruck's arm; she looked at me, smiling, with her head a little inclined, while, upon her shoulder, she made her open parasol revolve. 'Which is most improper, – to walk alone or to walk with gentlemen? I wish to do what is most improper.'

'What mysterious logic governs your conduct?' I inquired.

'He thinks you can't understand him when he talks like that,' said Miss Ruck. 'But I do understand you, always!'

'So I have always ventured to hope, my dear Miss Ruck.'

'Well, if I didn't, it wouldn't be much loss,' rejoined this young lady.

'Allons, en marche!' cried M. Pigeonneau, smiling still, and undiscouraged by her inhumanity. 'Let us make together the tour of the garden.' And he imposed his society upon Miss Ruck with a respectful, elderly grace which was evidently unable to see anything in her reluctance but modesty, and was sublimely conscious of a mission to place modesty at its ease. This ill-assorted couple walked in front, while Aurora Church and I strolled along together.

'I am sure this is more improper,' said my companion; 'this is delightfully improper. I don't say that as a compliment to you,' she added. 'I would say it to any man, no matter how stupid.'

'Oh, I am very stupid,' I answered, 'but this doesn't seem to me wrong.'

'Not for you, no; only for me. There is nothing that a man can do that is wrong, is there? En morale, you know, I mean. Ah, yes, he can steal; but I think there is nothing else, is there?'

'I don't know. One doesn't know those things until after one has done them. Then one is enlightened.'

'And you mean that you have never been enlightened? You make yourself out very good.'

'That is better than making one's self out bad, as you do.'

The young girl glanced at me a moment, and then, with her charming smile, 'That's one of the consequences of a false position.'

'Is your position false?' I inquired, smiling too at this large formula.

'Distinctly so.'

'In what way?'

'Oh, in every way. For instance, I have to pretend to be a *jeune fille*. I am not a jeune fille; no American girl is a jeune fille; an American girl is an intelligent, responsible creature. I have to pretend to be very innocent, but I am not very innocent.'

'You don't pretend to be very innocent; you pretend to be – what shall I call it? – very wise.'

'That's no pretence. I am wise.'

'You are not an American girl,' I ventured to observe.

My companion almost stopped, looking at me; there was a little flush in her cheek. 'Voilà!' she said. 'There's my false position. I want to be an American girl, and I'm not.'

'Do you want me to tell you?' I went on. 'An American girl wouldn't talk as you are talking now.'

'Please tell me,' said Aurora Church, with expressive eagerness. 'How would she talk?'

'I can't tell you all the things an American girl would say, but I think I can tell you the things she wouldn't say. She wouldn't reason out her conduct, as you seem to me to do.'

Aurora gave me the most flattering attention. 'I see. She would be simpler. To do very simple things that are not at all simple – that is the American girl!'

I permitted myself a small explosion of hilarity. 'I don't know whether you are a French girl, or what you are,' I said, 'but you are very witty.'

'Ah, you mean that I strike false notes!' cried Aurora Church, sadly. 'That's just what I want to avoid. I wish you would always tell me.'

The conversational union between Miss Ruck and her neighbour, in front of us, had evidently not become a close one. The young lady suddenly turned round to us with a question: 'Don't you want some ice cream?'

'*She* doesn't strike false notes,' I murmured.

There was a kind of pavilion or kiosk, which served as a café, and at which the delicacies procurable at such an establishment were dispensed. Miss Ruck pointed to the little green tables and chairs which were set out on the gravel; M. Pigeonneau, fluttering with a sense of dissipation, seconded the proposal, and we presently sat down and gave our order to a nimble attendant. I managed again to place myself next to Aurora Church; our companions were on the other side of the table.

My neighbour was delighted with our situation. 'This is best of all,' she said. 'I never believed I should come to a café with two strange men! Now, you can't persuade me this isn't wrong.'

'To make it wrong we ought to see your mother coming down that path.'

'Ah, my mother makes everything wrong,' said the young girl, attacking with a little spoon in the shape of a spade the apex of a pink ice. And then she returned to her idea of a moment before: 'You must promise to tell me – to warn me in some way – whenever I strike a false note. You must give a little cough, like that – ahem!'

'You will keep me very busy, and people will think I am in a consumption.'

'*Voyons*,' she continued, 'why have you never talked to me more? Is that a false note? Why haven't you been "attentive"? That's what American girls call it; that's what Miss Ruck calls it.'

I assured myself that our companions were out of ear-shot, and that Miss Ruck was much occupied with a large vanilla cream. 'Because you are always entwined with that young lady. There is no getting near you.'

Aurora looked at her friend while the latter devoted herself to her ice. 'You wonder why I like her so much, I suppose. So does mamma; elle s'y perd. I don't like her particularly; je n'en suis pas folle. But she gives me information; she tells me about America. Mamma has always tried to prevent my knowing anything about it, and I am all the more curious. And then Miss Ruck is very fresh.'

'I may not be so fresh as Miss Ruck,' I said, 'but in future, when you want information, I recommend you to come to me for it.'

'Our friend offers to take me to America; she invites me to go back with her, to stay with her. You couldn't do that, could you?' And the young girl looked at me a moment. '*Bon*, a false note! I can see it by your face; you remind me of a *maître de piano*.'

'You overdo the character – the poor American girl,' I said. 'Are you going to stay with that delightful family?'

'I will go and stay with any one that will take me or ask me. It's a real *nostalgie*. She says that in New York – in Thirty-Seventh Street – I should have the most lovely time.'

'I have no doubt you would enjoy it.'

'Absolute liberty to begin with.'

'It seems to me you have a certain liberty here,' I rejoined.

'Ah *this?* Oh, I shall pay for this. I shall be punished by mamma, and I shall be lectured by Madame Galopin.'

'The wife of the pasteur?'

'His *digne épouse*. Madame Galopin, for mamma, is the incarnation of European opinion. That's what vexes me with mamma, her thinking so much of people like Madame Galopin. Going to see Madame Galopin – mamma calls that being in European society. European society! I'm so sick of that expression; I have heard it since I was six years old. Who is Madame Galopin – who thinks anything of her here? She is nobody; she is perfectly third-rate. If I like America better than mamma, I also know Europe better.'

'But your mother, certainly,' I objected, a trifle timidly, for my young lady was excited, and had a charming little passion in her eye – 'your mother has a great many social relations all over the continent.'

'She thinks so, but half the people don't care for us. They are not so good as we, and they know it – I'll do them that justice – and they wonder why we should care for them. When we are polite to them, they think the less of us; there are plenty of people like that. Mamma thinks so much of them simply because they are foreigners. If I could tell you all the dull, stupid, second-rate people I have had to talk to, for no better reason than that they were *de leur pays*! – Germans, French, Italians, Turks, everything. When I complain, mamma always says that at any rate it's practice in the language. And she makes so much of the English, too; I don't know what that's practice in.'

Before I had time to suggest an hypothesis, as regards this latter point, I saw something that made me rise, with a certain solemnity, from my chair. This was nothing less than the neat little figure of Mrs Church – a perfect model of the *femme comme il faut* – approaching our table with an impatient step, and followed most unexpectedly in her advance by the pre-eminent form of Mr Ruck. She had evidently come in quest of her daughter, and if she had commanded this gentleman's attendance, it had been on no softer ground than that of his unenvied paternity to her guilty child's accomplice. My movement had given the alarm, and Aurora Church and M. Pigeonneau got up; Miss Ruck alone did not, in the local phrase, derange herself. Mrs Church, beneath her modest little bonnet, looked very serious, but not at all fluttered; she came straight to her daughter, who received her with a smile, and then she looked all round at the rest of us, very fixedly and tranquilly, without bowing. I must do both these ladies the justice to mention that neither of them made the least little 'scene'.

'I have come for you, dearest,' said the mother.

'Yes, dear mamma.'

'Come for you – come for you,' Mrs Church repeated, looking down at the relics of our little feast. 'I was obliged to ask Mr Ruck's assistance. I was puzzled; I thought a long time.'

'Well, Mrs Church, I was glad to see you puzzled once in your life!' said Mr Ruck, with friendly jocosity. 'But you came pretty straight for all that. I had hard work to keep up with you.'

'We will take a cab, Aurora,' Mrs Church went on, without heeding this pleasantry – 'a closed one. Come, my daughter.'

'Yes, dear mamma.' The young girl was blushing, yet she was still smiling; she looked round at us all, and, as her eyes met mine, I thought she was beautiful. 'Good-bye,' she said to us. 'I have had a *lovely time*.'

'We must not linger,' said her mother; 'it is five o'clock. We are to dine, you know, with Madame Galopin.'

'I had quite forgotten,' Aurora declared. 'That will be charming.'

'Do you want me to assist you to carry her back, ma'am?' asked Mr Ruck.

Mrs Church hesitated a moment, with her serene little gaze. 'Do you prefer, then, to leave your daughter to finish the evening with these gentlemen?'

Mr Ruck pushed back his hat and scratched the top of his head. 'Well, I don't know. How would you like that, Sophy?'

'Well, I never!' exclaimed Sophy, as Mrs Church marched off with her daughter.

8

I had half expected that Mrs Church would make me feel the weight of her disapproval of my own share in that little act of revelry in the English Garden. But she maintained her claim to being a highly reasonable woman – I could not but admire the justice of this pretension – by recognising my irresponsibility. I had taken her daughter as I found her, which was, according to Mrs Church's view, in a very equivocal position. The natural instinct of a young man, in such a situation, is not to protest but to profit; and it was clear to Mrs Church that I had had nothing to do with Miss Aurora's appearing in public under the insufficient chaperonage of Miss Ruck. Besides, she liked to converse, and she apparently did me the honour to believe that of all the members of the Pension Beaurepas I had the most cultivated understanding. I found her in the salon a couple of evenings after the incident I have just narrated, and I approached her with a view of making my peace with her, if this should prove necessary. But Mrs Church was as gracious as I could have desired; she put her marker into her book, and folded her plump little hands on the cover. She made no specific allusion to the English Garden; she embarked, rather, upon those general considerations in which her refined intellect was so much at home.

'Always at your studies, Mrs Church,' I ventured to observe.

'Que voulez-vous? To say studies is to say too much; one doesn't study in the parlour of a boarding-house. But I do what I can; I have always done what I can. That is all I have ever claimed.'

'No one can do more, and you seem to have done a great deal.'

'Do you know my secret?' she asked, with an air of brightening confidence. And she paused a moment before she imparted her secret – 'To care only for the best! To do the best, to know the best – to have, to desire, to recognise, only the best. That's what I have always done, in my quiet little way. I have gone through Europe on my devoted little errand, seeking, seeing, heeding, only the best. And it has not been for myself alone; it has been for my daughter. My daughter has had the best. We are not rich, but I can say that.'

'She has had you, madam,' I rejoined finely.

'Certainly, such as I am, I have been devoted. We have got something everywhere; a little here, a little there. That's the real secret – to get something everywhere; you always can if you *are* devoted. Sometimes it has been a little music, sometimes a little deeper insight into the history of art; every little counts you know. Sometimes it has been just a glimpse, a view, of a lovely landscape, an impression. We have always been on the look-out. Sometimes it has been valued friendship, a delightful social tie.'

'Here comes the "European society", the poor daughter's bugbear,' I said to myself. 'Certainly,' I remarked aloud – I admit, rather perversely – 'if you have lived a great deal in *pensions*, you must have got acquainted with lots of people.'

Mrs Church dropped her eyes a moment; and then, with considerable gravity, 'I think the European pension system in many respects remarkable, and in some satisfactory. But of the friendships that we have formed, few have been contracted in establishments of this kind.'

'I am sorry to hear that!' I said, laughing.

'I don't say it for you, though I might say it for some others. We have been interested in European *homes*.'

'Oh, I see!'

'We have the *éntree* of the old Genevese society. I like its tone. I prefer it to that of Mr Ruck,' added Mrs Church, calmly: 'to that of Mrs Ruck and Miss Ruck – of Miss Ruck, especially.'

'Ah, the poor Rucks haven't any tone at all,' I said. 'Don't take them more seriously than they take themselves.'

'Tell me this,' my companion rejoined, 'are they fair examples?'

'Examples of what?'

'Of our American tendencies.'

' "Tendencies" is a big word, dear lady; tendencies are difficult to calculate. And you shouldn't abuse those good Rucks, who have been very kind to your daughter. They have invited her to go and stay with them in Thirty-Seventh Street.'

'Aurora has told me. It might be very serious.'

'It might be very droll,' I said.

'To me,' declared Mrs Church, 'it is simply terrible. I think we shall have to leave the Pension Beaurepas. I shall go back to Madame Chamousset.'

'On account of the Rucks?' I asked.

'Pray, why don't they go themselves? I have given them some excellent addresses – written down the very hours of the trains. They were going to Appenzell; I thought it was arranged.'

'They talk of Chamouni now,' I said; 'but they are very helpless and undecided.'

'I will give them some Chamouni addresses. Mrs Ruck will send for a *chaise à porteurs*; I will give her the name of a man who lets them lower than you get them at the hotels. After that they *must* go.'

'Well, I doubt,' I observed, 'whether Mr Ruck will ever really be seen on the Mer de Glace – in a high hat. He's not like you; he doesn't value his European privileges. He takes no interest. He regrets Wall Street, acutely. As his wife says, he is very restless, but he has no curiosity about Chamouni. So you must not depend too much on the effect of your addresses.'

'Is it a frequent type?' asked Mrs Church, with an air of self-control.

'I am afraid so. Mr Ruck is a broken-down man of business. He is broken-down in health, and I suspect he is broken down in fortune. He has spent his whole life in buying and selling; he knows how to do nothing else. His wife and daughter have spent their lives, not in selling, but in buying; and they, on their side, know how to do nothing else. To get something in a shop that they can put on their backs – that is their one idea; they haven't another in their heads. Of course they spend no end of money, and they do it with an implacable persistence, with a mixture of audacity and of cunning. They do it in his teeth and they do it behind his back; the mother protects the daughter, and the daughter eggs on the mother. Between them they are bleeding him to death.'

'Ah, what a picture!' murmured Mrs Church. 'I am afraid they are very – uncultivated.'

'I share your fears. They are perfectly ignorant; they have no resources. The vision of fine clothes occupies their whole imagination. They have not an idea – even a worse one – to compete with it. Poor Mr Ruck, who is extremely good-natured and soft, seems to me a really tragic figure. He is getting bad news every day from home; his business is going to the dogs. He is unable to stop it; he has to stand and watch his fortunes ebb. He has been used to doing things in a big way, and he feels "mean" if he makes a fuss about bills. So the ladies keep sending them in.'

'But haven't they common sense? Don't they know they are ruining themselves?'

'They don't believe it. The duty of an American husband and father is to keep them going. If he asks them how, that's his own affair. So, by way of not being mean, of being a good American husband and father, poor Ruck stands staring at bankruptcy.'

Mrs Church looked at me a moment, in quickened meditation. 'Why, if Aurora were to go to stay with them, she might not even be properly fed!'

'I don't, on the whole, recommend,' I said, laughing, 'that your daughter should pay a visit to Thirty-Seventh Street.'

'Why should I be subjected to such trials – so sadly *éprouvée?* Why should a daughter of mine like that dreadful girl?'

'*Does* she like her?'

'Pray, do you mean,' asked my companion, softly, 'that Aurora is a hypocrite?'

I hesitated a moment. 'A little, since you ask me. I think you have forced her to be.'

Mrs Church answered this possibly presumptuous charge with a tranquil, candid exultation. 'I never force my daughter!'

'She is nevertheless in a false position,' I rejoined. 'She hungers and thirsts to go back to her own country; she wants to "come out" in New York, which is certainly, socially speaking, the El Dorado of young ladies. She likes any one, for the moment, who will talk to her of that, and serve as a connecting-link with her native shores. Miss Ruck performs this agreeable office.'

'Your idea is, then, that if she were to go with Miss Ruck to America she would drop her afterwards.'

I complimented Mrs Church upon her logical mind, but I repudiated this cynical supposition. 'I can't imagine her – when it should come to the point – embarking with the famille Ruck. But I wish she might go, nevertheless.'

Mrs Church shook her head serenely, and smiled at my inappropriate zeal. 'I trust my poor child may never be guilty of so fatal a mistake. She is completely in error; she is wholly unadapted to the peculiar conditions of American life. It would not please her. She would not sympathise. My daughter's ideal is not the ideal of the class of young women to which Miss Ruck belongs. I fear they are very numerous; they give the tone – they give the tone.'

'It is you that are mistaken,' I said; 'go home for six months and see.'

'I have not, unfortunately, the means to make costly experiments. My daughter has had great advantages – rare advantages – and I should be very sorry to believe that *au fond* she does not appreciate them. One thing is certain: I must remove her from this pernicious influence. We must part company with this deplorable family. If Mr Ruck and his ladies cannot be induced to go to Chamouni – a journey that no traveller with the smallest self-respect would omit – my daughter and I shall be obliged to retire. We shall go to Dresden.'

'To Dresden?'

'The capital of Saxony. I had arranged to go there for the autumn, but it will be simpler to go immediately. There are several works in the gallery with which my daughter has not, I think, sufficiently familiarised herself; it is especially strong in the seventeenth century schools.'

As my companion offered me this information I perceived Mr Ruck come lounging in, with his hands in his pockets, and his elbows making acute angles. He had his usual anomalous appearance of both seeking and avoiding society, and he wandered obliquely toward Mrs Church, whose last words he had overheard. 'The seventeenth century schools,' he said, slowly, as if he were weighing some very small object in a very large pair of scales. 'Now, do you suppose they *had* schools at that period?'

Mrs Church rose with a good deal of precision, making no answer to this incongruous jest. She clasped her large volume to her neat little bosom, and she fixed a gentle, serious eye upon Mr Ruck.

'I had a letter this morning from Chamouni,' she said.

'Well,' replied Mr Ruck, 'I suppose you've got friends all over.'

'I have friends at Chamouni, but they are leaving. To their great regret.' I had got up, too; I listened to this statement, and I wondered. I am almost ashamed to mention the subject of my agitation. I asked myself whether this was a sudden improvisation, consecrated by maternal devotion; but this point has never been elucidated. 'They are giving up some charming rooms; perhaps you would like them. I would suggest your telegraphing. The weather is glorious,' continued Mrs Church, 'and the highest peaks are now perceived with extraordinary distinctness.'

Mr Ruck listened, as he always listened, respectfully. 'Well,' he said, 'I don't know as I want to go up Mount Blank. That's the principal attraction, isn't it?'

'There are many others. I thought I would offer you an – an exceptional opportunity.'

'Well,' said Mr Ruck, 'you're right down friendly. But I seem to have more opportunities than I know what to do with. I don't seem able to take hold.'

'It only needs a little decision,' remarked Mrs Church, with an air which was an admirable example of this virtue. 'I wish you good-night, sir.' And she moved noiselessly away.

Mr Ruck, with his long legs apart, stood staring after her; then he transferred his perfectly quiet eyes to me. 'Does she own a hotel over there?' he asked. 'Has she got any stock in Mount Blank?'

9

The next day Madame Beaurepas handed me, with her own elderly fingers, a missive, which proved to be a telegram. After glancing at it, I informed her that it was apparently a signal for my departure; my brother had arrived in England, and proposed to me to meet him there; he had come on business and was to spend but three weeks in Europe. 'But my house empties itself!' cried the old woman. 'The famille Ruck talks of leaving me, and Madame Church *nous fait la révérence.*'

'Mrs Church is going away?'

'She is packing her trunk; she is a very extraordinary person. Do you know what she asked me this morning? To invent some combination by which the famille Ruck should move away. I informed her that I was not an inventor. That poor famille Ruck! "Oblige me by getting rid of them," said Madame Church, as she would have asked Célestine to remove a dish of cabbage. She speaks as if the world were made for Madame Church. I intimated to her that if she objected to the company there was a very simple remedy; and at present *elle fait ses paquets.*'

'She really asked you to get the Rucks out of the house?'

'She asked me to tell them that their rooms had been let, three months ago, to another family. She has an *aplomb!*'

Mrs Church's aplomb caused me considerable diversion; I am not sure that it was not, in some degree, to laugh over it at my leisure that I went out into the garden that evening to smoke a cigar. The night was dark and not particularly balmy, and most of my fellow-pensioners, after dinner, had remained in-doors. A long straight walk conducted from the door of the house to the ancient grille that I have described, and I stood here for some time, looking through the iron bars at the silent empty street. The prospect was not entertaining, and I presently turned away. At this moment I saw, in the distance, the door of the house open and throw a shaft of lamplight into the darkness. Into the lamplight there stepped the figure of a female, who presently closed the door behind her. She disappeared in the dusk of the garden, and I had seen her but for an instant, but I remained under the impression that Aurora Church, on the eve of her departure, had come out for a meditative stroll.

I lingered near the gate, keeping the red tip of my cigar turned toward the house, and before long a young lady emerged from among the shadows of the trees and encountered the light of a lamp that stood just outside the gate. It was in fact Aurora Church, but she seemed more bent upon conversation than upon meditation. She stood a moment looking at me, and then she said, –

'Ought I to retire – to return to the house?'

'If you ought, I should be very sorry to tell you so,' I answered.

'But we are all alone; there is no one else in the garden.'

'It is not the first time that I have been alone with a young lady. I am not at all terrified.'

'Ah, but I?' said the young girl. 'I have never been alone' – then, quickly, she interrupted herself. 'Good, there's another false note!'

'Yes, I am obliged to admit that one is very false.'

She stood looking at me. 'I am going away to-morrow; after that there will be no one to tell me.'

'That will matter little,' I presently replied. 'Telling you will do no good.'

'Ah, why do you say that?' murmured Aurora Church.

I said it partly because it was true; but I said it for other reasons, as well, which it was hard to define. Standing there bare-headed, in the night air, in the vague light, this young lady looked extremely interesting; and the interest of her appearance was not diminished by a suspicion on my own part that she had come into the garden knowing me to be there. I thought her a charming girl, and I felt very sorry for her; but as I looked at her, the terms in which Madame Beaurepas had ventured to characterise her recurred to me with a certain force. I had professed a contempt for them at the time, but it now came into my head that perhaps this unfortunately situated, this insidiously mutinous, young creature was looking out for a preserver. She was certainly not a girl to throw herself at a man's head, but it was possible that in her intense – her almost morbid – desire to put into effect an ideal which was perhaps after all charged with as many fallacies as her mother affirmed, she might do something reckless and irregular – something in which a sympathetic compatriot, as yet unknown, would find his profit. The image, unshaped though it was, of this sympathetic compatriot filled me with a sort of envy. For some moments I was silent, conscious of these things, and then I answered her question. 'Because some things – some differences – are felt, not learned. To you liberty is not natural; you are like a person who has bought a repeater, and, in his satisfaction, is constantly making it sound. To a real American girl her liberty is a very vulgarly-ticking old clock.'

'Ah, you mean, then,' said the poor girl, 'that my mother has ruined me?'

'Ruined you?'

'She has so perverted my mind that when I try to be natural I am necessarily immodest.'

'That again is a false note,' I said, laughing.

She turned away. 'I think you are cruel.'

'By no means,' I declared; 'because, for my own taste, I prefer you as – as –'

I hesitated, and she turned back. 'As what?'

'As you are.'

She looked at me a while again, and then she said, in a little reasoning voice that reminded me of her mother's, only that it was conscious and studied, 'I was not aware that I am under any particular obligation to please you!' And then she gave a clear laugh, quite at variance with her voice.

'Oh, there is no obligation,' I said, 'but one has preferences. I am very sorry you are going away.'

'What does it matter to you? You are going yourself.'

'As I am going in a different direction, that makes all the greater separation.'

She answered nothing; she stood looking through the bars of the tall gate at the empty, dusky street. 'This grille is like a cage,' she said at last.

'Fortunately, it is a cage that will open.' And I laid my hand on the lock.

'Don't open it,' and she pressed the gate back. 'If you should open it I would go out – and never return.'

'Where should you go?'

'To America.'

'Straight away?'

'Somehow or other. I would go to the American consul. I would beg him to give me money – to help me.'

I received this assertion without a smile; I was not in a smiling humour. On the contrary, I felt singularly excited, and I kept my hand on the lock of the gate. I believed (or I thought I believed) what my companion said, and I had – absurd as it may appear – an irritated vision of her throwing herself upon consular sympathy. It seemed to me, for a moment, that to pass out of that gate with this yearning, straining young creature would be to pass into some mysterious felicity. If I were only a hero of romance, I would offer, myself, to take her to America.

In a moment more, perhaps, I should have persuaded myself that I was one, but at this juncture I heard a sound that was not romantic. It proved to be the very realistic tread of Célestine, the cook, who stood grinning at us as we turned about from our colloquy.

'I ask *bien pardon*,' said Célestine. 'The mother of mademoiselle desires that mademoiselle should come in immediately. M. le Pasteur Galopin has come to make his adieux to *ces dames*.'

Aurora gave me only one glance, but it was a touching one. Then she slowly departed with Célestine.

The next morning, on coming into the garden, I found that Mrs Church and her daughter had departed. I was informed of this fact by old M. Pigeonneau, who sat there under a tree, having his coffee at a little green table.

'I have nothing to envy you,' he said; 'I had the last glimpse of that charming Miss Aurora.'

'I had a very late glimpse,' I answered, 'and it was all I could possibly desire.'

'I have always noticed,' rejoined M. Pigeonneau, 'that your desires are more moderate than mine. Que voulez-vous? I am of the old school. Je crois que la race se perd. I regret the departure of that young girl: she had an enchanting smile. Ce sera une femme d'esprit. For the mother, I can console myself. I am not sure that *she* was a femme d'esprit, though she wished to pass for one. Round, rosy, *potelée*, she yet had not the temperament of her appearance; she was a *femme austère*. I have often noticed that contradiction in American ladies. You see a plump little woman, with a speaking eye and the contour and complexion of a ripe peach, and if you venture to conduct yourself in the smallest degree in accordance with these *indices*, you discover a species of Methodist – of what do you call it? – of Quakeress. On the other hand, you encounter a tall, lean, angular person, without colour, without grace, all elbows and knees, and you find it's a nature of the tropics! The women of duty look like coquettes, and the others look like alpenstocks! However, we have still the handsome Madame Ruck – a real *femme de Rubens*, *celle-là*. It is very true that to talk to her one must know the Flemish tongue!'

I had determined, in accordance with my brother's telegram, to go away in the afternoon; so that, having various duties to perform, I left M. Pigeonneau to his international comparisons. Among other things, I went in the course of the morning to the banker's, to draw money for my journey, and there I found Mr Ruck, with a pile of crumpled letters in his lap, his chair tipped back and his eyes gloomily fixed on the fringe of the green plush table-cloth. I timidly expressed the hope that he had got better news from home; whereupon he gave me a look in which, considering his provocation, the absence of irritation was conspicuous.

He took up his letters in his large hand, and crushing them together held it out to me. 'That epistolary matter,' he said, 'is worth about five cents. But I guess,' he added, rising, 'I have taken it in by this time.' When I had drawn my money, I asked him to come and breakfast with me at the little *brasserie*, much favoured by students, to which I used to resort in the old town. 'I couldn't eat, sir,' he said, 'I couldn't eat. Bad news takes away the appetite. But I guess I'll go with you, so that I needn't go to table down there at the pension. The old woman down there is always accusing me of turning up my nose at her food. Well, I guess I shan't turn up my nose at anything now.'

We went to the little brasserie, where poor Mr Ruck made the lightest possible breakfast. But if he ate very little, he talked a great deal; he talked about business, going into a hundred details in which I was quite unable to follow him. His talk was not angry nor bitter; it was a long, meditative, melancholy monologue; if it had been a trifle less incoherent I should almost have called it philosophic. I was very sorry for him; I wanted to do something for him, but the only thing I could do was, when we had breakfasted, to see him safely back to the Pension Beaurepas. We went across the Treille and down the Corraterie, out of which we turned into the Rue du Rhône. In this latter street, as all the world knows, are many of those brilliant jewellers' shops for which Geneva is famous. I always admired their glittering windows, and never passed them without a lingering glance. Even on this occasion, preoccupied as I was with my impending departure and with my companion's troubles, I suffered my eyes to wander along the precious tiers that flashed and twinkled behind the huge, clear plates of glass. Thanks to this inveterate habit, I made a discovery. In the largest and most brilliant of these establishments I perceived two ladies, seated before the counter with an air of absorption which sufficiently proclaimed their identity. I hoped my companion would not see them, but as we came abreast of the door, a little beyond, we found it open to the warm summer air. Mr Ruck happened to glance in, and he immediately recognised his wife and daughter. He slowly stopped, looking at them; I wondered what he would do. The salesman was holding up a bracelet before them, on its velvet cushion, and flashing it about in an irresistible manner.

Mr Ruck said nothing, but he presently went in, and I did the same.

'It will be an opportunity,' I remarked, as cheerfully as possible, 'for me to bid good-bye to the ladies.'

They turned round when Mr Ruck came in, and looked at him without confusion. 'Well, you had better go home to breakfast,' remarked his wife. Miss Sophy made no remark, but she took the bracelet from the attendant and gazed at it very fixedly. Mr Ruck seated himself on an empty stool and looked round the shop.

'Well, you have been here before,' said his wife; 'you were here the first day we came.'

Miss Ruck extended the precious object in her hands towards me. 'Don't you think that sweet?' she inquired.

I looked at it a moment. 'No, I think it's ugly.'

She glanced at me a moment, incredulous. 'Well, I don't believe you have any taste.'

'Why, sir, it's just lovely,' said Mrs Ruck.

'You'll see it some day on me, any way,' her daughter declared.

'No, he won't,' said Mr Ruck quietly.

'It will be his own fault, then,' Miss Sophy observed.

'Well, if we are going to Chamouni we want to get something here,' said Mrs Ruck. 'We may not have another chance.'

Mr Ruck was still looking round the shop, whistling in a very low tone. 'We ain't going to Chamouni. We are going to New York city, straight.'

'Well, I'm glad to hear that,' said Mrs Ruck. 'Don't you suppose we want to take something home?'

'If we are going straight back I must have that bracelet,' her daughter declared. 'Only I don't want a velvet case; I want a satin case.'

'I must bid you good-bye,' I said to the ladies. 'I am leaving Geneva in an hour or two.'

'Take a good look at that bracelet, so you'll know it when you see it,' said Miss Sophy.

'She's bound to have something,' remarked her mother, almost proudly.

Mr Ruck was still vaguely inspecting the shop; he was still whistling a little. 'I am afraid he is not at all well,' I said, softly, to his wife.

She twisted her head a little, and glanced at him.

'Well, I wish he'd improve!' she exclaimed.

'A satin case, and a nice one!' said Miss Ruck to the shopman.

I bade Mr Ruck good-bye. 'Don't wait for me,' he said, sitting there on his stool, and not meeting my eye. 'I've got to see this thing through.'

I went back to the Pension Beaurepas, and when, an hour later, I left it with my luggage, the family had not returned.

Lady Barberina

I

It is well known that there are few sights in the world more brilliant than the main avenues of Hyde Park of a fine afternoon in June. This was quite the opinion of two persons who, on a beautiful day at the beginning of that month, four years ago, had established themselves under the great trees in a couple of iron chairs (the big ones with arms, for which, if I mistake not, you pay twopence), and sat there with the slow procession of the Drive behind them, while their faces were turned to the more vivid agitation of the Row. They were lost in the multitude of observers, and they belonged, superficially, at least, to that class of persons who, wherever they may be, rank rather with the spectators than with the spectacle. They were quiet, simple, elderly, of aspect somewhat neutral; you would have liked them extremely, but you would scarcely have noticed them. Nevertheless, in all that shining host, it is to them, obscure, that we must give our attention. The reader is begged to have confidence; he is not asked to make vain concessions. There was that in the faces of our friends which indicated that they were growing old together, and that they were fond enough of each other's company not to object (if it was a condition) even to that. The reader will have guessed that they were husband and wife; and perhaps while he is about it he will have guessed that they were of that nationality for which Hyde Park at the height of the season is most completely illustrative. They were familiar strangers, as it were; and people at once so initiated and so detached could only be Americans. This reflection, indeed, you would have made only after some delay; for it must be admitted that they carried few patriotic signs on the surface. They had the American turn of mind, but that was very subtle; and to your eye – if your eye had cared about it – they might have been of English, or even of Continental, parentage. It was as if it suited them to be colourless; their colour was all in their talk. They were not in the least verdant; they were gray, rather, of monotonous hue. If they were interested in the riders, the horses, the walkers, the great exhibition of English wealth and health, beauty, luxury and leisure, it was because all this referred itself to other impressions, because they had the key to almost everything that needed an answer – because, in a word, they were able to compare. They had not arrived, they had only returned; and recognition much more than surprise was expressed in their quiet gaze. It may as well be said outright that Dexter Freer and his wife belonged to that class of Americans who are constantly 'passing through' London. Possessors of a fortune of which, from any standpoint, the limits were plainly visible, they were unable to command that highest of luxuries – a habitation in their own country. They found it much more possible to economise at Dresden or Florence than at Buffalo or Minneapolis. The economy was as great, and the inspiration was greater. From Dresden, from Florence, moreover, they constantly made excursions which would not have been possible in those other cities; and it is even to be feared that they had some rather expensive methods of saving. They came to London to buy their portmanteaus, their tooth-brushes, their writing-paper; they occasionally even crossed the Atlantic to assure themselves that prices over there were still the same. They were eminently a social pair; their interests were mainly personal. Their point of view always was so distinctly human that they passed for being fond of gossip; and they certainly knew a good deal about the affairs of other people. They had friends in every country, in every town; and it was not their fault if people told them their secrets. Dexter Freer was a tall, lean man, with an interested eye, and a nose that rather aspired than drooped, yet was salient withal. He brushed his hair, which was streaked with white, forward over his ears in those locks which are represented in the portraits of clean-shaven gentlemen who flourished fifty years ago, and wore an old-fashioned neckcloth and gaiters. His wife, a small, plump person, of superficial freshness, with a white face, and hair that was still perfectly black, smiled perpetually, but had never laughed since the death of a son whom she had lost ten years after her marriage. Her husband, on the other hand, who was usually quite grave, indulged on great occasions in resounding mirth. People confided in her less than in him; but that mattered little, as she confided sufficiently in herself. Her dress, which was always black or dark gray, was so harmoniously simple that you could see she was fond of it; it was never smart by accident. She was full of intentions, of the most judicious sort; and though she was perpetually moving about the world she had the air of being perfectly stationary. She was celebrated for the promptitude with which she made her sitting-room at an inn, where she might be spending a night or two, look like an apartment long inhabited. With books, flowers, photographs, draperies, rapidly distributed – she had even a way, for the most part, of having a piano – the place seemed almost hereditary. The pair were just back from America, where they had spent three months, and now were able to face the world with something of the elation which people feel who have been justified in a prevision. They had found their native land quite ruinous.

'There he is again!' said Mr Freer, following with his eyes a young man who passed along the Row, riding slowly. 'That's a beautiful thoroughbred!'

Mrs Freer asked idle questions only when she wished for time to think. At present she had simply to look and see who it was her husband meant. 'The horse is too big,' she remarked, in a moment.

'You mean that the rider is too small,' her husband rejoined; 'he is mounted on his millions.'

'Is it really millions?'

'Seven or eight, they tell me.'

'How disgusting!' It was in this manner that Mrs Freer usually spoke of the large fortunes of the day. 'I wish he would see us,' she added.

'He does see us, but he doesn't like to look at us. He is too conscious; he isn't easy.'

'Too conscious of his big horse?'

'Yes, and of his big fortune; he is rather ashamed of it.'

'This is an odd place to come, then,' said Mrs Freer.

'I am not sure of that. He will find people here richer than himself, and other big horses in plenty, and that will cheer him up. Perhaps, too, he is looking for that girl.'

'The one we heard about? He can't be such a fool.'

'He isn't a fool,' said Dexter Freer. 'If he is thinking of her, he has some good reason.'

'I wonder what Mary Lemon would say.'

'She would say it was right, if he should do it. She thinks he can do no wrong. He is exceedingly fond of her.'

'I shan't be sure of that if he takes home a wife who will despise her.'

'Why should the girl despise her? She is a delightful woman.'

'The girl will never know it – and if she should, it would make no difference; she will despise everything.'

'I don't believe it, my dear; she will like some things very much. Every one will be very nice to her.'

'She will despise them all the more. But we are speaking as if it were all arranged; I don't believe in it at all,' said Mrs Freer.

'Well, something of the sort – in this case or in some other – is sure to happen sooner or later,' her husband replied, turning round a little toward the part of the delta which is formed, near the entrance to the Park, by the divergence of the two great vistas of the Drive and the Row.

Our friends had turned their backs, as I have said, to the solemn revolution of wheels and the densely-packed mass of spectators who had chosen that part of the show. These spectators were now agitated by a unanimous impulse: the pushing back of chairs, the shuffle of feet, the rustle of garments and the deepening murmur of voices sufficiently expressed it. Royalty was approaching – royalty had passed. Freer turned his head and his ear a little; but he failed to alter his position further, and his wife took no notice of the flurry. They had seen royalty pass, all over Europe, and they knew that it passed very quickly. Sometimes it came back; sometimes it didn't; for more than once they had seen it pass for the last time. They were veteran tourists, and they knew perfectly when to get up and when to remain seated. Mr Freer went on with his proposition: 'Some young fellow is certain to do it, and one of these girls is certain to take the risk. They must take risks, over here, more and more.'

'The girls, I have no doubt, will be glad enough; they have had very little chance as yet. But I don't want Jackson to begin.'

'Do you know I rather think I do?' said Dexter Freer; 'It will be very amusing.'

'For us, perhaps, but not for him; he will repent of it, and be wretched. He is too good for that.'

'Wretched, never! He has no capacity for wretchedness; and that's why he can afford to risk it.'

'He will have to make great concessions,' Mrs Freer remarked.

'He won't make one.'

'I should like to see.'

'You admit, then, that it will be amusing, which is all I contend for. But, as you say, we are talking as if it were settled, whereas there is probably nothing in it, after all. The best stories always turn out false. I shall be sorry in this case.'

They relapsed into silence, while people passed and re-passed them – continuous, successive, mechanical, with strange sequences of faces. They looked at the people, but no one looked at them, though every one was there so admittedly to see what was to be seen. It was all striking, all pictorial, and it made a great composition. The wide, long area of the Row, its red-brown surface dotted with bounding figures, stretched away into the distance and became suffused and misty in the bright, thick air. The deep, dark English verdure that bordered and overhung it, looked rich and old, revived and refreshed though it was by the breath of June. The mild blue of the sky was spotted with great silvery clouds, and the light drizzled down in heavenly shafts over the quieter spaces of the Park, as one saw them beyond the Row. All this, however, was only a background, for the scene was before everything personal; superbly so, and full of the gloss and lustre, the contrasted tones, of a thousand polished surfaces. Certain things were salient, pervasive – the shining flanks of the perfect horses, the twinkle of bits and spurs, the smoothness of fine cloth adjusted to shoulders and limbs, the sheen of hats and boots, the freshness of complexions, the expression of smiling, talking faces, the flash and flutter of rapid gallops. Faces were everywhere, and they were the great effect; above all, the fair faces of women on tall horses, flushed a little under their stiff black hats, with figures stiffened, in spite of much definition of curve, by their tight-fitting habits. Their hard little helmets; their neat, compact heads; their straight necks; their firm, tailor-made armour; their blooming, competent physique, made them look doubly like amazons about to ride a charge. The men, with their eyes before them, with hats of undulating brim, good profiles, high collars, white flowers on their chests, long legs and long feet, had an air more elaboratively decorative, as they jolted beside the ladies, always out of step. These were youthful types; but it was not all youth, for many a saddle was surmounted by a richer rotundity; and ruddy faces, with short white whiskers or with matronly chins, looked down comfortably from an equilibrium which was moral and social as well as physical. The walkers differed from the riders only in being on foot, and in looking at the riders more than these looked at them; for they would have done as well in the saddle and ridden as the others rode. The women had tight little bonnets and still tighter little knots of hair; their round chins rested on a close swathing of lace, or, in some cases, of silver chains and circlets. They had flat backs and small waists; they walked slowly, with their elbows out, carrying vast parasols, and turning their heads very little to the right or the left. They were amazons unmounted, quite ready to spring into the saddle. There was a great deal of beauty and a general look of successful development, which came from clear, quiet eyes, and from well-cut lips, on which syllables were liquid and sentences brief. Some of the young men, as well as the women, had the happiest proportions and oval faces, in which line and colour were pure and fresh and the idea of the moment was not very intense.

'They are very good-looking,' said Mr Freer, at the end of ten minutes; 'they are the finest whites.'

'So long as they remain white they do very well; but when they venture upon colour!' his wife replied. She sat with her eyes on a level with the skirts of the ladies who passed her; and she had been following the progress of a green velvet robe, enriched with ornaments of steel and much gathered up in the hands of its wearer, who, herself apparently in her teens, was accompanied by a young lady draped in scanty pink muslin, embroidered, æsthetically, with flowers that simulated the iris.

'All the same, in a crowd, they are wonderfully well turned out,' Dexter Freer went on; 'take the men, and women, and horses together. Look at that big fellow on the light chestnut: what could be more perfect? By the way, it's Lord Canterville,' he added in a moment, as if the fact were of some importance.

Mrs Freer recognised its importance to the degree of raising her glass to look at Lord Canterville. 'How do you know it's he?' she asked, with her glass still up.

'I heard him say something the night I went to the House of Lords. It was very few words, but I remember him. A man who was near me told me who he was.'

'He is not so handsome as you,' said Mrs Freer, dropping her glass.

'Ah, you're too difficult!' her husband murmured. 'What a pity the girl isn't with him,' he went on; 'we might see something.'

It appeared in a moment that the girl was with him. The nobleman designated had ridden slowly forward from the start, but just opposite our friends he pulled up to look behind him, as if he had been waiting for some one. At the same moment a gentleman in the Walk engaged his attention, so that he advanced to the barrier which protects the pedestrians, and halted there, bending a little from his saddle and talking with his friend, who leaned against the rail. Lord Canterville was indeed perfect, as his American admirer had said. Upwards of sixty, and of great stature and great presence, he was really a splendid apparition. In exquisite preservation, he had the freshness of middle life, and would have been young to the eye if the lapse of years were not needed to account for his considerable girth. He was clad from head to foot in garments of a radiant gray, and his fine florid countenance was surmounted with a white hat, of which the majestic curves were a triumph of good form. Over his mighty chest was spread a beard of the richest growth, and of a colour, in spite of a few streaks, vaguely grizzled, to which the coat of his admirable horse appeared to be a perfect match. It left no opportunity, in his uppermost button-hole, for the customary gardenia; but this was of comparatively little consequence, as the vegetation of the beard itself was tropical. Astride his great steed, with his big fist, gloved in pearl-gray, on his swelling thigh, his face lighted up with good-humoured indifference, and all his magnificent surface reflecting the mild sunshine, he was a very imposing man indeed, and visibly, incontestably, a personage. People almost lingered to look at him as they passed. His halt was brief, however, for he was almost immediately joined by two handsome girls, who were as well turned out, in Dexter Freer's phrase, as himself. They had been detained a moment at the entrance to the Row, and now advanced side by side, their groom close behind them. One was taller and older than the other, and it was apparent at a glance that they were sisters. Between them, with their charming shoulders, contracted waists, and skirts that hung without a wrinkle, like a plate of zinc, they represented in a singularly complete form the pretty English girl in the position in which she is prettiest.

'Of course they are his daughters,' said Dexter Freer, as they rode away with Lord Canterville; 'and in that case one of them must be Jackson Lemon's sweetheart. Probably the bigger; they said it was the eldest. She is evidently a fine creature.'

'She would hate it over there,' Mrs Freer remarked, for all answer to this cluster of inductions.

'You know I don't admit that. But granting she should, it would do her good to have to accommodate herself.'

'She wouldn't accommodate herself.'

'She looks so confoundedly fortunate, perched up on that saddle,' Dexter Freer pursued, without heeding his wife's rejoinder.

'Aren't they supposed to be very poor?'

'Yes, they look it!' And his eyes followed the distinguished trio as, with the groom, as distinguished in his way as any of them, they started on a canter.

The air was full of sound, but it was low and diffused; and when, near our friends, it became articulate, the words were simple and few.

'It's as good as the circus, isn't it, Mrs Freer?' These words correspond to that description, but they pierced the air more effectually than any our friends had lately heard. They were uttered by a young man who had stopped short in the path, absorbed by the sight of his compatriots. He was short and stout, he had a round, kind face, and short, stiff-looking hair, which was reproduced in a small bristling beard. He wore a double-breasted walking-coat, which was not, however, buttoned, and on the summit of his round head was perched a hat of exceeding smallness, and of the so-called 'pot' category. It evidently fitted him, but a hatter himself would not have known why. His hands were encased in new gloves, of a dark-brown colour, and they hung with an air of unaccustomed inaction at his sides. He sported neither umbrella nor stick. He extended one of his hands, almost with eagerness, to Mrs Freer, blushing a little as he became aware that he had been eager.

'Oh, Doctor Feeder!' she said, smiling at him. Then she repeated to her husband, 'Doctor Feeder, my dear!' and her husband said, 'Oh, Doctor, how d'ye do?' I have spoken of the composition of his appearance; but the items were not perceived by these two. They saw only one thing, his delightful face, which was both simple and clever, and unreservedly good. They had lately made the voyage from New York in his company, and it was plain that he would be very genial at sea. After he had stood in front of them a moment, a chair beside Mrs Freer became vacant, on which he took possession of it, and sat there telling her what he thought of the Park and how he liked London. As she knew every one she had known many of his people at home; and while she listened to him she remembered how large their contribution had been to the virtue and culture of Cincinnati. Mrs Freer's social horizon included even that city; she had been on terms almost familiar with several families from Ohio, and was acquainted with the position of the Feeders there. This family, very numerous, was interwoven into an enormous cousinship. She herself was quite out of such a system, but she could have told you whom Doctor Feeder's great-grandfather had married. Every one, indeed, had heard of the good deeds of the descendants of this worthy, who were generally physicians, excellent ones, and whose name expressed not inaptly their numerous acts of charity. Sidney Feeder, who had several cousins of this name established in the same line at Cincinnati, had transferred himself and his ambition to New York, where his practice, at the end of three years, had begun to grow. He had studied his profession at Vienna, and was impregnated with German science; indeed, if he had only worn spectacles, he might perfectly, as he sat there watching the riders in Rotten Row as if their proceedings were a successful demonstration, have passed for a young German of distinction. He had come over to London to attend a medical congress which met this year in the British capital; for his interest in the healing art was by no means limited to the cure of his patients; it embraced every form of experiment, and the expression of his honest eyes would almost have reconciled you to vivisection. It was the first time he had come to the Park; for social experiments he had little leisure. Being aware, however, that it was a very typical, and as it were symptomatic, sight, he had conscientiously reserved an afternoon, and had dressed himself carefully for the occasion. 'It's quite a brilliant show,' he said to Mrs Freer; 'it makes me wish I had a mount.' Little as he resembled Lord Canterville, he rode very well.

'Wait till Jackson Lemon passes again, and you can stop him and make him let you take a turn.' This was the jocular suggestion of Dexter Freer.

'Why, is he here? I have been looking out for him; I should like to see him.'

'Doesn't he go to your medical congress?' asked Mrs Freer.

'Well, yes, he attends; but he isn't very regular. I guess he goes out a good deal.'

'I guess he does,' said Mr Freer; 'and if he isn't very regular, I guess he has a good reason. A beautiful reason, a charming reason,' he went on, bending forward to look down toward the beginning of the Row. 'Dear me, what a lovely reason!'

Doctor Feeder followed the direction of his eyes, and after a moment understood his allusion. Little Jackson Lemon, on his big horse, passed along the avenue again, riding beside one of the young girls who had come that way shortly before in the company of Lord Canterville. His lordship followed, in conversation with the other, his younger daughter. As they advanced, Jackson Lemon turned his eyes toward the multitude under the trees, and it so happened that they rested upon the Dexter Freers. He smiled, and raised his hat with all possible friendliness; and his three companions turned to see to whom he was bowing with so much cordiality. As he settled his hat on his head he espied the young man from Cincinnati, whom he had at first overlooked; whereupon he smiled still more brightly and waved Sidney Feeder an airy salutation with his hand, reining in a little at the same time just for an instant, as if he half expected the Doctor to come and speak to him. Seeing him with strangers, however, Sidney Feeder hung back, staring a little as he rode away.

It is open to us to know that at this moment the young lady by whose side he was riding said to him, familiarly enough: 'Who are those people you bowed to?'

'Some old friends of mine – Americans,' Jackson Lemon answered.

'Of course they are Americans; there is nothing but Americans nowadays.'

'Oh yes, our turn's coming round!' laughed the young man.

'But that doesn't say who they are,' his companion continued. 'It's so difficult to say who Americans are,' she added, before he had time to answer her.

'Dexter Freer and his wife – there is nothing difficult about that; every one knows them.'

'I never heard of them,' said the English girl.

'Ah, that's your fault. I assure you everybody knows them.'

'And does everybody know the little man with the fat face whom you kissed your hand to?'

'I didn't kiss my hand, but I would if I had thought of it. He is a great chum of mine, – a fellow-student at Vienna.'

'And what's *his* name?'

'Doctor Feeder.'

Jackson Lemon's companion was silent a moment. 'Are *all* your friends doctors?' she presently inquired.

'No; some of them are in other businesses.'

'Are they all in some business?'

'Most of them; save two or three, like Dexter Freer.'

'Dexter Freer? I thought you said Doctor Freer.'

The young man gave a laugh. 'You heard me wrong. You have got doctors on the brain, Lady Barb.'

'I am rather glad,' said Lady Barb, giving the rein to her horse, who bounded away.

'Well, yes, she's very handsome, the reason,' Doctor Feeder remarked, as he sat under the trees.

'Is he going to marry her?' Mrs Freer inquired.

'Marry her? I hope not.'

'Why do you hope not?'

'Because I know nothing about her. I want to know something about the woman that man marries.'

'I suppose you would like him to marry in Cincinnati,' Mrs Freer rejoined lightly.

'Well, I am not particular where it is; but I want to know her first.' Doctor Feeder was very sturdy.

'We were in hopes you would know all about it,' said Mr Freer.

'No; I haven't kept up with him there.'

'We have heard from a dozen people that he has been always with her for the last month; and that kind of thing, in England, is supposed to mean something. Hasn't he spoken of her when you have seen him?'

'No, he has only talked about the new treatment of spinal meningitis. He is very much interested in spinal meningitis.'

'I wonder if he talks about it to Lady Barb,' said Mrs Freer.

'Who is she, any way?' the young man inquired.

'Lady Barberina Clement.'

'And who is Lady Barberina Clement?'

'The daughter of Lord Canterville.'

'And who is Lord Canterville?'

'Dexter must tell you that,' said Mrs Freer.

And Dexter accordingly told him that the Marquis of Canterville had been in his day a great sporting nobleman and an ornament to English society, and had held more than once a high post in her Majesty's household. Dexter Freer knew all these things – how his lordship had married a daughter of Lord Treherne, a very serious, intelligent and beautiful woman, who had redeemed him from the extravagance of his youth and presented him in rapid succession with a dozen little tenants for the nurseries at Pasterns – this being, as Mr Freer also knew, the name of the principal seat of the Cantervilles. The Marquis was a Tory, but very liberal for a Tory, and very popular in society at large; good-natured, good-looking, knowing how to be genial and yet remain a *grand seigneur*, clever enough to make an occasional speech, and much associated with the fine old English pursuits, as well as with many of the new improvements – the purification of the Turf, the opening of the museums on Sunday, the propagation of coffee-taverns, the latest ideas on sanitary reform. He disapproved of the extension of the suffrage, but he positively had drainage on the brain. It had been said of him at least once (and I think in print) that he was just the man to convey to the popular mind the impression that the British aristocracy is still a living force. He was not very rich, unfortunately (for a man who had to exemplify such truths), and of his twelve children no less than seven were daughters. Lady Barberina, Jackson Lemon's friend, was the second; the eldest had married Lord Beauchemin. Mr

Freer had caught quite the right pronunciation of this name: he called it Bitumen. Lady Louisa had done very well, for her husband was rich, and she had brought him nothing to speak of; but it was hardly to be expected that the others would do so well. Happily the younger girls were still in the school-room; and before they had come up, Lady Canterville, who was a woman of resources, would have worked off the two that were out. It was Lady Agatha's first season; she was not so pretty as her sister, but she was thought to be cleverer. Half a dozen people had spoken to him of Jackson Lemon's being a great deal at the Cantervilles. He was supposed to be enormously rich.

'Well, so he is,' said Sidney Feeder, who had listened to Mr Freer's little recital with attention, with eagerness even, but with an air of imperfect apprehension.

'Yes, but not so rich as they probably think.'

'Do they want his money? Is that what they're after?'

'You go straight to the point,' Mrs Freer murmured.

'I haven't the least idea,' said her husband. 'He is a very nice fellow in himself.'

'Yes, but he's a doctor,' Mrs Freer remarked.

'What have they got against that?' asked Sidney Feeder.

'Why, over here, you know, they only call them in to prescribe,' said Dexter Freer; 'the profession isn't – a – what you'd call aristocratic.'

'Well, I don't know it, and I don't know that I want to know it. How do you mean, aristocratic? What profession is? It would be rather a curious one. Many of the gentlemen at the congress there are quite charming.'

'I like doctors very much,' said Mrs Freer; 'my father was a doctor. But they don't marry the daughters of marquises.'

'I don't believe Jackson wants to marry that one.'

'Very possibly not – people are such asses,' said Dexter Freer. 'But he will have to decide. I wish you would find out, by the way; you can if you will.'

'I will ask him – up at the congress; I can do that. I suppose he has got to marry some one,' Sidney Feeder added, in a moment, 'and she may be a nice girl.'

'She is said to be charming.'

'Very well, then; it won't hurt him. I must say, however, I am not sure I like all that about her family.'

'What I told you? It's all to their honour and glory.'

'Are they quite on the square? It's like those people in Thackeray.'

'Oh, if Thackeray could have done this!' Mrs Freer exclaimed, with a good deal of expression.

'You mean all this scene?' asked the young man.

'No; the marriage of a British noblewoman and an American doctor. It would have been a subject for Thackeray.'

'You see you do want it, my dear,' said Dexter Freer quietly.

'I want it as a story, but I don't want it for Doctor Lemon.'

'Does he call himself "Doctor" still?' Mr Freer asked of young Feeder.

'I suppose he does; I call him so. Of course he doesn't practise. But once a doctor, always a doctor.'

'That's doctrine for Lady Barb!'

Sidney Feeder stared. 'Hasn't she got a title too? What would she expect him to be? President of the United States? He's a man of real ability; he might have stood at the head of his profession. When I think of that, I want to swear. What did his father want to go and make all that money for?'

'It must certainly be odd to them to see a "medical man" with six or eight millions,' Mr Freer observed.

'They use the same term as the Choctaws,' said his wife.

'Why, some of their own physicians make immense fortunes,' Sidney Feeder declared.

'Couldn't he be made a baronet by the Queen?' This suggestion came from Mrs Freer.

'Yes, then he would be aristocratic,' said the young man. 'But I don't see why he should want to marry over here; it seems to me to be going out of his way. However, if he is happy, I don't care. I like him very much; he has got lots of ability. If it hadn't been for his father he would have made a splendid doctor. But, as I say, he takes a great interest in medical science, and I guess he means to promote it all he can – with his fortune. He will always be doing something in the way of research. He thinks we *do* know something, and he is bound we shall know more. I hope she won't prevent him, the young marchioness – is that her rank? And I hope they are really good people. He ought to be very useful. I should want to know a good deal about the family I was going to marry into.'

'He looked to me, as he rode there, as if he knew a good deal about the Clements,' Dexter Freer said, rising, as his wife suggested that they ought to be going; 'and he looked to me pleased with the knowledge. There they come, down on the other side. Will you walk away with us, or will you stay?'

'Stop him and ask him, and then come and tell us – in Jermyn Street.' This was Mrs Freer's parting injunction to Sidney Feeder.

'He ought to come himself – tell him that,' her husband added.

'Well, I guess I'll stay,' said the young man, as his companions merged themselves in the crowd that now was tending toward the gates. He went and stood by the barrier, and saw Doctor Lemon and his friends pull up at the entrance to the Row, where they apparently prepared to separate. The separation took some time, and Sidney Feeder became interested. Lord Canterville and his younger daughter lingered to talk with two gentlemen, also mounted, who looked a good deal at the legs of Lady Agatha's horse. Jackson Lemon and Lady Barberina were face to face, very near each other; and she, leaning forward a little, stroked the overlapping neck of his glossy bay. At a distance he appeared to be talking, and she to be listening and saying nothing. 'Oh yes, he's making love to her,' thought Sidney Feeder. Suddenly her father turned away, to leave the Park, and she joined him and disappeared, while Doctor Lemon came up on the left again, as if for a final gallop. He had not gone far before he perceived his *confrère*, who awaited him at the rail; and he repeated the gesture which Lady Barberina had spoken of as a kissing of his hand, though it must be added that, to his friend's eyes, it had not quite that significance. When he reached the point where Feeder stood he pulled up.

'If I had known you were coming here I would have given you a mount,' he said. There was not in his person that irradiation of wealth and distinction which made Lord Canterville glow like a picture; but as he sat there with his little legs stuck out, he looked very bright and sharp and happy, wearing in his degree the aspect of one of Fortune's favourites. He had a thin, keen, delicate face, a nose very carefully finished, a rapid eye, a trifle hard in expression, and a small moustache, a good deal cultivated. He was not striking, but he was very positive, and it was easy to see that he was full of purpose.

'How many horses have you got – about forty?' his compatriot inquired, in response to his greeting.

'About five hundred,' said Jackson Lemon.

'Did you mount your friends – the three you were riding with?'

'Mount them? They have got the best horses in England.'

'Did they sell you this one?' Sidney Feeder continued in the same humorous strain.

'What do you think of him?' said his friend, not deigning to answer this question.

'He's an awful old screw; I wonder he can carry you.'

'Where did you get your hat?' asked Doctor Lemon, in return.

'I got it in New York. What's the matter with it?'

'It's very beautiful; I wish I had bought one like it.'

'The head's the thing – not the hat. I don't mean yours, but mine. There is something very deep in your question; I must think it over.'

'Don't – don't,' said Jackson Lemon; 'you will never get to the bottom of it. Are you having a good time?'

'A glorious time. Have you been up to-day?'

'Up among the doctors? No; I have had a lot of things to do.'

'We had a very interesting discussion. I made a few remarks.'

'You ought to have told me. What were they about?'

'About the intermarriage of races, from the point of view –' And Sidney Feeder paused a moment, occupied with the attempt to scratch the nose of his friend's horse.

'From the point of view of the progeny, I suppose?'

'Not at all; from the point of view of the old friends.'

'Damn the old friends!' Doctor Lemon exclaimed, with jocular crudity.

'Is it true that you are going to marry a young marchioness?'

The face of the young man in the saddle became just a trifle rigid, and his firm eyes fixed themselves on Doctor Feeder.

'Who has told you that?'

'Mr and Mrs Freer, whom I met just now.'

'Mr and Mrs Freer be hanged! And who told them?'

'Ever so many people; I don't know who.'

'Gad, how things are tattled!' cried Jackson Lemon, with some asperity.

'I can see it's true, by the way you say that.'

'Do Freer and his wife believe it?' Jackson Lemon went on impatiently.

'They want you to go and see them: you can judge for yourself.'

'I will go and see them, and tell them to mind their own business.'

'In Jermyn Street; but I forget the number. I am sorry the marchioness isn't American,' Sidney Feeder continued.

'If I should marry her, she would be,' said his friend. 'But I don't see what difference it can make to you.'

'Why, she'll look down on the profession; and I don't like that from your wife.'

'That will touch me more than you.'

'Then it *is* true?' cried Feeder, more seriously looking up at his friend.

'She won't look down; I will answer for that.'

'You won't care; you are out of it all now.'

'No, I am not; I mean to do a great deal of work.'

'I will believe that when I see it,' said Sidney Feeder, who was by no means perfectly incredulous, but who thought it salutary to take that tone. 'I am not sure that you have any right to work you oughtn't to have everything; you ought to leave the field to us. You must pay the penalty of being so rich. You would have been celebrated if you had continued to practise – more celebrated than any one. But you won't be now – you can't be. Some one else will be, in your place.'

Jackson Lemon listened to this, but without meeting the eyes of the speaker; not, however, as if he were avoiding them, but as if the long stretch of the Ride, now less and less obstructed, invited him and made his companion's talk a little retarding. Nevertheless, he answered, deliberately and kindly enough: 'I hope it will be you'; and he bowed to a lady who rode past.

'Very likely it will. I hope I make you feel badly – that's what I'm trying to do.'

'Oh, awfully!' cried Jackson Lemon; 'all the more that I am not in the least engaged.'

'Well, that's good. Won't you come up to-morrow?' Doctor Feeder went on.

'I'll try, my dear fellow; I can't be sure. By-by!'

'Oh, you're lost anyway!' cried Sidney Feeder, as the other started away.

2

It was Lady Marmaduke, the wife of Sir Henry Marmaduke, who
had introduced Jackson Lemon to Lady Beauchemin; after which
Lady Beauchemin had made him acquainted with her mother and
sisters. Lady Marmaduke was also transatlantic; she had been for
her conjugal baronet the most permanent consequence of a tour in
the United States. At present, at the end of ten years, she knew her
London as she had never known her New York, so that it had been
easy for her to be, as she called herself, Jackson Lemon's social
godmother. She had views with regard to his career, and these
views fitted into a social scheme which, if our space permitted, I
should be glad to lay before the reader in its magnitude. She wished
to add an arch or two to the bridge on which she had effected her
transit from America, and it was her belief that Jackson Lemon
might furnish the materials. This bridge, as yet a somewhat sketchy
and rickety structure, she saw (in the future) boldly stretching from
one solid pillar to another. It would have to go both ways, for
reciprocity was the keynote of Lady Marmaduke's plan. It was her
belief that an ultimate fusion was inevitable, and that those who
were the first to understand the situation would gain the most. The
first time Jackson Lemon had dined with her, he met Lady Beauchemin, who was her intimate friend. Lady Beauchemin was
remarkably gracious; she asked him to come and see her as if she
really meant it. He presented himself, and in her drawing-room met
her mother, who happened to be calling at the same moment. Lady
Canterville, not less friendly than her daughter, invited him down
to Pasterns for Easter week; and before a month had passed it
seemed to him that, though he was not what he would have called
intimate at any house in London, the door of the house of Clement
opened to him pretty often. This was a considerable good fortune,
for it always opened upon a charming picture. The inmates were
a blooming and beautiful race, and their interior had an aspect of
the ripest comfort. It was not the splendour of New York (as New

York had lately begun to appear to the young man), but a splendour in which there was an unpurchasable ingredient of age. He himself had a great deal of money, and money was good, even when it was new; but old money was the best. Even after he learned that Lord Canterville's fortune was more ancient than abundant, it was still the mellowness of the golden element that struck him. It was Lady Beauchemin who had told him that her father was not rich; having told him, besides this, many surprising things – things that were surprising in themselves or surprising on her lips. This struck him afresh later that evening – the day he met Sidney Feeder in the Park. He dined out, in the company of Lady Beauchemin, and afterward, as she was alone – her husband had gone down to listen to a debate – she offered to 'take him on'. She was going to several places, and he must be going to some of them. They compared notes, and it was settled that they should proceed together to the Trumpingtons', whither, also, it appeared at eleven o'clock that all the world was going, the approach to the house being choked for half a mile with carriages. It was a close, muggy night; Lady Beauchemin's chariot, in its place in the rank, stood still for long periods. In his corner beside her, through the open window, Jackson Lemon, rather hot, rather oppressed, looked out on the moist, greasy pavement, over which was flung, a considerable distance up and down, the flare of a public-house. Lady Beauchemin, however, was not impatient, for she had a purpose in her mind, and now she could say what she wished.

'Do you really love her?' That was the first thing she said.

'Well, I guess so,' Jackson Lemon answered, as if he did not recognise the obligation to be serious.

Lady Beauchemin looked at him a moment in silence; he felt her gaze, and turning his eyes, saw her face, partly shadowed, with the aid of a street-lamp. She was not so pretty as Lady Barberina; her countenance had a certain sharpness; her hair, very light in colour and wonderfully frizzled, almost covered her eyes, the expression of which, however, together with that of her pointed nose, and the glitter of several diamonds, emerged from the gloom. 'You don't seem to know. I never saw a man in such an odd state,' she presently remarked.

'You push me a little too much; I must have time to think of it,' the young man went on. 'You know in my country they allow us plenty of time.' He had several little oddities of expression, of which he was perfectly conscious, and which he found convenient, for they protected him in a society in which a lonely American was rather exposed; they gave him the advantage which corresponded with certain drawbacks. He had very few natural Americanisms, but the occasional use of one, discreetly chosen, made him appear simpler than he really was, and he had his reasons for wishing this result. He was not simple; he was subtle, circumspect, shrewd, and perfectly aware that he might make mistakes. There was a danger of his making a mistake at present – a mistake which would be immensely grave. He was determined only to succeed. It is true that for a great success he would take a certain risk; but the risk was to be considered, and he gained time while he multiplied his guesses and talked about his country.

'You may take ten years if you like,' said Lady Beauchemin. 'I am in no hurry whatever to make you my brother-in-law. Only you must remember that you spoke to me first.'

'What did I say?'

'You told me that Barberina was the finest girl you had seen in England.'

'Oh, I am willing to stand by that; I like her type.'

'I should think you might!'

'I like her very much – with all her peculiarities.'

'What do you mean by her peculiarities?'

'Well, she has some peculiar ideas,' said Jackson Lemon, in a tone of the sweetest reasonableness; 'and she has a peculiar way of speaking.'

'Ah, you can't expect us to speak as well as you!' cried Lady Beauchemin.

'I don't know why not; you do some things much better.'

'We have our own ways, at any rate, and we think them the best in the world. One of them is not to let a gentleman devote himself to a girl for three or four months without some sense of responsibility. If you don't wish to marry my sister you ought to go away.'

'I ought never to have come,' said Jackson Lemon.

'I can scarcely agree to that; for I should have lost the pleasure of knowing you.'

'It would have spared you this duty, which you dislike very much.'

'Asking you about your intentions? I don't dislike it at all; it amuses me extremely.'

'Should you like your sister to marry me?' asked Jackson Lemon, with great simplicity.

If he expected to take Lady Beauchemin by surprise he was disappointed; for she was perfectly prepared to commit herself. 'I should like it very much. I think English and American society ought to be but one – I mean the best of each – a great whole.'

'Will you allow me to ask whether Lady Marmaduke suggested that to you?'

'We have often talked of it.'

'Oh yes, that's her aim.'

'Well, it's my aim too. I think there's a great deal to be done.'

'And you would like me to do it?'

'To begin it, precisely. Don't you think we ought to see more of each other? – I mean the best in each country.'

Jackson Lemon was silent a moment. 'I am afraid I haven't any general ideas. If I should marry an English girl it wouldn't be for the good of the species.'

'Well, we want to be mixed a little; that I am sure of,' Lady Beauchemin said.

'You certainly got that from Lady Marmaduke.'

'It's too tiresome, your not consenting to be serious! But my father will make you so,' Lady Beauchemin went on. 'I may as well let you know that he intends in a day or two to ask you your intentions. That's all I wished to say to you. I think you ought to be prepared.'

'I am much obliged to you; Lord Canterville will do quite right.'

There was, to Lady Beauchemin, something really unfathomable in this little American doctor, whom she had taken up on grounds of large policy, and who, though he was assumed to have sunk the medical character, was neither handsome nor distinguished, but only immensely rich and quite original, for he was not insignificant. It was unfathomable, to begin with, that a medical man should be so rich, or that so rich a man should be medical; it was even, to an eye which was always gratified by suitability, rather irritating. Jackson Lemon himself could have explained it better than any one else, but this was an explanation that one could scarcely ask for. There were other things: his cool acceptance of certain situations: his general indisposition to explain; his way of taking refuge in jokes which at times had not even the merit of being American; his way, too, of appearing to be a suitor without being an aspirant. Lady Beauchemin, however, was, like Jackson Lemon, prepared to run a certain risk. His reserves made him slippery; but that was only when one pressed. She flattered herself that she could handle people lightly. 'My father will be sure to act with perfect tact,' she said; 'of course, if you shouldn't care to be questioned, you can go out of town.' She had the air of really wishing to make everything easy for him.

'I don't want to go out of town; I am enjoying it far too much here,' her companion answered. 'And wouldn't your father have a right to ask me what I meant by that?'

Lady Beauchemin hesitated; she was slightly perplexed. But in a moment she exclaimed: 'He is incapable of saying anything vulgar!'

She had not really answered his inquiry, and he was conscious of that; but he was quite ready to say to her, a little later, as he guided her steps from the brougham to the strip of carpet which, between a somewhat rickety border of striped cloth and a double row of waiting footmen, policemen and dingy amateurs of both sexes, stretched from the curbstone to the portal of the Trumping tons, 'Of course I shall not wait for Lord Canterville to speak to me.'

He had been expecting some such announcement as this from Lady Beauchemin, and he judged that her father would do no more than his duty. He knew that he ought to be prepared with an answer to Lord Canterville, and he wondered at himself for not yet having come to the point. Sidney Feeder's question in the Park had made him feel rather pointless; it was the first allusion that had been made to his possible marriage, except on the part of Lady Beauchemin. None of his own people were in London; he was perfectly independent, and even if his mother had been within reach he could not have consulted her on the subject. He loved her dearly, better than any one; but she was not a woman to consult, for she approved of whatever he did: it was her standard. He was careful not to be too serious when he talked with Lady Beauchemin; but he was very serious indeed as he thought over the matter within himself, which he did even among the diversions of the next half-hour, while he squeezed obliquely and slowly through the crush in Mrs Trumpington's drawing-room. At the end of the half-hour he came away, and at the door he found Lady Beauchemin, from whom he had separated on entering the house, and who, this time with a companion of her own sex, was awaiting her carriage and still 'going on'. He gave her his arm into the street, and as she stepped into the vehicle she repeated that she wished he would go out of town for a few days.

'Who, then, would tell me what to do?' he asked, for answer, looking at her through the window.

She might tell him what to do, but he felt free, all the same; and he was determined this should continue. To prove it to himself he jumped into a hansom and drove back to Brook Street, to his hotel, instead of proceeding to a bright-windowed house in Portland Place, where he knew that after midnight he should find Lady Canterville and her daughters. There had been a reference to the subject between Lady Barberina and himself during their ride, and she would probably expect him; but it made him taste his liberty not to go, and he liked to taste his liberty. He was aware that to taste it in perfection he ought to go to bed; but he did not go to bed, he did not even take off his hat. He walked up and down his sitting-room, with his head surmounted by this ornament, a good deal tipped back, and his hands in his pockets. There were a good many cards stuck into the frame of the mirror, over his chimney-piece, and every time he passed the place he seemed to see what was written on one of them – the name of the mistress of the house in Portland Place, his own name, and, in the lower left-hand corner, the words: 'A small Dance'. Of course, now, he must make up his mind; he would make it up to the next day: that was what he said to himself as he walked up and down; and according to his decision he would speak to Lord Canterville or he would take the night-express to Paris. It was better meanwhile that he should not see Lady Barberina. It was vivid to him, as he paused occasionally, looking vaguely at that card in the chimney-glass, that he had come pretty far; and he had come so far because he was under the charm – yes, he was in love with Lady Barb. There was no doubt whatever of that; he had a faculty for diagnosis, and he knew perfectly well what was the matter with him. He wasted no time in musing upon the mystery of this passion, in wondering whether he might not have escaped it by a little vigilance at first, or whether it would die out if he should go away. He accepted it frankly, for the sake of the pleasure it gave him – the girl was the delight of his eyes – and confined himself to considering whether such a marriage would square with his general situation. This would not at all necessarily follow from the fact that he was in love; too many other things would come in between. The most important of these was the change, not only of the geographical, but of the social, standpoint for his wife, and a certain readjustment that it would involve in his own relation to things. He was not inclined to readjustments, and there was no reason why he should be; his own position was in most respects so advantageous. But the girl tempted him almost irresistibly, satisfying his imagination both as a lover and as a student of the human organism; she was so blooming, so complete, of a type so rarely encountered in that degree of perfection. Jackson Lemon was not an Anglo-maniac, but he admired the physical conditions of the English – their complexion, their temperament, their tissue; and Lady Barberina struck him, in flexible, virginal form, as a wonderful compendium of these elements. There was something simple and robust in her beauty; it had the quietness of an old Greek statue, without the vulgarity of the modern simper or of contemporary prettiness. Her head was antique; and though her conversation was quite of the present period, Jackson Lemon had said to himself that there was sure to be in her soul a certain primitive sincerity which would match with her facial mould. He saw her as she might be in the future, the beautiful mother of beautiful children, in whom the look of race should be conspicuous. He should like his children to have the look of race, and he was not unaware that he must take his precautions accordingly. A great many people had it in England; and it was a pleasure to him to see it, especially as no one had it so unmistakably as the second daughter of Lord Canterville. It would be a great luxury to call such a woman one's own; nothing could be more evident than that, because it made no difference that she was not strikingly clever. Striking cleverness was not a part of harmonious form and the English complexion; it was associated with the modern simper, which was a result of modern nerves. If Jackson Lemon had wanted a nervous wife, of course he could have found her at home; but this tall, fair girl, whose character, like her figure, appeared mainly to have been formed by riding across country, was differently put together. All the same, would it suit his book, as they said in London, to marry her and transport her to New York? He came back to this question; came back to it with a persistency which, had she been admitted to a view of it, would have tried the patience of Lady Beauchemin. She had been irritated, more than once, at his appearing to attach himself so exclusively to this horn of the dilemma – as if it could possibly fail to be a good thing for a little American doctor to marry the daughter of an English peer. It would have been more becoming, in her ladyship's eyes, that he should take that for granted a little more, and the consent of her ladyship's – of their ladyships' – family a little less. They looked at the matter so differently! Jackson Lemon was conscious that if he should marry Lady Barberina Clement it would be because it suited him, and not because it suited his possible sisters-in-law. He believed that he acted in all things by his own will – an organ for which he had the highest respect.

It would have seemed, however, that on this occasion it was not working very regularly, for though he had come home to go to bed, the stroke of half-past twelve saw him jump, not into his couch, but into a hansom which the whistle of the porter had summoned to the door of his hotel, and in which he rattled off to Portland Place. Here he found – in a very large house – an assembly of three hundred people, and a band of music concealed in a bower of azaleas. Lady Canterville had not arrived; he wandered through the rooms and assured himself of that. He also discovered a very good conservatory, where there were banks and pyramids of azaleas. He watched the top of the staircase, but it was a long time before he saw what he was looking for, and his impatience at last was extreme. The reward, however, when it came, was all that he could have desired. It was a little smile from Lady Barberina, who stood behind her mother while the latter extended her finger-tips to the hostess. The entrance of this charming woman, with her beautiful daughters – always a noticeable incident – was effected with a certain brilliancy, and just now it was agreeable to Jackson Lemon to think that it concerned him more than any one else in the house.

Tall, dazzling, indifferent, looking about her as if she saw very little, Lady Barberina was certainly a figure round which a young man's fancy might revolve. She was very quiet and simple, had little manner and little movement; but her detachment was not a vulgar art. She appeared to efface herself, to wait till, in the natural course, she should be attended to; and in this there was evidently no exaggeration, for she was too proud not to have perfect confidence. Her sister, smaller, slighter, with a little surprised smile, which seemed to say that in her extreme innocence she was yet prepared for anything, having heard, indirectly, such extraordinary things about society, was much more impatient and more expressive, and projected across a threshold the pretty radiance of her eyes and teeth before her mother's name was announced. Lady Canterville was thought by many persons to be very superior to her daughters; she had kept even more beauty than she had given them; and it was a beauty which had been called intellectual. She had extraordinary sweetness, without any definite professions; her manner was mild almost to tenderness; there was even a kind of pity in it. Moreover, her features were perfect, and nothing could be more gently gracious than a way she had of speaking, or rather, of listening, to people, with her head inclined a little to one side. Jackson Lemon liked her very much, and she had certainly been most kind to him. He approached Lady Barberina as soon as he could do so without an appearance of precipitation, and said to her that he hoped very much she would not dance. He was a master of the art which flourishes in New York above every other, and he had guided her through a dozen waltzes with a skill which, as she felt, left absolutely nothing to be desired. But dancing was not his business to-night. She smiled a little at the expression of his hope.

'That is what mamma has brought us here for,' she said; 'she doesn't like it if we don't dance.'

'How does she know whether she likes it or not? You have always danced.'

'Once I didn't,' said Lady Barberina.

He told her that, at any rate, he would settle it with her mother, and persuaded her to wander with him into the conservatory, where there were coloured lights suspended among the plants, and a vault of verdure overhead. In comparison with the other rooms the conservatory was dusky and remote. But they were not alone; half a dozen other couples were in possession. The gloom was rosy with the slopes of azalea, and suffused with mitigated music, which made it possible to talk without consideration of one's neighbours. Nevertheless, though it was only in looking back on the scene later that Lady Barberina perceived this, these dispersed couples were talking very softly. She did not look at them; it seemed to her that, virtually, she was alone with Jackson Lemon. She said something about conservatories, about the fragrance of the air; for all answer to which he asked her, as he stood there before her, a question by which she might have been exceedingly startled.

'How do people who marry in England ever know each other before marriage? They have no chance.'

'I am sure I don't know,' said Lady Barberina; 'I never was married.'

'It's very different in my country. There a man may see much of a girl; he may come and see her, he may be constantly alone with her. I wish you allowed that over here.'

Lady Barberina suddenly examined the less ornamental side of her fan, as if it had never occurred to her before to look at it. 'It must be so very odd, America,' she murmured at last.

'Well, I guess in that matter we are right; over here it's a leap in the dark.'

'I am sure I don't know,' said the girl. She had folded her fan; she stretched out her arm mechanically and plucked a sprig of azalea.

'I guess it doesn't signify, after all,' Jackson Lemon remarked. 'They say that love is blind at the best.' His keen young face was bent upon hers; his thumbs were in the pockets of his trousers; he smiled a little, showing his fine teeth. She said nothing, but only pulled her azalea to pieces. She was usually so quiet that this small movement looked restless.

'This is the first time I have seen you in the least without a lot of people,' he went on.

'Yes, it's very tiresome,' she said.

'I have been sick of it; I didn't want to come here to-night.'

She had not met his eyes, though she knew they were seeking her own. But now she looked at him a moment. She had never objected to his appearance, and in this respect she had no repugnance to overcome. She liked a man to be tall and handsome, and Jackson Lemon was neither; but when she was sixteen, and as tall herself as she was to be at twenty, she had been in love (for three weeks) with one of her cousins, a little fellow in the Hussars, who was shorter even than the American, shorter consequently than herself. This proved that distinction might be independent of stature – not that she ever reasoned it out. Jackson Lemon's facial spareness, his bright little eye, which seemed always to be measuring things, struck her as original, and she thought them very cutting, which would do very well for a husband of hers. As she made this reflection, of course it never occurred to her that she herself might be cut; she was not a sacrificial lamb. She perceived that his features expressed a mind – a mind that would be rather effective. She would never have taken him for a doctor; though, indeed, when all was said, that was very negative and didn't account for the way he imposed himself.

'Why, then, did you come?' she asked, in answer to his last speech.

'Because it seems to me after all better to see you in this way than not to see you at all; I want to know you better.'

'I don't think I ought to stay here,' said Lady Barberina, looking round her.

'Don't go till I have told you I love you,' murmured the young man.

She made no exclamation, indulged in no start; he could not see even that she changed colour. She took his request with a noble simplicity, with her head erect and her eyes lowered.

'I don't think you have a right to tell me that.'

'Why not?' Jackson Lemon demanded. 'I wish to claim the right; I wish you to give it to me.'

'I can't – I don't know you. You have said it yourself.'

'Can't you have a little faith? That will help us to know each other better. It's disgusting, the want of opportunity; even at Pasterns I could scarcely get a walk with you. But I have the greatest faith in you. I feel that I love you, and I couldn't do more than that at the end of six months. I love your beauty – I love you from head to foot.

Don't move, please don't move.' He lowered his tone; but it went straight to her ear, and it must be believed that it had a certain eloquence. For himself, after he had heard himself say these words, all his being was in a glow. It was a luxury to speak to her of her beauty; it brought him nearer to her than he had ever been. But the colour had come into her face, and it seemed to remind him that her beauty was not all. 'Everything about you is sweet and noble,' he went on; 'everything is dear to me. I am sure you are good. I don't know what you think of me; I asked Lady Beauchemin to tell me, and she told me to judge for myself. Well, then, I judge you like me. Haven't I a right to assume that till the contrary is proved? May I speak to your father? That's what I want to know. I have been waiting; but now what should I wait for longer? I want to be able to tell him that you have given me some hope. I suppose I ought to speak to him first. I meant to, to-morrow, but meanwhile, to-night, I thought I would just put this in. In my country it wouldn't matter particularly. You must see all that over there for yourself. If you should tell me not to speak to your father, I wouldn't; I would wait. But I like better to ask your leave to speak to him than to ask his to speak to you.'

His voice had sunk almost to a whisper; but, though it trembled, his emotion gave it peculiar intensity. He had the same attitude, his thumbs in his trousers, his attentive head, his smile, which was a matter of course; no one would have imagined what he was saying. She had listened without moving, and at the end she raised her eyes. They rested on his a moment, and he remembered, a good while later, the look which passed her lids.

'You may say anything that you please to my father, but I don't wish to hear any more. You have said too much, considering how little idea you have given me before.'

'I was watching you,' said Jackson Lemon.

Lady Barberina held her head higher, looking straight at him. Then, quite seriously, 'I don't like to be watched,' she remarked.

'You shouldn't be so beautiful, then. Won't you give me a word of hope?' he added.

'I have never supposed I should marry a foreigner,' said Lady Barberina.

'Do you call me a foreigner?'

'I think your ideas are very different, and your country is different; you have told me so yourself.'

'I should like to show it to you; I would make you like it.'

'I am not sure what you would make me do,' said Lady Barberina, very honestly.

'Nothing that you don't want.'

'I am sure you would try,' she declared, with a smile.

'Well,' said Jackson Lemon, 'after all, I am trying now.'

To this she simply replied she must go to her mother, and he was obliged to lead her out of the conservatory. Lady Canterville was not immediately found, so that he had time to murmur as they went, 'Now that I have spoken, I am very happy.'

'Perhaps you are happy too soon,' said the girl.

'Ah, don't say that, Lady Barb.'

'Of course I must think of it.'

'Of course you must!' said Jackson Lemon. 'I will speak to your father to-morrow.'

'I can't fancy what he will say.'

'How can he dislike me?' the young man asked, in a tone which Lady Beauchemin, if she had heard him, would have been forced to attribute to his general affectation of the jocose. What Lady Beauchemin's sister thought of it is not recorded; but there is perhaps a clue to her opinion in the answer she made him after a moment's silence: 'Really, you know, you *are* a foreigner!' With this she turned her back upon him, for she was already in her mother's hands. Jackson Lemon said a few words to Lady Canterville; they were chiefly about its being very hot. She gave him her vague, sweet attention, as if he were saying something ingenious of which she missed the point. He could see that she was thinking of the doings of her daughter Agatha, whose attitude toward the contemporary young man was wanting in the perception of differences – a madness without method; she was evidently not occupied with Lady Barberina, who was more to be trusted. This young woman never met her suitor's eyes again; she let her own rest, rather ostentatiously, upon other objects. At last he was going away without a glance from her. Lady Canterville had asked him to come to lunch on the morrow, and he had said he would do so if she would promise him he should see his lordship. 'I can't pay you another visit until I have had some talk with him,' he said.

'I don't see why not; but if I speak to him I dare say he will be at home,' she answered.

'It will be worth his while!'

Jackson Lemon left the house reflecting that as he had never proposed to a girl before he could not be expected to know how women demean themselves in this emergency. He had heard, indeed, that Lady Barb had had no end of offers; and though he thought it probable that the number was exaggerated, as it always is, it was to be supposed that her way of appearing suddenly to have dropped him was but the usual behaviour for the occasion.

3

At her mother's the next day she was absent from luncheon, and Lady Canterville mentioned to him (he didn't ask) that she had gone to see a dear old great-aunt, who was also her godmother, and who lived at Roehampton. Lord Canterville was not present, but our young man was informed by his hostess that he had promised her he would come in exactly at three o'clock. Jackson Lemon lunched with Lady Canterville and the children, who appeared in force at this repast, all the younger girls being present, and two little boys, the juniors of the two sons who were in their teens. Jackson, who was very fond of children, and thought these absolutely the finest in the world – magnificent specimens of a magnificent brood, such as it would be so satisfactory in future days to see about his own knee – Jackson felt that he was being treated as one of the family, but was not frightened by what he supposed the privilege to imply. Lady Canterville betrayed no consciousness whatever of his having mooted the question of becoming her son-in-law, and he believed that her eldest daughter had not told her of their talk the night before. This idea gave him pleasure; he liked to think that Lady Barb was judging him for herself. Perhaps, indeed, she was taking counsel of the old lady at Roehampton: he believed that he was the sort of lover of whom a godmother would approve. Godmothers in his mind were mainly associated with fairy-tales (he had had no baptismal sponsors of his own); and that point of view would be favourable to a young man with a great deal of gold who had suddenly arrived from a foreign country – an apparition, surely, sufficiently elfish. He made up his mind that he should like Lady Canterville as a mother-in-law; she would be too well-bred to meddle. Her husband came in at three o'clock, just after they had left the table, and said to Jackson Lemon that it was very good in him to have waited.

'I haven't waited,' Jackson replied, with his watch in his hand; 'you are punctual to the minute.'

I know not how Lord Canterville may have judged his young friend, but Jackson Lemon had been told more than once in his life that he was a very good fellow, but rather too literal. After he had lighted a cigarette in his lordship's 'den', a large brown apartment on the ground-floor, which partook at once of the nature of an office and of that of a harness-room (it could not have been called in any degree a library), he went straight to the point in these terms: 'Well now, Lord Canterville, I feel as if I ought to let you know without more delay that I am in love with Lady Barb, and that I should like to marry her.' So he spoke, puffing his cigarette, with his conscious but unextenuating eye fixed on his host.

No man, as I have intimated, bore better being looked at than this noble personage; he seemed to bloom in the envious warmth of human contemplation, and never appeared so faultless as when he was most exposed. 'My dear fellow, my dear fellow,' he murmured, almost in disparagement, stroking his ambrosial beard from before the empty fireplace. He lifted his eyebrows, but he looked perfectly good-natured.

'Are you surprised, sir?' Jackson Lemon asked.

'Why, I suppose any one is surprised at a man wanting one of his children. He sometimes feels the weight of that sort of thing so much, you know. He wonders what the devil another man wants of them.' And Lord Canterville laughed pleasantly out of the copious fringe of his lips.

'I only want one of them,' said Jackson Lemon, laughing too, but with a lighter organ.

'Polygamy would be rather good for the parents. However, Louisa told me the other night that she thought you were looking the way you speak of.'

'Yes, I told Lady Beauchemin that I love Lady Barb, and she seemed to think it was natural.'

'Oh yes, I suppose there's no want of nature in it! But, my dear fellow, I really don't know what to say.'

'Of course you'll have to think of it.' Jackson Lemon, in saying this, felt that he was making the most liberal concession to the point of view of his interlocutor; being perfectly aware that in his own country it was not left much to the parents to think of.

'I shall have to talk it over with my wife.'

'Lady Canterville has been very kind to me; I hope she will continue.'

'My dear fellow, we are excellent friends. No one could appreciate you more than Lady Canterville. Of course we can only consider such a question on the – a – highest grounds. You would never want to marry without knowing, as it were, exactly what you are doing. I, on my side, naturally, you know, am bound to do the best I can for my own child. At the same time, of course, we don't want to spend our time in – a – walking round the horse. We want to keep to the main line.' It was settled between them after a little that the main line was that Jackson Lemon knew to a certainty the state of his affections and was in a position to pretend to the hand of a young lady who, Lord Canterville might say – of course, you know, without any swagger – had a right to expect to do well, as the women call it.

'I should think she had,' Jackson Lemon said, 'she's a beautiful type.'

Lord Canterville stared a moment. 'She is a clever, well-grown girl, and she takes her fences like a grasshopper. Does she know all this, by the way?' he added.

'Oh yes, I told her last night.'

Again Lord Canterville had the air, unusual with him, of returning his companion's scrutiny. 'I am not sure that you ought to have done that, you know.'

'I couldn't have spoken to you first – I couldn't,' said Jackson Lemon. 'I meant to, but it stuck in my crop.'

'They don't in your country, I guess,' his lordship returned, smiling

'Well, not as a general thing; however, I find it very pleasant to discuss with you now.' And in truth it was very pleasant. Nothing could be easier, friendlier, more informal, than Lord Canterville's manner, which implied all sorts of equality, especially that of age and fortune, and made Jackson Lemon feel at the end of three minutes almost as if he too were a beautifully preserved and somewhat straitened nobleman of sixty, with the views of a man of the world about his own marriage. The young American perceived that Lord Canterville waived the point of his having spoken first to the girl herself, and saw in this indulgence a just concession to the ardour of young affection. For Lord Canterville seemed perfectly to appreciate the sentimental side – at least so far as it was embodied in his visitor – when he said, without deprecation: 'Did she give you any encouragement?'

'Well, she didn't box my ears. She told me that she would think of it, but that I must speak to you. But, naturally, I shouldn't have said what I did to her if I hadn't made up my mind during the last fortnight that I am not disagreeable to her.'

'Ah, my dear young man, women are odd cattle!' Lord Canterville exclaimed, rather unexpectedly. 'But of course you know all that,' he added in an instant; 'you take the general risk.'

'I am perfectly willing to take the general risk; the particular risk is small.'

'Well, upon my honour I don't really know my girls. You see a man's time, in England, is tremendously taken up; but I dare say it's the same in your country. Their mother knows them – I think I had better send for their mother. If you don't mind I'll just suggest that she join us here.'

'I'm rather afraid of you both together, but if it will settle it any quicker –' said Jackson Lemon. Lord Canterville rang the bell, and, when a servant appeared, despatched him with a message to her ladyship. While they were waiting, the young man remembered that it was in his power to give a more definite account of his pecuniary basis. He had simply said before that he was abundantly able to marry; he shrank from putting himself forward as a billionaire. He had a fine taste, and he wished to appeal to Lord Canterville primarily as a gentleman. But now that he had to make a double impression, he bethought himself of his millions, for millions were always impressive. 'I think it only fair to let you know that my fortune is really very considerable,' he remarked.

'Yes, I dare say you are beastly rich,' said Lord Canterville.

'I have about seven millions.'

'Seven millions?'

'I count in dollars; upwards of a million and a half sterling.'

Lord Canterville looked at him from head to foot, with an air of cheerful resignation to a form of grossness which threatened to become common. Then he said, with a touch of that inconsequence of which he had already given a glimpse: 'What the deuce, then, possessed you to turn doctor?'

Jackson Lemon coloured a little, hesitated, and then replied, quickly: 'Because I had the talent for it.'

'Of course, I don't for a moment doubt of your ability; but don't you find it rather a bore?'

'I don't practise much. I am rather ashamed to say that.'

'Ah, well, of course, in your country it's different. I dare say you've got a door-plate, eh?'

'Oh yes, and a tin sign tied to the balcony!' said Jackson Lemon, smiling.

'What did your father say to it?'

'To my going into medicine? He said he would be hanged if he'd take any of my doses. He didn't think I should succeed; he wanted me to go into the house.'

'Into the House – a –' said Lord Canterville, hesitating a little. 'Into your Congress – yes, exactly.'

'Ah, no, not so bad as that. Into the store,' Jackson Lemon replied, in the candid tone in which he expressed himself when, for reasons of his own, he wished to be perfectly national.

Lord Canterville stared, not venturing, even for the moment, to hazard an interpretation; and before a solution had presented itself Lady Canterville came into the room.

'My dear, I thought we had better see you. Do you know he wants to marry our second girl?' It was in these simple terms that her husband acquainted her with the question.

Lady Canterville expressed neither surprise nor elation; she simply stood there, smiling, with her head a little inclined to the side, with all her customary graciousness. Her charming eyes rested on those of Jackson Lemon, and though they seemed to show that she had to think a little of so serious a proposition, his own discovered in them none of the coldness of calculation, 'Are you talking about Barberina?' she asked in a moment, as if her thoughts had been far away.

Of course they were talking about Barberina, and Jackson Lemon repeated to her ladyship what he had said to the girl's father. He had thought it all over, and his mind was quite made up. Moreover, he had spoken to Lady Barb.

'Did she tell you that, my dear?' asked Lord Canterville, while he lighted another cigar.

She gave no heed to this inquiry, which had been vague and accidental on his lordship's part, but simply said to Jackson Lemon that the thing was very serious, and that they had better sit down for a moment. In an instant he was near her on the sofa on which she had placed herself, still smiling and looking up at her husband with an air of general meditation, in which a sweet compassion for every one concerned was apparent.

'Barberina has told me nothing,' she said, after a little.

'That proves she cares for me!' Jackson Lemon exclaimed eagerly.

Lady Canterville looked as if she thought this almost too ingenious, almost professional; but her husband said cheerfully, jovially: 'Ah, well, if she cares for you, I don't object.'

This was a little ambiguous; but before Jackson Lemon had time to look into it, Lady Canterville asked gently: 'Should you expect her to live in America?'

'Oh, yes; that's my home, you know.'

'Shouldn't you be living sometimes in England?'

'Oh, yes, we'll come over and see you.' The young man was in love, he wanted to marry, he wanted to be genial, and to commend himself to the parents of Lady Barb; at the same time it was in his nature not to accept conditions, save in so far as they exactly suited him, to tie himself, or, as they said in New York, to give himself away. In any transaction he preferred his own terms to those of any one else. Therefore, the moment Lady Canterville gave signs of wishing to extract a promise, he was on his guard.

'She'll find it very different; perhaps she won't like it,' her ladyship suggested.

'If she likes me, she'll like my country,' said Jackson Lemon, with decision.

'He tells me he has got a plate on his door,' Lord Canterville remarked humorously.

'We must talk to her, of course; we must understand how she feels,' said his wife, looking more serious than she had done as yet.

'Please don't discourage her, Lady Canterville,' the young man begged, 'and give me a chance to talk to her a little more myself. You haven't given me much chance, you know.'

'We don't offer our daughters to people, Mr Lemon,' Lady Canterville was always gentle, but now she was a little majestic.

'She isn't like some women in London, you know,' said Jackson Lemon's host, who seemed to remember that to a discussion of such importance he ought from time to time to contribute a word of wisdom. And Jackson Lemon, certainly, if the idea had been presented to him, would have said that, No, decidedly, Lady Barberina had not been thrown at him.

'Of course not,' he declared, in answer to her mother's remark. 'But, you know, you mustn't refuse them too much, either; you mustn't make a poor fellow wait too long. I admire her, I love her, more than I can say; I give you my word of honour for that.'

'He seems to think that settles it,' said Lord Canterville, smiling down at the young American, very indulgently, from his place before the cold chimney-piece.

'Of course that's what we desire, Philip,' her ladyship returned, very nobly.

'Lady Barb believes it; I am sure she does!' Jackson Lemon exclaimed. 'Why should I pretend to be in love with her if I am not?'

Lady Canterville received this inquiry in silence, and her husband, with just the least air in the world of repressed impatience, began to walk up and down the room. He was a man of many engagements, and he had been closeted for more than a quarter of an hour with the young American doctor. 'Do you imagine you should come often to England?' Lady Canterville demanded, with a certain abruptness, returning to that important point.

'I'm afraid I can't tell you that; of course we shall do whatever seems best.' He was prepared to suppose they should cross the Atlantic every summer: that prospect was by no means displeasing to him; but he was not prepared to give any such pledge to Lady Canterville, especially as he did not believe it would really be necessary. It was in his mind, not as an overt pretension, but as a tacit implication, that he should treat with Barberina's parents on a footing of perfect equality; and there would somehow be nothing equal if he should begin to enter into engagements which didn't belong to the essence of the matter. They were to give their daughter, and he was to take her: in this arrangement there would be as much on one side as on the other. But beyond this he had nothing to ask of them; there was nothing he wished them to promise, and his own pledges, therefore, would have no equivalent. Whenever his wife should wish it, she should come over and see her people. Her home was to be in New York; but he was tacitly conscious that on the question of absences he should be very liberal. Nevertheless, there was something in the very grain of his character which forbade that he should commit himself at present in respect to times and dates.

Lady Canterville looked at her husband, but her husband was not attentive; he was taking a peep at his watch. In a moment, however, he threw out a remark to the effect that he thought it a capital thing that the two countries should become more united, and there was nothing that would bring it about better than a few of the best people on both sides pairing off together. The English, indeed, had begun it; a lot of fellows had brought over a lot of pretty girls, and it was quite fair play that the Americans should take their pick. They were all one race, after all; and why shouldn't they make one society – the best on both sides, of course? Jackson Lemon smiled as he recognised Lady Marmaduke's philosophy, and he was pleased to think that Lady Beauchemin had some influence with her father; for he was sure the old gentleman (as he mentally designated his host) had got all this from her, though he expressed himself less happily than the cleverest of his daughters. Our hero had no objection to make to it, especially if there was anything in it that would really help his case. But it was not in the least on these high grounds that he had sought the hand of Lady Barb. He wanted her not in order that her people and his (the best on both sides!) should make one society; he wanted her simply because he wanted her. Lady Canterville smiled; but she seemed to have another thought.

'I quite appreciate what my husband says; but I don't see why poor Barb should be the one to begin.'

'I dare say she'll like it,' said Lord Canterville, as if he were attempting a short cut. 'They say you spoil your women awfully.'

'She's not one of their women yet,' her ladyship remarked, in the sweetest tone in the world; and then she added, without Jackson Lemon's knowing exactly what she meant, 'It seems so strange.'

He was a little irritated; and perhaps these simple words added to the feeling. There had been no positive opposition to his suit, and Lord and Lady Canterville were most kind; but he felt that they held back a little, and though he had not expected them to throw themselves on his neck, he was rather disappointed, his pride was touched. Why should they hesitate? He considered himself such a good *parti*. It was not so much the old gentleman, it was Lady Canterville. As he saw the old gentleman look, covertly, a second time at his watch, he could have believed he would have been glad to settle the matter on the spot. Lady Canterville seemed to wish her daughter's lover to come forward more, to give certain assurances and guarantees. He felt that he was ready to say or do anything that was a matter of proper form; but he couldn't take the tone of trying to purchase her ladyship's consent, penetrated as he was with the conviction that such a man as he could be trusted to care for his wife rather more than an impecunious British peer and *his* wife could be supposed (with the lights he had acquired in English society) to care even for the handsomest of a dozen children. It was a mistake on Lady Canterville's part not to recognise that. He humoured her mistake to the extent of saying, just a little drily, 'My wife shall certainly have everything she wants.'

'He tells me he is disgustingly rich,' Lord Canterville added, pausing before their companion with his hands in his pockets.

'I am glad to hear it; but it isn't so much that,' she answered, sinking back a little on her sofa. If it was not that, she did not say what it was, though she had looked for a moment as if she were going to. She only raised her eyes to her husband's face, as if to ask for inspiration. I know not whether she found it, but in a moment she said to Jackson Lemon, seeming to imply that it was quite another point: 'Do you expect to continue your profession?'

He had no such intention, so far as his profession meant getting up at three o'clock in the morning to assuage the ills of humanity; but here, as before, the touch of such a question instantly stiffened him. 'Oh, my profession! I am rather ashamed of that matter. I have neglected my work so much, I don't know what I shall be able to do, once I am really settled at home.'

Lady Canterville received these remarks in silence; fixing her eyes again upon her husband's face. But this nobleman was really not helpful; still with his hands in his pockets, save when he needed to remove his cigar from his lips, he went and looked out of the window. 'Of course we know you don't practise, and when you're a married man you will have less time even than now. But I should really like to know if they call you Doctor over there.'

'Oh yes, universally. We are nearly as fond of titles as your people.'

'I don't call that a title.'

'It's not so good as duke or marquis, I admit; but we have to take what we have got.'

'Oh, bother, what does it signify?' Lord Canterville demanded, from his place at the window. 'I used to have a horse named Doctor, and a devilish good one too.'

'You may call me bishop, if you like,' said Jackson Lemon, laughing.

Lady Canterville looked grave, as if she did not enjoy this pleasantry. 'I don't care for any titles,' she observed; 'I don't see why a gentleman shouldn't be called Mr.'

It suddenly appeared to Jackson Lemon that there was something helpless, confused, and even slightly comical, in the position of this noble and amiable lady. The impression made him feel kindly; he too, like Lord Canterville, had begun to long for a short cut. He relaxed a moment, and leaning toward his hostess, with a smile and his hands on his little knees, he said softly, 'It seems to me a question of no importance; all I desire is that you should call me your son-in-law.'

Lady Canterville gave him her hand, and he pressed it almost affectionately. Then she got up, remarking that before anything was decided she must see her daughter, she must learn from her own lips the state of her feelings. 'I don't like at all her not having spoken to me already,' she added.

'Where has she gone – to Roehampton? I dare say she has told it all to her godmother,' said Lord Canterville.

'She won't have much to tell, poor girl!' Jackson Lemon exclaimed. 'I must really insist upon seeing with more freedom the person I wish to marry.'

'You shall have all the freedom you want, in two or three days,' said Lady Canterville. She smiled with all her sweetness; she appeared to have accepted him, and yet still to be making tacit asssumptions. 'Are there not certain things to be talked of first?'

'Certain things, dear lady?'

Lady Canterville looked at her husband, and though he was still at his window, this time he felt it in her silence, and had to come away and speak. 'Oh, she means settlements, and that kind of thing.' This was an allusion which came with a much better grace from him.

Jackson Lemon looked from one of his companions to the other; he coloured a little, and gave a smile that was perhaps a trifle fixed. 'Settlements? We don't make them in the United States. You may be sure I shall make a proper provision for my wife.'

'My dear fellow, over here – in our class, you know, it's the custom,' said Lord Canterville, with a richer brightness in his face at the thought that the discussion was over.

'I have my own ideas,' Jackson answered, smiling.

'It seems to me it's a question for the solicitors to discuss,' Lady Canterville suggested.

'They may discuss it as much as they please,' said Jackson Lemon, with a laugh. He thought he saw his solicitors discussing it! He had indeed his own ideas. He opened the door for Lady Canterville, and the three passed out of the room together, walking into the hall in a silence in which there was just a tinge of awkwardness. A note had been struck which grated and scratched a little. A pair of brilliant footmen, at their approach, rose from a bench to a great altitude, and stood there like sentinels presenting arms. Jackson Lemon stopped, looking for a moment into the interior of his hat, which he had in his hand. Then, raising his keen eyes, he fixed them a moment on those of Lady Canterville, addressing her, instinctively, rather than her husband. 'I guess you and Lord Canterville had better leave it to me!'

'We have our traditions, Mr Lemon,' said her ladyship, with nobleness. 'I imagine you don't know –' she murmured.

Lord Canterville laid his hand on the young man's shoulder. 'My dear boy, those fellows will settle it in three minutes.'

'Very likely they will!' said Jackson Lemon. Then he asked of Lady Canterville when he might see Lady Barb.

She hesitated a moment, in her gracious way. 'I will write you a note.'

One of the tall footmen, at the end of the impressive vista, had opened wide the portals, as if even he were aware of the dignity to which the little visitor had virtually been raised. But Jackson lingered a moment; he was visibly unsatisfied, though apparently so little unconscious that he was unsatisfying. 'I don't think you understand me.'

'Your ideas are certainly different,' said Lady Canterville.

'If the girl understands you, that's enough!' Lord Canterville exclaimed in a jovial, detached, irrelevant way.

'May not *she* write to me?' Jackson asked of her mother. 'I certainly must write to her, you know, if you won't let me see her.'

'Oh yes, you may write to her, Mr Lemon.'

There was a point for a moment in the look that he gave Lady Canterville, while he said to himself that if it were necessary he would transmit his notes through the old lady at Roehampton. 'All right, good-bye; you know what I want, at any rate.' Then, as he was going, he turned and added: 'You needn't be afraid that I won't bring her over in the hot weather!'

'In the hot weather?' Lady Canterville murmured, with vague visions of the torrid zone, while the young American quitted the house with the sense that he had made great concessions.

His host and hostess passed into a small morning-room, and (Lord Canterville having taken up his hat and stick to go out again) stood there a moment, face to face.

'It's clear enough he wants her,' said his lordship, in a summary manner.

'There's something so odd about him,' Lady Canterville answered. 'Fancy his speaking so about settlements!'

'You had better give him his head; he'll go much quieter.'

'He's so obstinate – very obstinate; it's easy to see that. And he seems to think a girl in your daughter's position can be married from one day to the other – with a ring and a new frock – like a housemaid.'

'Well, of course, over there, that's the kind of thing. But he seems really to have a most extraordinary fortune; and every one does say their women have *carte blanche*.'

'*Carte blanche* is not what Barb wishes; she wishes a settlement. She wants a definite income; she wants to be safe.'

Lord Canterville stared a moment. 'Has she told you so? I thought you said –' And then he stopped. 'I beg your pardon,' he added.

Lady Canterville gave no explanation of her inconsistency. She went on to remark that American fortunes were notoriously insecure; one heard of nothing else; they melted away like smoke. It was their duty to their child to demand that something should be fixed.

'He has a million and a half sterling,' said Lord Canterville. 'I can't make out what he does with it.'

'She ought to have something very handsome,' his wife remarked.

'Well, my dear, you must settle it: you must consider it; you must send for Hilary. Only take care you don't put him off; it may be a very good opening, you know. There is a great deal to be done out there; I believe in all that,' Lord Canterville went on, in the tone of a conscientious parent.

'There is no doubt that he *is* a doctor – in those places,' said Lady Canterville, musingly.

'He may be a pedlar for all I care.'

'If they should go out, I think Agatha might go with them,' her ladyship continued, in the same tone, a little disconnectedly.

'You may send them all out if you like. Good-bye!' And Lord Canterville kissed his wife.

But she detained him a moment, with her hand on his arm. 'Don't you think he is very much in love?'

'Oh yes, he's very bad; but he's a clever little beggar.'

'She likes him very much,' Lady Canterville announced, rather formally, as they separated.

4

Jackson Lemon had said to Sidney Feeder in the Park that he would
call on Mr and Mrs Freer; but three weeks elapsed before he knocked
at their door in Jermyn Street. In the meantime he had met them
at dinner, and Mrs Freer had told him that she hoped very much
he would find time to come and see her. She had not reproached
him, nor shaken her finger at him; and her clemency, which was
calculated, and very characteristic of her, touched him so much (for
he was in fault; she was one of his mother's oldest and best friends),
that he very soon presented himself. It was a fine Sunday afternoon,
rather late, and the region of Jermyn Street looked forsaken and
inanimate; the native dulness of the landscape appeared in all its
purity. Mrs Freer, however, was at home, resting on a lodging-
house sofa – an angular couch, draped in faded chintz – before she
went to dress for dinner. She made the young man very welcome;
she told him she had been thinking of him a great deal; she had
wished to have a chance to talk with him. He immediately perceived
what she had in mind, and then he remembered that Sidney Feeder
had told him what it was that Mr and Mrs Freer took upon themselves to say. This had provoked him at the time, but he had
forgotten it afterward; partly because he became aware, that same
evening, that he did wish to marry the 'young marchioness', and
partly because since then he had had much greater annoyances.
Yes, the poor young man, so conscious of liberal intensions, of a
large way of looking at the future, had had much to irritate and
disgust him. He had seen the mistress of his affections but three or
four times, and he had received letters from Mr Hilary, Lord Canterville's solicitor, asking him, in terms the most obsequious, it is true,
to designate some gentleman of the law with whom the preliminaries of his marriage to Lady Barberina Clement might be
arranged. He had given Mr Hilary the name of such a functionary,
but he had written by the same post to his own solicitor (for whose
services in other matters he had had much occasion, Jackson Lemon

being distinctly contentious), instructing him that he was at liberty to meet Mr Hilary, but not at liberty to entertain any proposals as to this odious English idea of a settlement. If marrying Jackson Lemon were not settlement enough, then Lord and Lady Canterville had better alter their point of view. It was quite out of the question that he should alter his. It would perhaps be difficult to explain the strong aversion that he entertained to the introduction into his prospective union of this harsh diplomatic element; it was as if they mistrusted him, suspected him; as if his hands were to be tied, so that he could not handle his own fortune as he thought best. It was not the idea of parting with his money that displeased him, for he flattered himself that he had plans of expenditure for his wife beyond even the imagination of her distinguished parents. It struck him even that they were fools not to have perceived that they should make a much better thing of it by leaving him perfectly free. This intervention of the solicitor was a nasty little English tradition – totally at variance with the large spirit of American habits – to which he would not submit. It was not his way to submit when he disapproved: why should he change his way on this occasion, when the matter lay so near him? These reflections, and a hundred more, had flowed freely through his mind for several days before he called in Jermyn Street, and they had engendered a lively indignation and a really bitter sense of wrong. As may be imagined, they had infused a certain awkwardness into his relations with the house of Canterville, and it may be said of these relations that they were for the moment virtually suspended. His first interview with Lady Barb, after his conference with the old couple, as he called her august elders, had been as tender as he could have desired. Lady Canterville, at the end of three days, had sent him an invitation – five words on a card – asking him to dine with them to-morrow, quite *en famille*. This had been the only formal intimation that his engagement to Lady Barb was recognised; for even at the family banquet, which included half a dozen outsiders, there had been no allusion on the part either of his host or his hostess to the subject of their conversation in Lord Canterville's den. The only allusion was a wandering ray, once or twice, in Lady Barberina's eyes. When, however, after dinner, she strolled away with him into the music-room, which was lighted and empty, to play for him something out of *Carmen*, of which he had spoken at table, and when the young couple were allowed to enjoy for upwards of an hour, unmolested, the comparative privacy of this rich apartment, he felt that Lady Canterville definitely counted upon him. She didn't believe in any serious difficulties. Neither did he, then; and that was why it was a nuisance there should be a vain appearance of them. The arrangements, he supposed Lady Canterville would have said, were pending, and indeed they were; for he had already given orders in Bond Street for the setting of an extraordinary number of diamonds. Lady Barb, at any rate, during that hour he spent with her, had had nothing to say about arrangements; and it had been an hour of pure satisfaction. She had seated herself at the piano and had played perpetually, in a soft incoherent manner, while he leaned over the instrument, very close to her, and said everything that came into his head. She was very bright and serene, and she looked at him as if she liked him very much.

This was all he expected of her, for it did not belong to the cast of her beauty to betray a vulgar infatuation. That beauty was more delightful to him than ever; and there was a softness about her which seemed to say to him that from this moment she was quite his own. He felt more than ever the value of such a possession; it came over him more than ever that it had taken a great social outlay to produce such a mixture. Simple and girlish as she was, and not particularly quick in the give and take of conversation, she seemed to him to have a part of the history of England in her blood; she was a *résumé* of generations of privileged people, and of centuries of rich country-life. Between these two, of course, there was no allusion to the question which had been put into the hands of Mr Hilary, and the last thing that occurred to Jackson Lemon was that Lady Barb had views as to his settling a fortune upon her before their marriage. It may appear singular, but he had not asked himself whether his money operated upon her in any degree as a bribe; and this was because, instinctively, he felt that such a speculation was idle, – the point was not to be ascertained, – and because he was willing to assume that it was agreeable to her that she should continue to live in luxury. It was eminently agreeable to him that he might enable her to do so. He was acquainted with the mingled character of human motives, and he was glad that he was rich enough to pretend to the hand of a young woman who, for the best of reasons, would be very expensive. After that happy hour in the music-room he had ridden with her twice; but he had not found her otherwise accessible. She had let him know, the second time they rode, that Lady Canterville had directed her to make, for the moment, no further appointment with him; and on his presenting himself, more than once at the house, he had been told that neither the mother nor the daughter was at home; it had been added that Lady Barberina was staying at Roehampton. On giving him that information in the Park, Lady Barb had looked at him with a mute reproach there was always a certain superior dumbness in her eyes – as if he were exposing her to an annoyance that she ought to be spared; as if he were taking an eccentric line on a question that all well-bred people treated in the conventional way. His induction from this was not that she wished to be secure about his money, but that, like a dutiful English daughter, she received her opinions (on points that were indifferent to her) ready-made from a mamma whose fallibility had never been exposed. He knew by this that his solicitor had answered Mr Hilary's letter, and that Lady Canterville's coolness was the fruit of this correspondence. The effect of it was not in the least to make him come round, as he phrased it; he had not the smallest intention of doing that. Lady Canterville had spoken of the traditions of her family; but he had no need to go to his family for his own. They resided within himself; anything that he had definitely made up his mind to, acquired in an hour a kind of legendary force. Meanwhile, he was in the detestable position of not knowing whether or no he were engaged. He wrote to Lady Barb to inquire – it being so strange that she should not receive him; and she answered in a very pretty little letter, which had to his mind a sort of bygone quality, an old-fashioned freshness, as if it might have been written in the last century by Clarissa or Amelia: she answered that she did not in the least understand the situation; that, of course, she would never give him up; that her mother had said that there were the best reasons for their not going too fast; that, thank God, she was yet young, and could wait as long as he would; but that she begged he wouldn't write her anything about money-matters, as she could never comprehend them. Jackson felt that he was in no danger whatever of making this last mistake; he only noted how

Lady Barb thought it natural that there should be a discussion; and this made it vivid to him afresh that he had got hold of a daughter of the Crusaders. His ingenious mind could appreciate this hereditary assumption perfectly, at the same time that, to light his own footsteps, it remained entirely modern. He believed – or he thought he believed – that in the end he should marry Barberina Clement on his own terms; but in the interval there was a sensible indignity in being challenged and checked. One effect of it, indeed, was to make him desire the girl more keenly. When she was not before his eyes in the flesh, she hovered before him as an image; and this image had reasons of its own for being a radiant picture. There were moments, however, when he wearied of looking at it; it was so impalpable and thankless, and then Jackson Lemon, for the first time in his life, was melancholy. He felt alone in London, and very much out of it, in spite of all the acquaintances he had made, and the bills he had paid; he felt the need of a greater intimacy than any he had formed (save, of course, in the case of Lady Barb). He wanted to vent his disgust, to relieve himself, from the American point of view. He felt that in engaging in a contest with the great house of Canterville he was, after all, rather single. That singleness was, of course, in a great measure an inspiration; but it pinched him a little at moments. Then he wished his mother had been in London, for he used to talk of his affairs a great deal with this delightful parent, who had a soothing way of advising him in the sense he liked best. He had even gone so far as to wish he had never laid eyes on Lady Barb and had fallen in love with some transatlantic maiden of a similar composition. He presently came back, of course, to the knowledge that in the United States there was – and there could be – nothing similar to Lady Barb; for was it not precisely as a product of the English climate and the British constitution that he valued her? He had relieved himself, from his American point of view, by speaking his mind to Lady Beauchemin, who confessed that she was very much vexed with her parents. She agreed with him that they had made a great mistake; they ought to have left him free; and she expressed her confidence that that freedom would be for her family, as it were, like the silence of the sage, golden. He must excuse them; he must remember that what was asked of him had been their custom for centuries. She did not mention her authority as to the origin of customs, but she assured him that she would say three words to her father and mother which would make it all right. Jackson answered that customs were all very well, but that intelligent people recognised, when they saw it, the right occasion for departing from them; and with this he awaited the result of Lady Beauchemin's remonstrance. It had not as yet been perceptible, and it must be said that this charming woman was herself much bothered. When, on her venturing to say to her mother that she thought a wrong line had been taken with regard to her sister's *prétendant,* Lady Canterville had replied that Mr Lemon's unwillingness to settle anything was in itself a proof of what they had feared, the unstable nature of his fortune (for it was useless to talk – this gracious lady could be very decided – there could be no serious reason but that one): on meeting this argument, as I say, Jackson's protectress felt considerably baffled. It was perhaps true, as her mother said, that if they didn't insist upon proper guarantees Barberina might be left in a few years with nothing but the stars and stripes (this odd phrase was a quotation from Mr Lemon) to cover her. Lady Beauchemin tried to reason it out with Lady Marmaduke; but these were complications unforeseen by Lady Marmaduke in her project of an Anglo-American society. She was obliged to confess that Mr Lemon's fortune could not have the solidity of long-established things; it was a very new fortune indeed. His father had made the greater part of it all in a lump, a few years before his death, in the extraordinary way in which people made money in America; that, of course, was why the son had those singular professional attributes. He had begun to study to be a doctor very young, before his expectations were so great. Then he had found he was very clever, and very fond of it; and he had kept on, because, after all, in America, where there were no country-gentlemen, a young man had to have something to do, don't you know? And Lady Marmaduke, like an enlightened woman, intimated that in such a case she thought it much better taste not to try to sink anything. 'Because, in America, don't you see,' she reasoned, 'you can't sink it – nothing *will* sink. Everything is floating about – in the newspapers.' And she tried to console her friend by remarking that if Mr Lemon's fortune was precarious, it was at all events so big. That was just the trouble for Lady Beauchemin; it was so big, and yet they were going to lose it. He was as obstinate as a mule; she was sure he would never come round. Lady Marmaduke declared that he would come round; she even offered to bet a dozen pair of *gants de Suède* on it; and she added that this consummation lay quite in the hands of Barberina. Lady Beauchemin promised herself to converse with her sister; for it was not for nothing that she herself had felt the international contagion.

Jackson Lemon, to dissipate his chagrin, had returned to the sessions of the medical congress, where, inevitably, he had fallen into the hands of Sidney Feeder, who enjoyed in this disinterested assembly a high popularity. It was Doctor Feeder's earnest desire that his old friend should share it, which was all the more easy as the medical congress was really, as the young physician observed, a perpetual symposium. Jackson Lemon entertained the whole body – entertained it profusely, and in a manner befitting one of the patrons of science rather than its humbler votaries; but these dissipations only made him forget for a moment that his relations with the house of Canterville were anomalous. His great difficulty punctually came back to him, and Sidney Feeder saw it stamped upon his brow. Jackson Lemon with his acute inclination to open himself, was on the point, more than once, of taking the sympathetic Sidney into his confidence. His friend gave him easy opportunity; he asked him what it was he was thinking of all the time, and whether the young marchioness had concluded she couldn't swallow a doctor. These forms of speech were displeasing to Jackson Lemon, whose fastidiousness was nothing new; but it was for even deeper reasons that he said to himself that, for such complicated cases as his, there was no assistance in Sidney Feeder. To understand his situation one must know the world; and the child of Cincinnati didn't know the world – at least the world with which his friend was now concerned.

'Is there a hitch in your marriage? Just tell me that,' Sidney Feeder had said, taking everything for granted, in a manner which was in itself a proof of great innocence. It is true he had added that he supposed he had no business to ask; but he had been anxious about it ever since hearing from Mr and Mrs Freer that the British aristocracy was down on the medical profession. 'Do they want you to give it up? Is that what the hitch is about? Don't desert your colours,

Jackson. The elimination of pain, the mitigation of misery, constitute surely the noblest profession in the world.'

'My dear fellow, you don't know what you are talking about,' Jackson observed, for answer to this. 'I haven't told any one I was going to be married; still less have I told any one that any one objected to my profession. I should like to see them do it. I have got out of the swim to-day, but I don't regard myself as the sort of person that people object to. And I do expect to do something, yet.'

'Come home, then, and do it. And excuse me if I say that the facilities for getting married are much greater over there.'

'You don't seem to have found them very great.'

'I have never had time. Wait till my next vacation, and you will see.'

'The facilities over there are too great. Nothing is good but what is difficult,' said Jackson Lemon, in a tone of artificial sententiousness that quite tormented his interlocutor.

'Well, they have got their backs up, I can see that. I'm glad you like it. Only if they despise your profession, what will they say to that of your friends? If they think you are queer, what would they think of me?' asked Sidney Feeder, the turn of whose mind was not, as a general thing, in the least sarcastic, but who was pushed to this sharpness by a conviction that (in spite of declarations which seemed half an admission and half a denial) his friend was suffering himself to be bothered for the sake of a good which might be obtained elsewhere without bother. It had come over him that the bother was of an unworthy kind.

'My dear fellow, all that is idiotic.' That had been Jackson Lemon's reply; but it expressed but a portion of his thoughts. The rest was inexpressible, or almost; being connected with a sentiment of rage at its having struck even so genial a mind as Sidney Feeder's that, in proposing to marry a daughter of the highest civilisation, he was going out of his way – departing from his natural line. Was he then so ignoble, so pledged to inferior things, that when he saw a girl who (putting aside the fact that she had not genius, which was rare, and which, though he prized rarity, he didn't want) seemed to him the most complete feminine nature he had known, he was to think himself too different, too incongruous, to mate with her? He would mate with whom he chose; that was the upshot of Jackson Lemon's

reflections. Several days elapsed, during which everybody – even
the pure-minded, like Sidney Feeder – seemed to him very abject.

I relate all this to show why it was that in going to see Mrs Freer
he was prepared much less to be angry with people who, like the
Dexter Freers, a month before, had given it out that he was engaged
to a peer's daughter, than to resent the insinuation that there were
obstacles to such a prospect. He sat with Mrs Freer alone for half
an hour in the sabbatical stillness of Jermyn Street. Her husband
had gone for a walk in the Park; he always walked in the Park on
Sunday. All the world might have been there, and Jackson and Mrs
Freer in sole possession of the district of St James's. This perhaps had
something to do with making him at last rather confidential; the
influences were conciliatory, persuasive. Mrs Freer was extremely
sympathetic; she treated him like a person she had known from the
age of ten; asked his leave to continue recumbent; talked a great deal
about his mother; and seemed almost for a while to perform the
kindly functions of that lady. It had been wise of her from the first
not to allude, even indirectly, to his having neglected so long to call;
her silence on this point was in the best taste. Jackson Lemon had
forgotten that it was a habit with her, and indeed a high accom-
plishment, never to reproach people with these omissions. You
might have left her alone for two years, her greeting was always
the same; she was never either too delighted to see you or not
delighted enough. After a while, however, he perceived that her
silence had been to a certain extent a reference; she appeared to take
for granted that he devoted all his hours to a certain young lady.
It came over him for a moment that his country people took a great
deal for granted; but when Mrs Freer, rather abruptly, sitting up on
her sofa, said to him, half simply, half solemnly, 'And now, my dear
Jackson, I want you to tell me something!' – he perceived that after
all she didn't pretend to know more about the impending matter
than he himself did. In the course of a quarter of an hour – so
appreciatively she listened – he had told her a good deal about it.
It was the first time he had said so much to any one, and the process
relieved him even more than he would have supposed. It made
certain things clear to him, by bringing them to a point – above all,
the fact that he had been wronged. He made no allusion whatever
to its being out of the usual way that, as an American doctor, he

should sue for the hand of a marquis's daughter; and this reserve was not voluntary, it was quite unconscious. His mind was too full of the offensive conduct of the Cantervilles, and the sordid side of their want of confidence. He could not imagine that while he talked to Mrs Freer – and it amazed him afterward that he should have chattered so; he could account for it only by the state of his nerves – she should be thinking only of the strangeness of the situation he sketched for her. She thought Americans as good as other people, but she didn't see where, in American life, the daughter of a marquis would, as she phrased it, work in. To take a simple instance, – they coursed through Mrs Freer's mind with extraordinary speed – would she not always expect to go in to dinner first? As a novelty, over there, they might like to see her do it, at first; there might be even a pressure for places for the spectacle. But with the increase of every kind of sophistication that was taking place in America, the humorous view to which she would owe her safety might not continue to be taken; and then where would Lady Barberina be? This was but a small instance; but Mrs Freer's vivid imagination – much as she lived in Europe, she knew her native land so well – saw a host of others massing themselves behind it. The consequence of all of which was that after listening to him in the most engaging silence, she raised her clasped hands, pressed them against her breast, lowered her voice to a tone of entreaty, and, with her perpetual little smile, uttered three words: 'My dear Jackson, don't don't don't.'

'Don't what?' he asked, staring.

'Don't neglect the chance you have of getting out of it; it would never do.'

He knew what she meant by his chance of getting out of it; in his many meditations he had, of course, not overlooked that. The ground the old couple had taken about settlements (and the fact that Lady Beauchemin had not come back to him to tell him, as she promised, that she had moved them, proved how firmly they were rooted) would have offered an all-sufficient pretext to a man who should have repented of his advances. Jackson Lemon knew that; but he knew at the same time that he had not repented. The old couple's want of imagination did not in the least alter the fact that Barberina was, as he had told her father, a beautiful type. Therefore he simply said to Mrs Freer that he didn't in the least wish to get out of it; he was as much in it as ever, and he intended to remain there. But what did she mean, he inquired in a moment, by her statement that it would never do? Why wouldn't it do? Mrs Freer replied by another inquiry – Should he really like her to tell him? It wouldn't do, because Lady Barb would not be satisfied with her place at dinner. She would not be content – in a society of commoners – with any but the best; and the best she could not expect (and it was to be supposed that he did not expect her) always to have.

'What do you mean by commoners?' Jackson Lemon demanded, looking very serious.

'I mean you, and me, and my poor husband, and Dr Feeder,' said Mrs Freer.

'I don't see how there can be commoners where there are not lords. It is the lord that makes the commoner; and *vice versa*.'

'Won't a lady do as well? Lady Barberina – a single English girl – can make a million inferiors.'

'She will be, before anything else, my wife; and she will not talk about inferiors any more than I do. I never do; it's very vulgar.'

'I don't know what she'll talk about, my dear Jackson, but she will think; and her thoughts won't be pleasant – I mean for others. Do you expect to sink her to your own rank?'

Jackson Lemon's bright little eyes were fixed more brightly than ever upon his hostess. 'I don't understand you; and I don't think you understand yourself.' This was not absolutely candid, for he did understand Mrs Freer to a certain extent; it has been related that, before he asked Lady Barb's hand of her parents, there had been moments when he himself was not very sure that the flower of the British aristocracy would flourish in American soil. But an intimation from another person that it was beyond his power to pass off his wife – whether she were the daughter of a peer or of a shoemaker – set all his blood on fire. It quenched on the instant his own perception of difficulties of detail, and made him feel only that he was dishonoured – he, the heir of all the ages – by such insinuations. It was his belief – though he had never before had occasion to put it forward – that his position, one of the best in the world, was one of those positions that make everything possible. He had had the best education the age could offer, for if he had rather wasted his time at Harvard, where he entered very young, he had, as he believed, been tremendously serious at Heidelberg and at Vienna. He had devoted himself to one of the noblest professions – a profession recognised as such everywhere but in England – and he had inherited a fortune far beyond the expectation of his earlier years, the years when he cultivated habits of work which alone – or rather in combination with talents that he neither exaggerated nor minimised – would have conduced to distinction. He was one of the most fortunate inhabitants of an immense, fresh, rich country, a country whose future was admitted to be incalculable, and he moved with perfect ease in a society in which he was not overshadowed by others. It seemed to him, therefore, beneath his dignity to wonder whether he could afford, socially speaking, to marry according to his taste. Jackson Lemon pretended to be strong; and what was the use of being strong if you were not prepared to undertake things that timid people might find difficult? It was his plan to marry the woman he liked, and not to be afraid of her afterward. The effect of Mrs Freer's doubt of his success was to represent to him that his own character would not cover his wife's; she couldn't have made him feel otherwise if she had told him that he was marrying beneath him, and would have to ask for indulgence. 'I don't believe you know how much I think that any woman who marries me will be doing very well,' he added, directly.

'I am very sure of that; but it isn't so simple – one's being an American,' Mrs Freer rejoined, with a little philosophic sigh.

'It's whatever one chooses to make it.'

'Well, you'll make it what no one has done yet, if you take that young lady to America and make her happy there.'

'Do you think it's such a very dreadful place?'

'No, indeed; but she will.'

Jackson Lemon got up from his chair, and took up his hat and stick. He had actually turned a little pale, with the force of his emotion; it had made him really quiver that his marriage to Lady Barberina should be looked at as too high a flight. He stood a moment leaning against the mantelpiece, and very much tempted to say to Mrs Freer that she was a vulgar-minded old woman. But he said something that was really more to the point: 'You forget that she will have her consolations.'

'Don't go away, or I shall think I have offended you. You can't console a wounded marchioness.'

'How will she be wounded? People will be charming to her.'

'They will be charming to her – charming to her!' These words fell from the lips of Dexter Freer, who had opened the door of the room and stood with the knob in his hand, putting himself into relation to his wife's talk with their visitor. This was accomplished in an instant. 'Of course I know whom you mean,' he said, while he exchanged greetings with Jackson Lemon. 'My wife and I – of course you know we are great busybodies – have talked of your affair, and we differ about it completely: she sees only the dangers and I see the advantages.'

'By the advantages he means the fun for us,' Mrs Freer remarked, settling her sofa-cushions.

Jackson looked with a certain sharp blankness from one of these disinterested judges to the other; and even yet they did not perceive how their misdirected familiarities wrought upon him. It was hardly more agreeable to him to know that the husband wished to see Lady Barb in America, than to know that the wife had a dread of such a vision; for there was that in Dexter Freer's face which seemed to say that the thing would take place somehow for the benefit of the spectators. 'I think you both see too much – a great deal too much. he answered, rather coldly.

'My dear young man, at my age I can take certain liberties,' said Dexter Freer. 'Do it – I beseech you to do it: it has never been done before.' And then, as if Jackson's glance had challenged this last assertion, he went on: 'Never, I assure you, this particular thing. Young female members of the British aristocracy have married coachmen and fishmongers, and all that sort of thing: but they have never married you and me.'

'They certainly haven't married you.' said Mrs Freer.

'I am much obliged to you for your advice.' It may be thought that Jackson Lemon took himself rather seriously: and indeed I am afraid that if he had not done so there would have been no occasion for my writing this little history. But it made him almost sick to hear his engagement spoken of as a curious and ambiguous phenomenon. He might have his own ideas about it – one always had about one's engagement; but the ideas that appeared to have peopled the imagination of his friends ended by kindling a little hot spot in each of his cheeks. 'I would rather not talk any more about my little plans.' he added to Dexter Freer. 'I have been saying all sorts of absurd things to Mrs Freer.'

'They have been most interesting, that lady declared. You have been very stupidly treated.'

'May she tell me when you go?' her husband asked of the young man.

'I am going now; she may tell you whatever she likes.'

'I am afraid we have displeased you,' said Mrs Freer; 'I have said too much what I think. You must excuse me. it's all for your mother.'

'It's she whom I want Lady Barberina to see!' Jackson Lemon exclaimed, with the inconsequence of filial affection.

'Deary me!' murmured Mrs Freer.

'We shall go back to America to see how you get on,' her husband said; 'and if you succeed, it will be a great precedent.'

'Oh, I shall succeed!' And with this he took his departure. He walked away with the quick step of a man labouring under a certain excitement; walked up to Piccadilly and down past Hyde Park Corner. It relieved him to traverse these distances, for he was thinking hard, under the influence of irritation; and locomotion helped him to think. Certain suggestions that had been made him in the last half hour rankled in his mind, all the more that they seemed to have a kind of representative value. to be an echo of the common voice. If his prospects wore that face to Mrs Freer, they would probably wear it to others; and he felt a sudden need of showing such others that they took a pitiful measure of his position. Jackson Lemon walked and walked till he found himself on the highway of Hammersmith. I have represented him as a young man of much strength of purpose, and I may appear to undermine this plea when I relate that he wrote that evening to his solicitor that Mr Hilary was to be informed that he would agree to any proposals for settlements that Mr Hilary should make. Jackson's strength of purpose was shown in his deciding to marry Lady Barberina on any terms. It seemed to him. under the influence of his desire to prove that he was not afraid – so odious was the imputation – that terms of any kind were very superficial things. What was fundamental, and of the essence of the matter, would be to marry Lady Barb and carry everything out.

5

'On Sundays, now, you might be at home,' Jackson Lemon said to his wife in the following month of March, more than six months after his marriage.

'Are the people any nicer on Sundays than they are on other days?' Lady Barberina replied, from the depths of her chair, without looking up from a stiff little book.

He hesitated a single instant before answering: 'I don't know whether they are, but I think they might be.'

'I am as nice as I know how to be. You must take me as I am. You knew when you married me that I was not an American.'

Jackson Lemon stood before the fire, towards which his wife's face was turned and her feet were extended; stood there some time, with his hands behind him and his eyes dropped a little obliquely upon the bent head and richly-draped figure of Lady Barberina. It may be said without delay that he was irritated, and it may be added that he had a double cause. He felt himself to be on the verge of the first crisis that had occurred between himself and his wife – the reader will perceive that it had occurred rather promptly – and he was annoyed at his annoyance. A glimpse of his state of mind before his marriage has been given to the reader, who will remember that at that period Jackson Lemon somehow regarded himself as lifted above possibilities of irritation. When one was strong, one was not irritable; and a union with a kind of goddess would of course be an element of strength. Lady Barb was a goddess still, and Jackson Lemon admired his wife as much as the day he led her to the altar· but I am not sure that he felt so strong.

'How do you know what people are?' he said in a moment. 'You have seen so few; you are perpetually denying yourself. If you should leave New York to-morrow you would know wonderfully little about it.'

'It's all the same,' said Lady Barb; 'the people are all exactly alike.'

'How can you tell? You never see them.'

'Didn't I go out every night for the first two months we were here?'

'It was only to about a dozen houses – always the same; people, moreover, you had already met in London. You have got no general impressions.'

'That's just what I have got; I had them before I came. Every one is just the same; they have the same names – just the same manners.'

Again, for an instant, Jackson Lemon hesitated; then he said, in that apparently artless tone of which mention has already been made, and which he sometimes used in London during his wooing: 'Don't you like it over here?'

Lady Barb raised her eyes from her book. 'Did you expect me to like it?'

'I hoped you would, of course. I think I told you so.'

'I don't remember. You said very little about it; you seemed to make a kind of mystery. I knew, of course, you expected me to live here, but I didn't know you expected me to like it.'

'You thought I asked of you the sacrifice, as it were.'

'I am sure I don't know,' said Lady Barb. She got up from her chair and tossed the volume she had been reading into the empty seat. 'I recommend you to read that book,' she added.

'Is it interesting?'

'It's an American novel.'

'I never read novels.'

'You had better look at that one; it will show you the kind of people you want me to know.'

'I have no doubt it's very vulgar,' said Jackson Lemon; 'I don't see why you read it.'

'What else can I do? I can't always be riding in the Park; I hate the Park,' Lady Barb remarked.

'It's quite as good as your own,' said her husband.

She glanced at him with a certain quickness, her eyebrows slightly lifted. 'Do you mean the park at Pasterns?'

'No; I mean the park in London.'

'I don't care about London. One was only in London a few weeks.'

'I suppose you miss the country,' said Jackson Lemon. It was his idea of life that he should not be afraid of anything, not be afraid, in any situation, of knowing the worst that was to be known about it; and the demon of a courage with which discretion was not properly commingled prompted him to take soundings which were perhaps not absolutely necessary for safety, and yet which revealed unmistakable rocks. It was useless to know about rocks if he couldn't avoid them; the only thing was to trust to the wind.

'I don't know what I miss. I think I miss everything!' This was his wife's answer to his too curious inquiry. It was not peevish for that is not the tone of a goddess; but it expressed a good deal – a good deal more than Lady Barb, who was rarely eloquent, had expressed before. Nevertheless, though his question had been precipitate, Jackson Lemon said to himself that he might take his time to think over what his wife's little speech contained; he could not help seeing that the future would give him abundant opportunity for that. He was in no hurry to ask himself whether poor Mrs Freer, in Jermyn Street, might not, after all, have been right in saying that, in regard to marrying the product of an English caste, it was not so simple to be an American doctor – might avail little even, in such a case, to be the heir of all the ages. The transition was complicated, but in his bright mind it was rapid, from the brush of a momentary contact with such ideas to certain considerations which led him to say, after an instant, to his wife, 'Should you like to go down into Connecticut?'

'Into Connecticut?'

'That's one of our States; it's about as large as Ireland. I'll take you there if you like.'

'What does one do there?'

'We can try and get some hunting.'

'You and I alone?'

'Perhaps we can get a party to join us.'

'The people in the State?'

'Yes; we might propose it to them.'

'The tradespeople in the towns?'

'Very true; they will have to mind their shops,' said Jackson Lemon. 'But we might hunt alone.'

'Are there any foxes?'

'No; but there are a few old cows.'

Lady Barb had already perceived that her husband took it into his head once in a while to laugh at her and she was aware that the present occasion was neither worse nor better than some others. She didn't mind it particularly now, though in England it would have disgusted her; she had the consciousness of virtue – an immense comfort – and flattered herself that she had learned the lesson of an altered standard of fitness; there were, moreover, so many more disagreeable things in America than being laughed at by one's husband. But she pretended to mind it, because it made him stop, and above all it stopped discussion, which with Jackson was so often jocular. and none the less tiresome for that. 'I only want to be left alone,' she said, in answer – though, indeed, it had not the manner of an answer – to his speech about the cows. With this she wandered away to one of the windows which looked out on the Fifth Avenue. She was very fond of these windows, and she had taken a great fancy to the Fifth Avenue, which, in the high-pitched winter weather, when everything sparkled, was a spectacle full of novelty. It will be seen that she was not wholly unjust to her adoptive country: she found it delightful to look out of the window. This was a pleasure she had enjoyed in London only in the most furtive manner: it was not the kind of thing that girls did in England. Besides, in London, in Hill Street, there was nothing particular to see; but in the Fifth Avenue everything and every one went by, and observation was made consistent with dignity by the masses of brocade and lace in which the windows were draped, which, some-how, would not have been tidy in England, and which made an ambush without concealing the brilliant day. Hundreds of women – the curious women of New York, who were unlike any that Lady Barb had hitherto seen – passed the house every hour, and her ladyship was infinitely entertained and mystified by the sight of their clothes. She spent a good deal more time than she was aware of in this amusement; and if she had been addicted to returning upon herself, or asking herself for an account of her conduct – an inquiry which she did not, indeed, completely neglect, but treated very cursorily – it would have made her smile sadly to think what she appeared mainly to have come to America for, conscious though she was that her tastes were very simple, and that so long as she didn't hunt, it didn't much matter what she did.

Her husband turned about to the fire, giving a push with his foot to a log that had fallen out of its place. Then he said – and the connection with the words she had just uttered was apparent enough – 'You really must be at home on Sundays, you know. I used to like that so much in London. All the best women here do it. You had better begin to-day. I am going to see my mother· if I meet any one I will tell them to come.'

'Tell them not to talk so much,' said Lady Barb, among her lace curtains.

'Ah, my dear,' her husband replied, 'it isn't every one that has your concision!' And he went and stood behind her in the window, putting his arm round her waist. It was as much of a satisfaction to him as it had been six months before, at the time the solicitors were settling the matter, that this flower of an ancient stem should be worn upon his own breast; he still thought its fragrance a thing quite apart, and it was as clear as day to him that his wife was the handsomest woman in New York. He had begun, after their arrival, by telling her this very often; but the assurance brought no colour to her cheek, no light to her eyes; to be the handsomest woman in New York evidently did not seem to her a position in life. Moreover, the reader may be informed that, oddly enough, Lady Barb did not particularly believe this assertion. There were some very pretty women in New York, and without in the least wishing to be like them she had seen no woman in America whom she desired to resemble – she envied some of their elements. It is probable that her own finest points were those of which she was most unconscious. But her husband was aware of all of them; nothing could exceed the minuteness of his appreciation of his wife. It was a sign of this that after he had stood behind her a moment he kissed her very tenderly. 'Have you any message for my mother?' he asked.

'Please give her my love. And you might take her that book.'

'What book?'

'That nasty one I have been reading.'

'Oh, bother your books,' said Jackson Lemon, with a certain irritation, as he went out of the room.

There had been a good many things in her life in New York that cost Lady Barb an effort; but sending her love to her mother-in-law was not one of these. She liked Mrs Lemon better than any one she had seen in America; she was the only person who seemed to Lady

Barb really simple, as she understood that quality. Many people had struck her as homely and rustic, and many others as pretentious and vulgar; but in Jackson's mother she had found the golden mean of a simplicity which, as she would have said, was really nice. Her sister, Lady Agatha, was even fonder of Mrs Lemon; but then Lady Agatha had taken the most extraordinary fancy to every one and everything, and talked as if America were the most delightful country in the world. She was having a lovely time (she already spoke the most beautiful American), and had been, during the winter that was just drawing to a close, the most prominent girl in New York. She had gone out at first with her sister; but for some weeks past Lady Barb had let so many occasions pass, that Agatha threw herself into the arms of Mrs Lemon, who found her extraordinarily quaint and amusing and was delighted to take her into society. Mrs Lemon, as an old woman, had given up such vanities; but she only wanted a motive, and in her good nature she ordered a dozen new caps and sat smiling against the wall while her little English maid, on polished floors, to the sound of music, cultivated the American step as well as the American tone. There was no trouble, in New York, about going out, and the winter was not half over before the little English maid found herself an accomplished diner, rolling about, without any chaperon at all, to banquets where she could count upon a bouquet at her plate. She had had a great deal of correspondence with her mother on this point, and Lady Canterville at last withdrew her protest, which in the meantime had been perfectly useless. It was ultimately Lady Canterville's feeling that if she had married the handsomest of her daughters to an American doctor, she might let another become a professional *raconteuse* (Agatha had written to her that she was expected to talk so much), strange as such a destiny seemed for a girl of nineteen. Mrs Lemon was even a much simpler woman than Lady Barberina thought her; for she had not noticed that Lady Agatha danced much oftener with Herman Longstraw than with any one else. Jackson Lemon, though he went little to balls, had discovered this truth, and he looked slightly preoccupied when, after he had sat five minutes with his mother on the Sunday afternoon through which I have invited the reader to trace so much more than (I am afraid) is easily apparent of the progress of this simple story, he learned that his sister-in-law was entertaining Mr Longstraw in the library. He had called half an hour before, and she had taken him into the other room to show him the seal of the Cantervilles, which she had fastened to one of her numerous trinkets (she was adorned with a hundred bangles and chains), and the proper exhibition of which required a taper and a stick of wax. Apparently he was examining it very carefully, for they had been absent a good while. Mrs Lemon's simplicity was further shown by the fact that she had not measured their absence; it was only when Jackson questioned her that she remembered.

Herman Longstraw was a young Californian who had turned up in New York the winter before, and who travelled on his moustache, as they were understood to say in his native State. This moustache, and some of the accompanying features, were very ornamental; several ladies in New York had been known to declare that they were as beautiful as a dream. Taken in connection with his tall stature, his familiar good-nature, and his remarkable Western vocabulary, they constituted his only social capital; for of the two great divisions, the rich Californians and the poor Californians, it was well known to which he belonged. Jackson Lemon looked at him as a slightly mitigated cowboy, and was somewhat vexed at his dear mother, though he was aware that she could scarcely figure to herself what an effect such an accent as that would produce in the halls of Canterville. He had no desire whatever to play a trick on the house to which he was allied, and knew perfectly that Lady Agatha had not been sent to America to become entangled with a Californian of the wrong denomination. He had been perfectly willing to bring her; he thought, a little vindictively, that this would operate as a hint to her parents as to what he might have been inclined to do if they had not sent Mr Hilary after him. Herman Longstraw, according to the legend, had been a trapper, a squatter, a miner, a pioneer – had been everything that one could be in the romantic parts of America, and had accumulated masses of experience before the age of thirty. He had shot bears in the Rockies and buffaloes on the plains; and it was even believed that he had brought down animals of a still more dangerous kind, among the haunts of men. There had been a story that he owned a cattle-ranch in Arizona; but a later and apparently more authentic version of it, though it represented him as looking after the cattle, did not depict him as their proprietor. Many of the stories told about him were false; but there is no doubt that his moustache, his good-nature and his accent were genuine. He danced very badly; but Lady Agatha had frankly told several persons that that was nothing new to her; and she liked (this, however, she did not tell) Mr Herman Longstraw. What she enjoyed in America was the revelation of freedom; and there was no such proof of freedom as conversation with a gentleman who dressed in skins when he was not in New York, and who, in his usual pursuits, carried his life (as well as that of other people) in his hand. A gentleman whom she had sat next to at a dinner in the early part of her stay in New York, remarked to her that the United States were the paradise of women and mechanics; and this had seemed to her at the time very abstract, for she was not conscious, as yet, of belonging to either class. In England she had been only a girl; and the principal idea connected with that was simply that, for one's misfortune, one was not a boy. But presently she perceived that New York was a paradise; and this helped her to know that she must be one of the people mentioned in the axiom of her neighbour – people who could do whatever they wanted, had a voice in everything, and made their taste and their ideas felt. She saw that it was great fun to be a woman in America, and that this was the best way to enjoy the New York winter – the wonderful, brilliant New York winter, the queer, long-shaped, glittering city, the heterogeneous hours, among which you couldn't tell the morning from the afternoon or the night from either of them, the perpetual liberties and walks, the rushings-out and the droppings-in, the intimacies, the endearments, the comicalities, the sleigh-bells, the cutters, the sunsets on the snow, the ice-parties in the frosty clearness, the bright, hot, velvety houses, the bouquets, the bonbons, the little cakes, the big cakes, the irrepressible inspirations of shopping, the innumerable luncheons and dinners that were offered to youth and innocence, the quantities of chatter of quantities of girls, the perpetual motion of the German, the suppers at restaurants after the play, the way in which life was pervaded by Delmonico and Delmonico by the sense that though one's hunting was lost and this so different, it was almost as good – and in all, through all, a kind of suffusion of bright, loud, friendly sound, which was very local, but very human.

Lady Agatha at present was staying, for a little change, with Mrs Lemon, and such adventures as that were part of the pleasure of her American season. The house was too close; but physically the girl could bear anything, and it was all she had to complain of; for Mrs Lemon, as we know, thought her a bonnie little damsel, and had none of the old-world scruples in regard to spoiling young people to which Lady Agatha now perceived that she herself, in the past, had been unduly sacrificed. In her own way – it was not at all her sister's way – she liked to be of importance; and this was assuredly the case when she saw that Mrs Lemon had apparently nothing in the world to do (after spending a part of the morning with her servants) but invent little distractions (many of them of the edible sort) for her guest. She appeared to have certain friends, but she had no society to speak of, and the people who came into her house came principally to see Lady Agatha. This, as we have seen, was strikingly the case with Herman Longstraw. The whole situation gave Lady Agatha a great feeling of success – success of a new and unexpected kind. Of course, in England, she had been born successful, in a manner, in coming into the world in one of the most beautiful rooms at Pasterns; but her present triumph was achieved more by her own effort (not that she had tried very hard) and by her merit. It was not so much what she said (for she could never say half as much as the girls in New York), as the spirit of enjoyment that played in her fresh young face, with its pointless curves, and shone in her gray English eyes. She enjoyed everything, even the street-cars, of which she made liberal use; and more than everything she enjoyed Mr Longstraw and his talk about buffaloes and bears. Mrs Lemon promised to be very careful, as soon as her son had begun to warn her; and this time she had a certain understanding of what she promised. She thought people ought to make the matches they liked; she had given proof of this in her late behaviour to Jackson, whose own union was, in her opinion, marked with all the arbitrariness of pure love. Nevertheless, she could see that Herman Longstraw would probably be thought rough in England; and it was not simply that he was so inferior to Jackson, for, after all, certain things were not to be expected. Jackson Lemon was not oppressed with his mother-in-law having taken his precautions against such a danger; but he was aware that he should give Lady Canterville a permanent advantage over him if, while she was in America, her daughter Agatha should attach herself to a mere moustache.

It was not always, as I have hinted, that Mrs Lemon entered completely into the views of her son, though in form she never failed to subscribe to them devoutly. She had never yet, for instance, apprehended his reason for marrying Lady Barberina Clement. This was a great secret, and Mrs Lemon was determined that no one should ever know it. For herself, she was sure that, to the end of time, she should not discover Jackson's reason. She could never ask about it, for that of course would betray her. From the first she had told him she was delighted; there being no need of asking for explanation then, as the young lady herself, when she should come to know her, would explain. But the young lady had not yet explained; and after this, evidently, she never would. She was very tall, very handsome, she answered exactly to Mrs Lemon's prefigurement of the daughter of a lord, and she wore her clothes, which were peculiar, but, to her, remarkably becoming, very well. But she did not elucidate; we know ourselves that there was very little that was explanatory about Lady Barb. So Mrs Lemon continued to wonder, to ask herself, 'Why that one, more than so many others, who would have been more natural?' The choice appeared to her, as I have said, very arbitrary. She found Lady Barb very different from other girls she had known, and this led her almost immediately to feel sorry for her daughter-in-law. She said to herself that Barb was to be pitied if she found her husband's people as peculiar as his mother found *her*; for the result of that would be to make her very lonesome. Lady Agatha was different, because she seemed to keep nothing back; you saw all there was of her, and she was evidently not home-sick. Mrs Lemon could see that Barberina was ravaged by this last passion and was too proud to show it. She even had a glimpse of the ultimate truth; namely, that Jackson's wife had not the comfort of crying, because that would have amounted to a confession that she had been idiotic enough to believe in advance that, in an American town, in the society of doctors, she should escape such pangs. Mrs Lemon treated her with the greatest gentleness – all the gentleness that was due to a young woman who was in the unfortunate position of having been married one couldn't tell why. The world, to Mrs Lemon's view, contained two great departments – that of persons, and that of things; and she believed that you must take an interest either in one or the other. The incomprehensible thing in Lady Barb was that she cared for neither side of the show. Her house apparently inspired her with no curiosity and no enthusiasm, though it had been thought magnificent enough to be described in successive columns of the American newspapers; and she never spoke of her furniture or her domestics, though she had a prodigious supply of such possessions. She was the same with regard to her acquaintance, which was immense, inasmuch as every one in the place had called on her. Mrs Lemon was the least critical woman in the world; but it had sometimes exasperated her just a little that her daughter-in-law should receive every one in New York in exactly the same way. There were differences, Mrs Lemon knew, and some of them were of the highest importance; but poor Lady Barb appeared never to suspect them. She accepted every one and everything, and asked no questions. She had no curiosity about her fellow-citizens, and as she never assumed it for a moment, she gave Mrs Lemon no opportunity to enlighten her. Lady Barb was a person with whom you could do nothing unless she gave you an opening; and nothing would have been more difficult than to enlighten her against her will. Of course she picked up a little knowledge; but she confounded and transposed American attributes in the most extraordinary way. She had a way of calling every one Doctor; and Mrs Lemon could scarcely convince her that this distinction was too precious to be so freely bestowed. She had once said to her mother-in-law that in New York there was nothing to know people by, their names were so very monotonous; and Mrs Lemon had entered into this enough to see that there was something that stood out a good deal in Barberina's own prefix. It is probable that during her short stay in New York complete justice was not done Lady Barb; she never got credit, for instance, for repressing her annoyance at the aridity of the social nomenclature, which seemed to her hideous. That little speech to her mother was the most reckless sign she gave of it; and there were few things that contributed more to the good conscience she habitually enjoyed, than her self-control on this particular point.

Jackson Lemon was making some researches, just now, which took up a great deal of his time; and, for the rest, he passed his hours abundantly with his wife. For the last three months, therefore, he had seen his mother scarcely more than once a week. In spite of researches, in spite of medical societies, where Jackson, to her knowledge, read papers, Lady Barb had more of her husband's company than she had counted upon at the time she married. She had never known a married pair to be so much together as she and Jackson; he appeared to expect her to sit with him in the library in the morning. He had none of the occupations of gentlemen and noblemen in England, for the element of politics appeared to be as absent as the hunting. There were politics in Washington, she had been told, and even at Albany, and Jackson had proposed to introduce her to these cities; but the proposal, made to her once at dinner before several people, had excited such cries of horror that it fell dead on the spot. 'We don't want you to see anything of that kind,' one of the ladies had said, and Jackson had appeared to be discouraged – that is if, in regard to Jackson, one could really tell.

'Pray, what is it you want me to see?' Lady Barb had asked on this occasion.

'Well, New York; and Boston, if you want to very much – but not otherwise; and Niagara: and, more than anything, Newport.'

Lady Barb was tired of their eternal Newport; she had heard of it a thousand times, and felt already as if she had lived there half her life; she was sure, moreover, that she should hate it. This is perhaps as near as she came to having a lively conviction on any American subject. She asked herself whether she was then to spend her life in the Fifth Avenue, with alternations of a city of villas (she detested villas), and wondered whether that was all the great American country had to offer her. There were times when she thought that she should like the backwoods, and that the Far West might be a resource; for she had analysed her feelings just deep enough to discover that when she had – hesitating a good deal – turned over the question of marrying Jackson Lemon, it was not in the least of American barbarism that she was afraid; her dread was of American civilisation. She believed the little lady I have just quoted was a goose; but that did not make New York any more interesting. It would be reckless to say that she suffered from an overdose of Jackson's company, because she had a view of the fact that he was much her most important social resource. She could talk to him about England; about her own England, and he understood more or less what she wished to say, when she wished to say anything, which was not frequent. There were plenty of other people who talked about England; but with them the range of allusion was always the hotels, of which she knew nothing, and the shops, and the opera, and the photographs: they had a mania for photographs. There were other people who were always wanting her to tell them about Pasterns, and the manner of life there, and the parties; but if there was one thing Lady Barb disliked more than another, it was describing Pasterns. She had always lived with people who knew, of themselves, what such a place would be, without demanding these pictorial efforts, proper only, as she vaguely felt, to persons belonging to the classes whose trade was the arts of expression. Lady Barb, of course, had never gone into it; but she knew that in her own class the business was not to express, but to enjoy; not to represent, but to be represented – though, indeed, this latter liability might convey offence; for it may be noted that even for an aristocrat Jackson Lemon's wife was aristocratic.

Lady Agatha and her visitor came back from the library in course of time, and Jackson Lemon felt it his duty to be rather cold to Herman Longstraw. It was not clear to him what sort of a husband his sister-in-law would do well to look for in America – if there were to be any question of husbands; but as to this he was not bound to be definite, provided he should rule out Mr Longstraw. This gentleman, however, was not given to perceive shades of manner; he had little observation, but very great confidence.

'I think you had better come home with me,' Jackson said to Lady Agatha; 'I guess you have stayed here long enough.'

'Don't let him say that, Mrs Lemon!' the girl cried. 'I like being with you so very much.'

'I try to make it pleasant,' said Mrs Lemon. 'I should really miss you now; but perhaps it's your mother's wish.' If it was a question of defending her guest from ineligible suitors, Mrs Lemon felt, of course, that her son was more competent than she; though she had a lurking kindness for Herman Longstraw, and a vague idea that he was a gallant, genial specimen of young America.

'Oh, mamma wouldn't see any difference!' Lady Agatha exclaimed, looking at Jackson with pleading blue eyes. 'Mamma
wants me to see every one; you know she does. That's what she sent
me to America for; she knew it was not like England. She wouldn't
like it if I didn't sometimes stay with people; she always wanted us
to stay at other houses. And she knows all about you, Mrs Lemon,
and she likes you immensely. She sent you a message the other day,
and I am afraid I forgot to give it you – to thank you for being so
kind to me and taking such a lot of trouble. Really she did, but I
forgot it. If she wants me to see as much as possible of America, it's
much better I should be here than always with Barb – it's much less
like one's own country. I mean it's much nicer – for a girl,' said Lady
Agatha, affectionately, to Mrs Lemon, who began also to look at
Jackson with a kind of tender argumentativeness.

'If you want the genuine thing, you ought to come out on the
plains,' Mr Longstraw interposed, with smiling sincerity. 'I guess
that was your mother's idea. Why don't you all come out?' He had
been looking intently at Lady Agatha while the remarks I have just
repeated succeeded each other on her lips – looking at her with a
kind of fascinated approbation, for all the world as if he had been
a slightly slow-witted English gentleman and the girl had been a
flower of the West – a flower that knew how to talk. He made no
secret of the fact that Lady Agatha's voice was music to him, his
ear being much more susceptible than his own inflections would
have indicated. To Lady Agatha those inflections were not displeasing, partly because, like Mr Herman himself, in general, she
had not a perception of shades; and partly because it never occurred
to her to compare them with any other tones. He seemed to her to
speak a foreign language altogether – a romantic dialect, through
which the most comical meanings gleamed here and there.

'I should like it above all things,' she said, in answer to his last
observation.

'The scenery's superior to anything round here,' Mr Longstraw
went on.

Mrs Lemon, as we know, was the softest of women; but, as an old
New Yorker, she had no patience with some of the new fashions.
Chief among these was the perpetual reference, which had become
common only within a few years, to the outlying parts of the

country, the States and Territories of which children, in her time, used to learn the names, in their order, at school, but which no one ever thought of going to or talking about. Such places, in Mrs Lemon's opinion, belonged to the geography-books, or at most to the literature of newspapers, but not to society nor to conversation; and the change – which, so far as it lay in people's talk, she thought at bottom a mere affectation – threatened to make her native land appear vulgar and vague. For this amiable daughter of Manhattan, the normal existence of man, and, still more, of woman, had been 'located', as she would have said, between Trinity Church and the beautiful Reservoir at the top of the Fifth Avenue – monuments of which she was personally proud; and if we could look into the deeper parts of her mind, I am afraid we should discover there an impression that both the countries of Europe and the remainder of her own continent were equally far from the centre and the light.

'Well, scenery isn't everything,' she remarked, mildly, to Mr Longstraw; 'and if Lady Agatha should wish to see anything of that kind, all she has got to do is to take the boat up the Hudson.'

Mrs Lemon's recognition of this river, I should say, was all that it need have been; she thought that it existed for the purpose of supplying New Yorkers with poetical feelings, helping them to face comfortably occasions like the present, and, in general, meet foreigners with confidence – part of the oddity of foreigners being their conceit about their own places.

'That's a good idea, Lady Agatha; let's take the boat,' said Mr Longstraw. 'I've had great times on the boats.'

Lady Agatha looked at her cavalier a little with those singular, charming eyes of hers – eyes of which it was impossible to say, at any moment, whether they were the shyest or the frankest in the world; and she was not aware, while this contemplation lasted, that her brother-in-law was observing her. He was thinking of certain things while he did so, of things he had heard about the English; who still, in spite of his having married into a family of that nation, appeared to him very much through the medium of hearsay. They were more passionate than the Americans, and they did things that would never have been expected; though they seemed steadier and less excitable, there was much social evidence to show that they were more impulsive.

'It's so very kind of you to propose that, Lady Agatha said in a moment to Mrs Lemon. 'I think I have never been in a ship – except, of course, coming from England. I am sure mamma would wish me to see the Hudson. We used to go in immensely for boating in England.'

'Did you boat in a ship?' Herman Longstraw asked, showing his teeth hilariously, and pulling his moustaches.

'Lots of my mother's people have been in the navy.' Lady Agatha perceived vaguely and good-naturedly that she had said something which the odd Americans thought odd, and that she must justify herself. Her standard of oddity was getting dreadfully dislocated.

'I really think you had better come back to us,' said Jackson; 'your sister is very lonely without you.'

'She is much more lonely with me. We are perpetually having differences. Barb is dreadfully vexed because I like America, instead of – instead of –' And Lady Agatha paused a moment; for it just occurred to her that this might be a betrayal.

'Instead of what?' Jackson Lemon inquired.

'Instead of perpetually wanting to go to England, as she does, she went on, only giving her phrase a little softer turn; for she felt the next moment that her sister could have nothing to hide, and must, of course, have the courage of her opinions. 'Of course England's best, but I dare say I like to be bad,' said Lady Agatha, artlessly.

'Oh, there's no doubt you are awfully bad!' Mr Longstraw exclaimed, with joyous eagerness. Of course he could not know that what she had principally in mind was an exchange of opinions that had taken place between her sister and herself just before she came to stay with Mrs Lemon. This incident, of which Longstraw was the occasion, might indeed have been called a discussion, for it had carried them quite into the realms of the abstract. Lady Barb had said she didn't see how Agatha could look at such a creature as that – an odious, familiar, vulgar being, who had not about him the rudiments of a gentleman. Lady Agatha had replied that Mr Longstraw was familiar and rough, and that he had a twang, and thought it amusing to talk of her as 'the Princess'; but that he was a gentleman for all that, and that at any rate he was tremendous fun. Her sister to this had rejoined that if he was rough and familiar he couldn't be a gentleman, inasmuch as that was just what a gentleman meant – a man who was civil, and well-bred, and well-born. Lady Agatha had argued that this was just where she differed; that a man might perfectly be a gentleman, and yet be rough, and even ignorant, so long as he was really nice. The only thing was that he should be really nice, which was the case with Mr Longstraw, who, moreover, was quite extraordinarily civil – as civil as a man could be. And then Lady Agatha made the strongest point she had ever made in her life (she had never been so inspired) in saying that Mr Longstraw was rough, perhaps, but not rude – a distinction altogether wasted on her sister, who declared that she had not come to America, of all places, to learn what a gentleman was. The discussion, in short, had been lively. I know not whether it was the tonic effect on them, too, of the fine winter weather, or, on the other hand, that of Lady Barb's being bored and having nothing else to do; but Lord Canterville's daughters went into the question with the moral earnestness of a pair of Bostonians. It was part of Lady Agatha's view of her admirer that he, after all, much resembled other tall people, with smiling eyes and moustaches, who had ridden a good deal in rough countries, and whom she had seen in other places. If he was more familiar, he was also more alert; still, the difference was not in himself, but in the way she saw him – the way she saw everybody in America. If she should see the others in the same way, no doubt they would be quite the same; and Lady Agatha sighed a little over the possibilities of life; for this peculiar way, especially regarded in connection with gentlemen, had become very pleasant to her.

She had betrayed her sister more than she thought, even though Jackson Lemon did not particularly show it in the tone in which he said: 'Of course she knows that she is going to see your mother in the summer.' His tone, rather, was that of irritation at the repetition of a familiar idea.

'Oh, it isn't only mamma,' replied Lady Agatha.

'I know she likes a cool house,' said Mrs Lemon, suggestively.

'When she goes, you had better bid her good-bye,' the girl went on.

'Of course I shall bid her good-bye,' said Mrs Lemon, to whom, apparently, this remark was addressed.

'I shall never bid you good-bye, Princess,' Herman Longstraw interposed. 'I can tell you that you never will see the last of me.'

'Oh, it doesn't matter about me, for I shall come back; but if Barb once gets to England she will never come back.'

'Oh, my dear child,' murmured Mrs Lemon, addressing Lady Agatha, but looking at her son.

Jackson looked at the ceiling, at the floor; above all, he looked very conscious.

'I hope you don't mind my saying that, Jackson dear,' Lady Agatha said to him, for she was very fond of her brother-in-law.

'Ah, well, then, she shan't go, then,' he remarked, after a moment, with a dry little laugh.

'But you promised mamma, you know,' said the girl, with the confidence of her affection.

Jackson looked at her with an eye which expressed none even of his very moderate hilarity. 'Your mother, then, must bring her back.'

'Get some of your navy people to supply an ironclad!' cried Mr Longstraw.

'It would be very pleasant if the Marchioness could come over,' said Mrs Lemon.

'Oh, she would hate it more than poor Barb,' Lady Agatha quickly replied. It did not suit her mood at all to see a marchioness inserted into the field of her vision.

'Doesn't she feel interested, from what you have told her?' Herman Longstraw asked of Lady Agatha. But Jackson Lemon did not heed his sister-in-law's answer; he was thinking of something else. He said nothing more, however, about the subject of his thought, and before ten minutes were over he took his departure, having, meanwhile, neglected also to revert to the question of Lady Agatha's bringing her visit to his mother to a close. It was not to speak to him of this (for, as we know, she wished to keep the girl, and somehow could not bring herself to be afraid of Herman Longstraw) that when Jackson took leave she went with him to the door of the house, detaining him a little, while she stood on the steps, as people had always done in New York in her time, though it was another of the new fashions she did not like, not to come out of the parlour. She placed her hand on his arm to keep him on the 'stoop', and looked up and down into the brilliant afternoon and the beautiful city – its chocolate-coloured houses, so extraordinarily smooth – in which it seemed to her that even the most fastidious people ought to be glad to live. It was useless to attempt to conceal it; her son's marriage had made a difference, had put up a kind of barrier. It had brought with it a problem much more difficult than his old problem of how to make his mother feel that she was still, as she had been in his childhood, the dispenser of his rewards. The old problem had been easily solved; the new one was a visible preoccupation. Mrs Lemon felt that her daughter-in-law did not take her seriously; and that was a part of the barrier. Even if Barberina liked her better than any one else, this was mostly because she liked every one else so little. Mrs Lemon had not a grain of resentment in her nature; and it was not to feed a sense of wrong that she permitted herself to criticise her son's wife. She could not help feeling that his marriage was not altogether fortunate if his wife didn't take his mother seriously. She knew she was not otherwise remarkable than as being his mother; but that position, which was no merit of hers (the merit was all Jackson's, in being her son), seemed to her one which, familiar as Lady Barb appeared to have been in England with positions of various kinds, would naturally strike the girl as a very high one, to be accepted as freely as a fine morning. If she didn't think of his mother as an indivisible part of him, perhaps she didn't think of other things either; and Mrs Lemon vaguely felt that, remarkable as Jackson was, he was made up of parts, and that it would never do that these parts should depreciate one by one, for there was no knowing what that might end in. She feared that things were rather cold for him at home when he had to explain so much to his wife – explain to her, for instance, all the sources of happiness that were to be found in New York. This struck her as a new kind of problem altogether for a husband. She had never thought of matrimony without a community of feeling in regard to religion and country; one took those great conditions for granted, just as one assumed that one's food was to be cooked; and if Jackson should have to discuss them with his wife, he might, in spite of his great abilities, be carried into regions where he would get entangled and embroiled – from which, even, possibly, he would not come back at all. Mrs Lemon had a horror of losing him in some way; and this fear was in her eyes as she stood on the steps of her house, and, after she had glanced up and down the street, looked at him a moment in silence. He simply kissed her again, and said she would take cold.

'I am not afraid of that, I have a shawl!' Mrs Lemon, who was very small and very fair, with pointed features and an elaborate cap, passed her life in a shawl, and owed to this habit her reputation for being an invalid – an idea which she scorned, naturally enough, inasmuch as it was precisely her shawl that (as she believed) kept her from being one. 'Is it true Barberina won't come back?' she asked of her son.

'I don't know that we shall ever find out; I don't know that I shall take her to England.'

'Didn't you promise, dear?'

'I don't know that I promised; not absolutely.'

'But you wouldn't keep her here against her will?' said Mrs Lemon, inconsequently.

'I guess she'll get used to it,' Jackson answered, with a lightness he did not altogether feel.

Mrs Lemon looked up and down the street again, and gave a little sigh. 'What a pity she isn't American!' She did not mean this as a reproach, a hint of what might have been; it was simply embarrassment resolved into speech.

'She couldn't have been American,' said Jackson, with decision.

'Couldn't she, dear?' Mrs Lemon spoke with a kind of respect; she felt that there were imperceptible reasons in this.

'It was just as she is that I wanted her,' Jackson added.

'Even if she won't come back?' his mother asked, with a certain wonder.

'Oh, she has got to come back!' Jackson said, going down the steps.

6

Lady Barb, after this, did not decline to see her New York acquaintances on Sunday afternoons, though she refused for the present to
enter into a project of her husband's, who thought it would be a
pleasant thing that she should entertain his friends on the evening
of that day. Like all good Americans, Jackson Lemon devoted much
consideration to the great question how, in his native land, society
should be brought into being. It seemed to him that it would help
the good cause, for which so many Americans are ready to lay down
their lives, if his wife should, as he jocularly called it, open a saloon.
He believed, or he tried to believe, the *salon* now possible in New
York, on condition of its being reserved entirely for adults; and in
having taken a wife out of a country in which social traditions were
rich and ancient, he had done something towards qualifying his
own house – so splendidly qualified in all strictly material respects
– to be the scene of such an effort. A charming woman, accustomed
only to the best in each country, as Lady Beauchemin said, what
might she not achieve by being at home (to the elder generation)
in an easy, early, inspiring, comprehensive way, on the evening in
the week on which worldly engagements were least numerous? He
laid this philosophy before Lady Barb, in pursuance of a theory that
if she disliked New York on a short acquaintance, she could not fail
to like it on a long one. Jackson Lemon believed in the New York
mind – not so much, indeed, in its literary, artistic, or political
achievements, as in its general quickness and nascent adaptability.
He clung to this belief, for it was a very important piece of material
in the structure that he was attempting to rear. The New York mind
would throw its glamour over Lady Barb if she would only give it
a chance; for it was exceedingly bright, entertaining, and sympathetic. If she would only have a *salon*, where this charming organ
might expand, and where she might inhale its fragrance in the most
convenient and luxurious way, without, as it were, getting up from
her chair; if she would only just try this graceful, good-natured

experiment (which would make every one like *her* so much too),
he was sure that all the wrinkles in the gilded scroll of his fate would
be smoothed out. But Lady Barb did not rise at all to his conception,
and had not the least curiosity about the New York mind. She
thought it would be extremely disagreeable to have a lot of
people tumbling in on Sunday evening without being invited; and
altogether her husband's sketch of the Anglo-American saloon
seemed to her to suggest familiarity. high-pitched talk (she had
already made a remark to him about 'screeching women'), and
exaggerated laughter. She did not tell him – for this. somehow, it
was not in her power to express. and, strangely enough, he never
completely guessed it – that she was singularly deficient in any
natural, or indeed acquired, understanding of what a saloon might
be. She had never seen one, and for the most part she never thought
of things she had not seen. She had seen great dinners, and balls.
and meets, and runs, and races; she had seen garden-parties. and
a lot of people, mainly women (who. however. didn't screech). at
dull, stuffy teas. and distinguished companies collected in splendid
castles; but all this gave her no idea of a tradition of conversation,
of a social agreement that the continuity of talk, its accumulations
from season to season, should not be lost. Conversation, in Lady
Barb's experience, had never been continuous; in such a case it
would surely have been a bore. It had been occasional and frag-
mentary. a trifle jerky with allusions that were never explained: it
had a dread of detail; it seldom pursued anything very far. or kept
hold of it very long.

There was something else that she did not say to her husband in
reference to his visions of hospitality, which was, that if she should
open a saloon (she had taken up the joke as well, for Lady Barb was
eminently good-natured), Mrs Vanderdecken would straightway
open another. and Mrs Vanderdecken's would be the more successful of the two. This lady. for reasons that Lady Barb had not yet
explored, was supposed to be the great personage in New York;
there were legends of her husband's family having behind them
a fabulous antiquity. When this was alluded to, it was spoken
of as something incalculable. and lost in the dimness of time.
Mrs Vanderdecken was young, pretty, clever, absurdly pretentious (Lady Barb thought), and had a wonderfully artistic house.

Ambition, also, was expressed in every rustle of her garments; and if she was the first person in America (this had an immense sound) it was plain that she intended to remain so. It was not till after she had been several months in New York that it came over Lady Barb that this brilliant, bristling native had flung down the glove; and when the idea presented itself, lighted up by an incident which I have no space to relate, she simply blushed a little (for Mrs Vander-decken), and held her tongue. She had not come to America to bandy words about precedence with such a woman as that. She had ceased to think about it much (of course one thought about it in England); but an instinct of self-preservation led her not to expose herself to occasions on which her claim might be tested. This, at bottom, had much to do with her having, very soon after the first flush of the honours paid her on her arrival, and which seemed to her rather grossly overdone, taken the line of scarcely going out. 'They can't keep *that* up!' she had said to herself; and, in short, she would stay at home. She had a feeling that whenever she should go forth she would meet Mrs Vanderdecken, who would withhold, or deny, or contest something – poor Lady Barb could never imagine what. She did not try to, and gave little thought to all this; for she was not prone to confess to herself fears, especially fears from which terror was absent. But, as I have said, it abode within her as a presentiment that if she should set up a drawing-room in the foreign style (it was curious, in New York, how they tried to be foreign), Mrs Vanderdecken would be beforehand with her. The continuity of conversation, oh! that idea she would certainly have; there was no one so continuous as Mrs Vanderdecken. Lady Barb, as I have related, did not give her husband the surprise of telling him of these thoughts, though she had given him some other surprises. He would have been very much astonished, and perhaps, after a bit, a little encouraged, at finding that she was liable to this particular form of irritation.

On the Sunday afternoon she was visible; and on one of these occasions, going into her drawing-room late, he found her entertaining two ladies and a gentleman. The gentleman was Sidney Feeder, and one of the ladies was Mrs Vanderdecken, whose ostensible relations with Lady Barb were of the most cordial nature. If she intended to crush her (as two or three persons, not conspicuous for

a narrow accuracy, gave out that she privately declared), Mrs
Vanderdecken wished at least to study the weak points of the
invader, to penetrate herself with the character of the English girl.
Lady Barb, indeed, appeared to have a mysterious fascination for the
representative of the American patriciate. Mrs Vanderdecken could
not take her eyes off her victim; and whatever might be her estimate
of her importance, she at least could not let her alone. 'Why does
she come to see me?' poor Lady Barb asked herself. 'I am sure I don't
want to see her; she has done enough for civility long ago.' Mrs
Vanderdecken had her own reasons; and one of them was simply
the pleasure of looking at the Doctor's wife, as she habitually called
the daughter of the Cantervilles. She was not guilty of the folly of
depreciating this lady's appearance, and professed an unbounded
admiration for it, defending it on many occasions against superficial
people who said there were fifty women in New York that were
handsomer. Whatever might have been Lady Barb's weak points,
they were not the curve of her cheek and chin, the setting of her
head on her throat, or the quietness of her deep eyes, which were
as beautiful as if they had been blank, like those of antique busts.
'The head is enchanting – perfectly enchanting,' Mrs Vanderdecken
used to say irrelevantly, as if there were only one head in the place.
She always used to ask about the Doctor; and that was another
reason why she came. She brought up the Doctor at every turn;
asked if he were often called up at night; found it the greatest of
luxuries, in a word, to address Lady Barb as the wife of a medical
man, more or less *au courant* of her husband's patients. The other
lady, on this Sunday afternoon, was a certain little Mrs Chew,
whose clothes looked so new that she had the air of a walking
advertisement issued by a great shop, and who was always asking
Lady Barb about England, which Mrs Vanderdecken never did. The
latter visitor conversed with Lady Barb on a purely American basis,
with that continuity (on her own side) of which mention has
already been made, while Mrs Chew engaged Sidney Feeder on
topics equally local. Lady Barb liked Sidney Feeder; she only hated
his name, which was constantly in her ears during the half-hour
the ladies sat with her, Mrs Chew having the habit, which annoyed
Lady Barb, of repeating perpetually the appellation of her interlocutor.

Lady Barb's relations with Mrs Vanderdecken consisted mainly in wondering, while she talked, what she wanted of her, and in looking, with her sculptured eyes, at her visitor's clothes, in which there was always much to examine. 'Oh, Doctor Feeder!' 'Now, Doctor Feeder!' 'Well, Doctor Feeder,' – these exclamations, on the lips of Mrs Chew, were an undertone in Lady Barb's consciousness. When I say that she liked her husband's *confrère*, as he used to call himself, I mean that she smiled at him when he came, and gave him her hand, and asked him if he would have some tea. There was nothing nasty (as they said in London) in Lady Barb, and she would have been incapable of inflicting a deliberate snub upon a man who had the air of standing up so squarely to any work that he might have in hand. But she had nothing to say to Sidney Feeder. He apparently had the art of making her shy, more shy than usual; for she was always a little so; she discouraged him, discouraged him completely. He was not a man who wanted drawing out, there was nothing of that in him, he was remarkably copious; but Lady Barb appeared unable to follow him, and half the time, evidently, did not know what he was saying. He tried to adapt his conversation to her needs; but when he spoke of the world, of what was going on in society, she was more at sea even than when he spoke of hospitals and laboratories, and the health of the city, and the progress of science. She appeared, indeed, after her first smile, when he came in, which was always charming, scarcely to see him, looking past him, and above him, and below him, and everywhere but at him, until he got up to go again, when she gave him another smile, as expressive of pleasure and of casual acquaintance as that with which she had greeted his entry; it seemed to imply that they had been having delightful talk for an hour. He wondered what the deuce Jackson Lemon could find interesting in such a woman, and he believed that his perverse, though gifted colleague, was not destined to feel that she illuminated his life. He pitied Jackson, he saw that Lady Barb, in New York, would neither assimilate nor be assimilated; and yet he was afraid to betray his incredulity, thinking it might be depressing to poor Lemon to show him how his marriage – now so dreadfully irrevocable – struck others. Sidney Feeder was a man of a strenuous conscience, and he did his duty overmuch by his old friend and his wife, from the simple fear that he should not do it enough. In order not to appear to neglect them, he called upon Lady Barb heroically, in spite of pressing engagements, week after week, enjoying his virtue himself as little as he made it fruitful for his hostess, who wondered at last what she had done to deserve these visitations. She spoke of them to her husband, who wondered also what poor Sidney had in his head, and yet was unable, of course, to hint to him that he need not think it necessary to come so often. Between Doctor Feeder's wish not to let Jackson see that his marriage had made a difference, and Jackson's hesitation to reveal to Sidney that his standard of friendship was too high, Lady Barb passed a good many of those numerous hours during which she asked herself if she had come to America for that. Very little had ever passed between her and her husband on the subject of Sidney Feeder; for an instinct told her that if they were ever to have scenes, she must choose the occasion well; and this odd person was not an occasion. Jackson had tacitly admitted that his friend Feeder was anything she chose to think him; he was not a man to be guilty, in a discussion, of the disloyalty of damning him with praise that was faint. If Lady Agatha had usually been with her sister, Doctor Feeder would have been better entertained; for the younger of the English visitors prided herself, after several months of New York, on understanding everything that was said, and catching every allusion, it mattered not from what lips it fell. But Lady Agatha was never at home; she had learned how to describe herself perfectly by the time she wrote to her mother that she was always 'on the go'. None of the innumerable victims of old-world tyranny who have fled to the United States as to a land of freedom, have ever offered more lavish incense to that goddess than this emancipated London *débutante*. She had enrolled herself in an amiable band which was known by the humorous name of 'the Tearers' – a dozen young ladies of agreeable appearance, high spirits and good wind, whose most general characteristic was that, when wanted, they were to be sought anywhere in the world but under the roof that was supposed to shelter them. They were never at home; and when Sidney Feeder, as sometimes happened, met Lady Agatha at other houses, she was in the hands of the irrepressible Longstraw. She had come back to her sister, but Mr Longstraw had followed her to the door. As to passing it, he had received direct discouragement from her brother-in-law; but he could at least hang about and wait for her. It may be confided to the reader. at the risk of diminishing the effect of the only incident which in the course of this very level narrative may startle him, that he never had to wait very long.

When Jackson Lemon came in, his wife's visitors were on the point of leaving her; and he did not ask even Sidney Feeder to remain, for he had something particular to say to Lady Barb.

'I haven't asked you half what I wanted – I have been talking so much to Doctor Feeder,' the dressy Mrs Chew said, holding the hand of her hostess in one of her own, and toying with one of Lady Barb's ribbons with the other.

'I don't think I have anything to tell you; I think I have told people everything,' Lady Barb answered, rather wearily.

'You haven't told *me* much!' Mrs Vanderdecken said. smiling brightly.

'What could one tell you? – you know everything,' Jackson Lemon interposed.

'Ah, no; there are some things that are great mysteries for me,' the lady returned. 'I hope you are coming to me on the 17th,' she added, to Lady Barb.

'On the 17th? I think we are going somewhere.'

'Do go to Mrs Vanderdecken's,' said Mrs Chew; 'you will see the cream of the cream.'

'Oh, gracious!' Mrs Vanderdecken exclaimed.

'Well, I don't care; she will, won't she, Doctor Feeder? – the very pick of American society.' Mrs Chew stuck to her point.

'Well, I have no doubt Lady Barb will have a good time,' said Sidney Feeder. 'I'm afraid you miss the bran,' he went on, with ir- relevant jocosity, to Lady Barb. He always tried the jocose when other elements had failed.

'The bran?' asked Lady Barb, staring.

'Where you used to ride, in the Park.'

'My dear fellow, you speak as if it were the circus,' Jackson Lemon said, smiling; 'I haven't married a mountebank!'

'Well, they put some stuff on the road,' Sidney Feeder explained, not holding much to his joke.

'You must miss a great many things,' said Mrs Chew, tenderly.

'I don't see what,' Mrs Vanderdecken remarked, 'except the fogs and the Queen. New York is getting more and more like London. It's a pity; you ought to have known us thirty years ago.'

'You are the queen, here,' said Jackson Lemon; 'but I don't know what you know about thirty years ago.'

'Do you think she doesn't go back? – she goes back to the last century!' cried Mrs Chew.

'I dare say I should have liked that,' said Lady Barb; 'but I can't imagine.' And she looked at her husband – a look she often had – as if she vaguely wished him to do something.

He was not called upon, however, to take any violent steps, for Mrs Chew presently said: 'Well, Lady Barberina, good-bye'; and Mrs Vanderdecken smiled in silence at her hostess, and addressed a farewell, accompanied very audibly with his title, to her host; and Sidney Feeder made a joke about stepping on the trains of the ladies' dresses as he accompanied them to the door. Mrs Chew had always a great deal to say at the last; she talked till she was in the street, and then she did not cease. But at the end of five minutes Jackson Lemon was alone with his wife; and then he told her a piece of news. He prefaced it, however, by an inquiry as he came back from the hall.

'Where is Agatha, my dear?'

'I haven't the least idea. In the streets somewhere, I suppose.'

'I think you ought to know a little more.'

'How can I know about things here? I have given her up; I can do nothing with her. I don't care what she does.'

'She ought to go back to England,' Jackson Lemon said, after a pause.

'She ought never to have come.'

'It was not my proposal, God knows!' Jackson answered, rather sharply.

'Mamma could never know what it really is,' said his wife.

'No, it has not been as yet what your mother supposed! Herman Longstraw wants to marry her. He has made me a formal proposal. I met him half an hour ago in Madison Avenue, and he asked me to come with him into the Columbia Club. There, in the billiard-room, which to-day is empty, he opened himself – thinking evidently that in laying the matter before me he was behaving with extraordinary propriety. He tells me he is dying of love. and that she is perfectly willing to go and live in Arizona.'

'So she is,' said Lady Barb. 'And what did you tell him?'

'I told him that I was sure it would never do, and that at any rate I could have nothing to say to it. I told him explicitly, in short, what I had told him virtually before. I said that we should send Agatha straight back to England, and that if they have the courage they must themselves broach the question over there.'

'When shall you send her back?' asked Lady Barb.

'Immediately; by the very first steamer.'

Alone, like an American girl?'

'Don't be rough, Barb,' said Jackson Lemon. 'I shall easily find some people; lots of people are sailing now.'

'I must take her myself,' Lady Barb declared in a moment. 'I brought her out, and I must restore her to my mother's hands.'

Jackson Lemon had expected this. and he believed he was prepared for it. But when it came he found his preparation was not complete: for he had no answer to make – none, at least, that seemed to him to go to the point. During these last weeks it had come over him, with a quiet, irresistible, unmerciful force, that Mrs Dexter Freer had been right when she said to him, that Sunday afternoon in Jermyn Street, the summer before, that he would find it was not so simple to be an American. Such an identity was complicated, in just the measure that she had foretold. by the difficulty of domesticating one's wife. The difficulty was not dissipated by his having taken a high tone about it; it pinched him from morning till night. like a misfitting shoe. His high tone had given him courage when he took the great step; but he began to perceive that the highest tone in the world cannot change the nature of things. His ears tingled when he reflected that if the Dexter Freers. whom he had thought alike ignoble in their hopes and their fears, had been by ill-luck spending the winter in New York, they would have found his predicament as entertaining as they could desire. Drop by drop the conviction had entered his mind – the first drop had come in the form of a word from Lady Agatha – that if his wife should return to England she would never again cross the Atlantic to the West. That word from Lady Agatha had been the touch from the outside, at which, often, one's fears crystallise. What she would do, how she would resist – this he was not yet prepared to tell himself; but he felt, every time he looked at her, that this beautiful woman whom he had adored was filled with a dumb, insuperable, ineradicable purpose. He knew that if she should plant herself, no power on earth would move her; and her blooming, antique beauty, and the general loftiness of her breeding, came to seem to him – rapidly – but the magnificent expression of a dense, patient, imperturbable obstinacy. She was not light, she was not supple, and after six months of marriage he had made up his mind that she was not clever; but nevertheless she would elude him. She had married him, she had come into his fortune and his consideration – for who was she, after all? Jackson Lemon was once so angry as to ask himself, reminding himself that in England Lady Claras and Lady Florences were as thick as blackberries – but she would have nothing to do, if she could help it, with his country. She had gone in to dinner first in every house in the place, but this had not satisfied her. It *had* been simple to be an American, in this sense that no one else in New York had made any difficulties; the difficulties had sprung from her peculiar feelings, which were after all what he had married her for, thinking they would be a fine temperamental heritage for his brood. So they would, doubtless, in the coming years, after the brood should have appeared; but meanwhile they interfered with the best heritage of all – the nationality of his possible children. Lady Barb would do nothing violent; he was tolerably certain of that. She would not return to England without his consent; only, when she should return, it would be once for all. His only possible line, then, was not to take her back – a position replete with difficulties, because, of course, he had, in a manner, given his word, while she had given no word at all, beyond the general promise she had murmured at the altar. She had been general, but he had been specific; the settlements he had made were a part of that. His difficulties were such as he could not directly face. He must tack in approaching so uncertain a coast. He said to Lady Barb presently that it would be very inconvenient for him to leave New York at that moment: she must remember that their plans had been laid for a later departure. He could not think of letting her make the voyage without him, and, on the other hand, they must pack her sister off without delay. He would therefore make instant inquiry for a chaperon, and he relieved his irritation by expressing considerable disgust at Herman Longstraw.

Lady Barb did not trouble herself to denounce this gentleman; her manner was that of having for a long time expected the worst. She simply remarked dryly, after having listened to her husband for some minutes in silence: 'I would as lief she should marry Doctor Feeder!'

The day after this, Jackson Lemon closeted himself for an hour with Lady Agatha, taking great pains to set forth to her the reasons why she should not unite herself with her Californian. Jackson was kind, he was affectionate; he kissed her and put his arm round her waist, he reminded her that he and she were the best of friends, and that she had always been awfully nice to him; therefore he counted upon her. She would break her mother's heart, she would deserve her father's curse, and she would get him, Jackson, into a pickle from which no human power could ever disembroil him. Lady Agatha listened and cried, and returned his kiss very affectionately, and admitted that her father and mother would never consent to such a marriage; and when he told her that he had made arrangements for her to sail for Liverpool (with some charming people) the next day but one, she embraced him again and assured him that she could never thank him enough for all the trouble he had taken about her. He flattered himself that he had convinced, and in some degree comforted her, and reflected with complacency that even should his wife take it into her head, Barberina would never get ready to embark for her native land between a Monday and a Wednesday. The next morning Lady Agatha did not appear at breakfast; but as she usually rose very late, her absence excited no alarm. She had not rung her bell, and she was supposed still to be sleeping. But she had never yet slept later than midday; and as this hour approached her sister went to her room. Lady Barb then discovered that she had left the house at seven o'clock in the morning, and had gone to meet Herman Longstraw at a neighbouring corner. A little note on the table explained it very succinctly, and put beyond the power of Jackson Lemon and his wife to doubt that by the time this news reached them their wayward sister had been united to the man of her preference as closely as the

laws of the State of New York could bind her. Her little note set forth
that as she knew she should never be permitted to marry him, she
had determined to marry him without permission, and that directly
after the ceremony, which would be of the simplest kind, they were
to take a train for the far West. Our history is concerned only with
the remote consequences of this incident, which made, of course,
a great deal of trouble for Jackson Lemon. He went to the far West
in pursuit of the fugitives, and overtook them in California; but he
had not the audacity to propose to them to separate, as it was easy
for him to see that Herman Longstraw was at least as well married
as himself. Lady Agatha was already popular in the new States,
where the history of her elopement, emblazoned in enormous
capitals, was circulated in a thousand newspapers. This question of
the newspapers had been for Jackson Lemon one of the most definite
results of his sister-in-law's *coup de tête*. His first thought had been
of the public prints, and his first exclamation a prayer that they
should not get hold of the story. But they did get hold of it, and they
treated the affair with their customary energy and eloquence. Lady
Barb never saw them; but an affectionate friend of the family,
travelling at that time in the United States, made a parcel of some
of the leading journals, and sent them to Lord Canterville. This
missive elicited from her ladyship a letter addressed to Jackson
Lemon which shook the young man's position to the base. The
phials of an unnameable vulgarity had been opened upon the house
of Canterville, and his mother-in-law demanded that in compensa-
tion for the affronts and injuries that were being heaped upon her
family, and bereaved and dishonoured as she was, she should at
least be allowed to look on the face of her other daughter. 'I suppose
you will not, for very pity, be deaf to such a prayer as that,' said Lady
Barb; and though shrinking from recording a second act of weakness on the part of a man who had such pretensions to be strong,
I must relate that poor Jackson, who blushed dreadfully over the
newspapers, and felt afresh, as he read them, the force of Mrs Freer's
terrible axiom – poor Jackson paid a visit to the office of the
Cunarders. He said to himself afterward that it was the newspapers
that had done it; he could not bear to appear to be on their side; they
made it so hard to deny that the country was vulgar, at a time when
one was in such need of all one's arguments. Lady Barb, before

sailing, definitely refused to mention any week or month as the date of their pre-arranged return to New York. Very many weeks and months have elapsed since then, and she gives no sign of coming back. She will never fix a date. She is much missed by Mrs Vander-decken, who still alludes to her – still says the line of the shoulders was superb; putting the statement, pensively, in the past tense. Lady Beauchemin and Lady Marmaduke are much disconcerted; the international project has not, in their view, received an impetus.

Jackson Lemon has a house in London, and he rides in the park with his wife, who is as beautiful as the day, and a year ago presented him with a little girl, with features that Jackson already scans for the look of race – whether in hope or fear, to-day, is more than my muse has revealed. He has occasional scenes with Lady Barb, during which the look of race is very visible in her own countenance; but they never terminate in a visit to the Cunarders. He is exceedingly restless, and is constantly crossing to the Conti-nent; but he returns with a certain abruptness, for he cannot bear to meet the Dexter Freers, and they seem to pervade the more comfortable parts of Europe. He dodges them in every town. Sidney Feeder feels very badly about him; it is months since Jackson has sent him any 'results'. The excellent fellow goes very often, in a consolatory spirit, to see Mrs Lemon; but he has not yet been able to answer her standing question: 'Why that girl more than another?' Lady Agatha Longstraw and her husband arrived a year ago in England, and Mr Longstraw's personality had immense success during the last London season. It is not exactly known what they live on, though it is perfectly known that he is looking for something to do. Meanwhile it is as good as known that Jackson Lemon supports them.